A Murder
in Mayfair

Also from Robert Barnard

A Murder
in Mayfair

Robert Barnard

Poisoned Pen Press

Poisoned Pen Press
6962 E. First Ave. Ste. 103
Scottsdale, AZ 85251
www.poisonedpenpress.com
info@poisonedpenpress.com
Printed in the United States of America

Author's Note

This is not a political novel, but the quest of Colin Pinnock to discover his own origins. Nevertheless, he is a politician—an MP and a junior government minister—and there are one or two aspects of British practice that may puzzle American readers.

When a party wins a general election in Britain, its leader goes to the Queen the next morning and is asked to form a government. He immediately sets to work to choose the most important members of that government, the Cabinet. The less important members of the government will be chosen and begin work in the subsequent couple of days. Colin Pinnock is a junior member of the government, with special responsibilities within a larger Ministry, the Department of Education.

Many MPs have no particular connection with

the constituencies they are elected for. Some, indeed, even today, show a marked disinclination even to visit the area they are MP for. Colin Pinnock is lucky to sit as MP for a constituency in the area where he grew up and was educated.

CHAPTER ONE

Office

I spent May 2, hungover, waiting by the telephone. Practically every one in the Parliamentary party did the same. Even newly elected MPs, callow youths of twenty-three who against every possible expectation of pundit or psephologist had taken seats from crusted and crusty sitting members, sat by their phones if they had them, wondering if their stunning victories had somehow caught the new Prime Minister's eye, and he would ring them and offer them something. Only the party's gadflies, too pleased with themselves and their careers as comic irritants, kept up the victory celebrations and let the phone go hang—and even one or two of them by the next day had received a call and had had to be paged in alcoholic dens or discreetly fetched from houses of ill-repute.

Because it was the next day that mattered, of course. May 2 was for cabinet posts and for important noncabinet jobs in the Foreign Office or the Treasury. May 3 was for the lesser jobs in the lesser ministries—posts that people like me, four years in Parliament and an occasional Opposition front-bench spokesman, might hope for. And how we did hope! How we did watch the television, dash out for an evening newspaper and dash back to the phone, ring our friends for hurried conversations about who was in, who had heard nothing yet, who was sure to hear before long.

At ten past two the phone rang. And it wasn't a friend, wasn't a constituent congratulating me or a local newspaper wanting a quote. It was Downing Street, inquiring whether it would be convenient for me to come and see the Prime Minister. Suppressing any inclination to irony or witticism, I murmured respectfully that it was quite convenient and that I would be there as soon as possible. I put the phone down reverently, but with a sudden rush of blood to the head I burst out into Cavaradossi's "Vittoria! Vittoria!"—the cry of triumph turning into a horrible shriek on the high C as I ran to the door of my flat, straightening my tie in the hall mirror. I was already wearing my only suit.

I wonder what it felt like for those who didn't get a call, taking off their suits at night.

Twenty minutes later it was over. The scenario was this: drive from my Pimlico flat to the House, walk across Parliament Square to Downing Street, greet the policeman on the door and be ushered in (*first time ever*), brief wait, then into the PM's office, get the offer, restrain extravagant thanks (he'll have had enough of those, with nearly a hundred jobs to fill—already the grin is a bit strained), then back to the front door, and out into Downing Street again.

There were still flushed and happy crowds at the gates that lead into Whitehall. As I'd gone through them I had heard people ask, "Who's that?" As I stood for a moment on the step, with the odd camera flashing, I wanted to go over to them and say: "I'm Colin Pinnock, and I'm the new junior minister in the Department of Education and Training, with special responsibility for the handicapped and the disadvantaged." On second thought it didn't seem like a good idea—politicians have to have a quick nose for the potentially ridiculous—and with one more smile to the much-diminished band of photographers, who were snapping as much for the record as for the newspapers, I walked directly to my new department in the tall, gloomy building in Great Smith Street.

They knew I was coming, of course. They'd been alerted from Downing Street as soon as I'd accepted. I was the fourth new minister they had received in two days.

"Welcome to the Department, Minister," said the doorman, and gestured to a little knot of welcomers, including the civil servant who was to be my private secretary and several members of his staff. After routine, slightly wary greetings all round they led me to the obscure part of the building from which our section functioned, and to my private office, where I was to assume responsibility for the halt and the blind, the slow learners and the underachievers, the late developers and the kids with special needs, the dyslexics and the inner-city dropouts.

"Let's get down to work," I said to my private secretary. "That means you briefing me."

Five hours later, in mid-evening, I decided to call it a day. I had learned volumes in that time. I decided I liked my private secretary, Patrick Lat-terby—liked him in a trusting, low-keyed kind of way: I would no doubt have a drink with him from time to time, but it was never going to be a socializing, buddy-pal kind of relationship. He was straightforward, dependable, unexciting. Would anybody want an exciting civil servant (supposing one could be found) as his private secretary? I decided I was lucky.

I realized quite quickly that my predecessor had been a career politician with no interest in his particular responsibilities at the Ministry. All the initiatives and projects had come from his civil servants, and Patrick went over not only these but also various other options which had been discarded or put on the back burner and which he thought I might want to revive. We discussed the parameters of my job, the possibilities of it—and, most usefully, the dangers. I was taken to meet the permanent secretary, a woman close to retirement age called Margaret Stevens, and we had a getting-to-know-you chat. She is the Secretary of State's principal adviser, a great force in the Depart-ment, practically a god. She dropped by into my little portion of her kingdom later on—a most unusual occurrence, but changes in government bring exceptional necessities with them, and this dropping in brought the only oddity of my first day at the Department.

Patrick and I were going over papers, and I was conscious of the door opening. I glanced up, only to see her start. It was a tiny jump—almost imperceptible, yet I perceived it, in the fraction of a second before my eyes tactfully went back to my papers again. Then she came forward and I rose to welcome her. She was entirely self-possessed by now, and put a folder down in front of Patrick.

"Potential land mine," she said. "Utmost secrecy and action soonest."

"Nothing to do with my appointment, I hope," I said smiling.

"Nothing at all. A matter your predecessor said he'd seen to six months ago but hadn't, and it could blow up in our faces. Patrick will fix it. You concentrate on the future."

That was all, and I put it out of my mind, and that tiny start as well. At eight o'clock we wound things up.

"You'll want to get back to your family," I said to Patrick, "and all I want to do at the moment is get back to my flat, pour myself a drink, feel chuffed with myself for an hour or two, then have an early night."

"Sounds sensible," Patrick Latterby said. "You're sure there's nothing else you want from me?"

"Nothing that can't wait till tomorrow."

He went off like a man who's beginning to think he's in luck with his new boss. I packed a pile of papers into my nice new red box and walked back to fetch my car from the Palace of Westminster parking lot. I'd told Patrick I wouldn't want an official car and driver until next morning. The policeman on the gate gave me a broad grin.

"Got yourself a nice new job...sir?"

PC Marrit was always perky and always friendly. He had been complained about several times by ministers in the former government who equated friendliness with lack of respect. No doubt some of our people, with time, would contract the disease of self-importance.

"Department of Education. Couldn't have asked for anything more to my taste. Dealing with the handicapped and the deprived."

"Well, I'll expect results for my daughter, then."

"Is your daughter handicapped?"

"Not really—only by the school she goes to.

They don't expect anything from the kids so they don't get anything out of them."

I nodded.

"London schools are going to be one of our problems, or our challenges I suppose I should say."

I stayed talking to him for a minute or two, and then went to get my car. Even now, the evening after our election victory, driving was still that bit hazardous around Westminster—there were people milling around, some of them drunkenly lurching off onto the road, camera crews still interviewing new MPs and in the interval sampling vox pop. I made it home, though—in any case the intoxication of victory would not register on a Breathalyzer.

My flat is in a block called Ruskin Terrace that used to be all Council tenants. Some of them had been sold to tenants by Westminster City Council, and the man who sold me his made a breathtaking profit on the deal. It's on the third floor, has a view of the river, and is a good-sized family flat. I should feel guilty about living there, but mostly I just don't think about it. Someone farther along the balcony clapped as I approached my flat, and I grinned and waved like royalty. I took the lift up, let myself into the flat, stepping over a small mountain of post, and switched on the lights. The living room was clean and welcoming—I had tidied up in the morning, while waiting for that phone call. I went into the kitchen, pulled out from the freezer a frozen portion of Bolognese sauce, then put it into a saucepan on the hot plate and began boiling water for the spaghetti. I stood for a moment savoring normality in the midst of tremendous upheaval. I opened a bottle of red wine, poured a good-sized glass, and went back to the living room.

Alone. Alone as a member of the government. Alone as a minister of the Crown. Alone as the minister responsible for children and adults who'd had a raw deal. The opportunities! The challenges! The dangers! I was high on the future, high on my career. I felt my life had been leading up to this, every tiny event a step forward, culminating in that handshake in Downing Street. I wondered if it would have felt even sweeter if I'd still had Susan to share it with me. Being honest with myself I didn't see how it could have been.

Music. I needed music. Not anything raucous and triumphal now—something gentle, ruminative. Maybe something English. English music isn't usually one of my things, but I found Vaughan Williams's Fifth and put it on the CD player. Then I went back to the hall to pick up my post.

Most of it wasn't post. The normal business of living and working and sending bills somehow gets suspended in Britain at election time. The real post at the bottom of the pile, which had been there when I left the flat that afternoon, was dwarfed by the cards, notes, scruffy pieces of paper that had been stuffed through my letterbox by neighbors and by friends who lived in the vicinity. Somehow or other the news of my appointment had got around. The cards and notes were congratulatory, hortatory, humorous, or satirical. Only one was a little snide—not bad by the standards of political life. An Australian research assistant I'd used, a young student with the most exquisite English accent, had scrawled "Good on yer, Cobber" on a National Portrait Gallery card of Clem Attlee. I chuckled, suspended operations for the moment, and went to put on the spaghetti. Then I came back to continue going through the pile.

The top one was an old-fashioned plain postcard, rather grubby round the edges. It had a stamp on it, but the stamp hadn't been postmarked. The address was correct, in easily legible, rather old-fashioned handwriting which somehow suggested to me that the sender didn't do a great deal of writing these days. I turned the card over. On the blank reverse there was written, in capitals, one stark question:

WHO DO YOU THINK YOU ARE?

CHAPTER TWO

Back to My Roots

I can't pretend I thought much about the postcard and its message during the rest of the evening. The euphoria gripping me was too powerful for that. Yesterday I had been a newly reelected MP known to few, tonight I was a minister of the Crown. A minister of the Crown known to few, I told myself, in a vain attempt to keep my feet on the ground. But there were enormous opportunities to do good, and to be seen to be doing good, and promotion in a year or two's time was a definite possibility. My state was like what people always say champagne induces, though it only seems to induce flatulence in me.

So if I thought about it at all, it was as an attempt to cut me down to size, tell me I was getting a lot too big for my boots. It did seem to me that it was awfully early for a condemnation of this kind: getting above yourself usually takes time. But perhaps it was a prophecy more than a judgment. Someone could have heard of my appointment (how? on the radio? in the *Evening Standard?*) and decided to give me a dour warning. Someone jealous, presumably. Then, also presumably, someone who knew me. But with a politician that "knew" could be wide, covering a variety of different kinds of knowing. It could be a constituent, for example, who had taken against me—perhaps over something I'd done for him, or failed to do. It could be someone whom I'd been involved with years ago in student politics. It could be someone who'd been a rival for the nomination when I got my Milton seat. Equally it could be someone who knew me well, someone, even, whom I liked, without realizing their jealousy of me.

I didn't give it much more thought than that. As I sluiced my plate under the hot tap I realized the Vaughan Williams had failed to calm me. I put on *Showboat* instead. To hell with calming down. I needed something to match my excitement.

But I did think of that card again in the early hours, when I was drowsing between sleep and waking, wanting to go in to start work in earnest but knowing I couldn't do that at 5 A.M. At one transition from sleeping to waking my half-conscious mind said to me: "That was not what the writer meant."

It came into my mind, apparently from nowhere. He was not telling me I was too big for my boots. Otherwise he would have made it more explicit: YOU'RE GETTING ABOVE YOURSELF. WHO DO YOU THINK YOU ARE? But he (or she) didn't. The writer just asked the bleak question, in capitals for dramatic effect: WHO DO YOU THINK YOU ARE? Put baldly like that, it was almost like asking you what you thought the point of existence was. At a more specific level it seemed to want me to focus on how I had come into the world.

I lay there, luxuriously, thinking about the postcard. It was stamped, with no postmark. That meant it could have come through the post—it happened quite frequently these days. But if that was the case, it would mean that it was posted before I had been given my job in the new government. As far as I could remember it lay in the midst of personal messages posted through the letterbox by people in the flats or living nearby. Since there was no second post on a Saturday, it seemed likely it was pushed through the door by the sender. Why? A change of mind? Or because the postcard was already stamped for another use, and he/she then decided to use it on me?

That seemed unprofitable speculation. So did consideration of the grubbiness of the card. More interesting was the fact that there was apparently no attempt to disguise the handwriting, beyond the use of capitals. The writer had no fear that I would recognize it. Or did not care whether I did or not.

I put the thoughts from me. What a daft thing to mull over on a wonderful day. Seven o'clock. Soon the wonderful day would start in earnest. I shaved, showered, and slotted two pieces of toast into the toaster.

"Oh, what a beautiful morning!" I sang.

Oklahoma, the best musical there ever was. No, the second-best. After *Showboat*.

It was a Sunday, a silly day to begin work. Patrick Latterby had told me that I could get into the Ministry from nine o'clock onward, and had promised that he would come in for a couple of hours around eleven, to point me in the direction of the first substantial issues I was likely to face. I rang to cancel the official car and set off to walk to work. Grosvenor Street and Millbank were warm, with a haze that was just lifting. I could still sense excitement in the air. That's a politician for you. What's the betting that a new minister in a Tory government reelected for the fourth time also felt excitement in the air on his way to work? You sense around you what you feel inside you. I dawdled along, had a cigarette in Victoria Gardens, and promptly at nine o'clock was at the door of the Ministry.

"Well, you're keen," said the doorman, smiling in an I've-seen-it-all way.

"I suppose new young ministers are always keen," I said. "Sorry to bring you in on a Sunday."

"No sweat. Double time suits me fine," he said, grinning. "Always happens when there's a new government with new faces. Now, can you find your way?"

I assured him I could find my way, and I spent the next couple of hours partly in rereading the stuff I'd gone through sketchily the day before, partly in walking round the Ministry and finding where every subsection was. When Patrick came in we had a good, hard session dealing with problems on the horizon and discussing the prioritization of several possible contributions of my section to any government legislative program. At a quarter to one I asked him if he had time for a drink, and he nodded.

"Have to be a quick one, though."

We went to the Bull and Barrel, and I managed to get a thickly filled sandwich with my pint. We stood drinking companionably by a window, talking with a degree of ease, but keeping off issues we shouldn't be discussing in a public place. He told me about his background, about where his children went to school, and what his wife was thinking of doing when they were a bit older. We were just getting to a transition point when he would ask me for matching personal details when, out of the blue it seemed, I heard myself asking:

"Do you know if my appointment got any coverage in the media?"

Patrick smiled secretively, apparently registering that I was not immune to the vanity of politicians.

"There was a picture in the *Evening Standard*. They had a whole page of junior ministerial appointees, so you were one of twelve or so, all photographed arriving at No. 10 or leaving it."

"I see."

"Are you wanting a photograph to send your parents?"

"I've only got a father, and I'm afraid he's past registering. What about television?"

"I don't know. My wife didn't mention seeing my new minister. I'd doubt it. With television news these days you'd be lucky to be mentioned on a quick run-through of junior posts. Why?"

I decided to go carefully here. If someone was wanting me to focus on my own background there might be reasons to keep other people out of the matter.

"Oh, I just got rather an odd postcard yesterday, and I wondered what sparked it off."

"Can't be the *Standard* photograph if you got it yesterday."

"I suspect it was put through the door."

"What kind of thing was it?"

I took a swill of my beer.

"Seemed to think I was getting above myself."

Patrick laughed.

"In record time! You could say that in time every government minister gets above himself, but on the first day!"

"When the process does start you'll have to give me a warning."

"Oh, we always do, in subtle little ways. Most politicians find subtle little ways of ignoring the warnings. But you're worried about this postcard, aren't you?"

"I just wonder what kind of person would send something like that on my first day as a minister."

"Some kind of nutter, I imagine. We can screen nutters at the Department. Most of them are totally harmless. A nutter who has your home address and access to your letterbox is a bit more worrying. You could inform the police at the Houses of Parliament, but I think I'd wait before doing that."

"Oh, sure. I've no evidence it's anything other than a harmless crank. You seem to have a lot of experience of the type."

Patrick took a pull at his pint before he replied.

"I do, but the type may change with the new government. The previous lot had been in a long time, so people had had time to develop personal obsessions: they had conceived a desperate passion for Michael Heseltine, for example, convinced themselves that Michael Portillo was the father of their unborn child."

"*Real* nutters," I commented. Patrick smiled a Civil Service sort of smile. He was telling me that jokes about our opponents were out of bounds.

"But hardly any of the new men are widely known on a personal level," he went on. "By that I mean few have become public personalities whom people feel they know. So I would guess that your correspondent either *does* know you personally, or else his or her grievance is political: someone who really feels it an affront for you people to get into power at all."

"Plenty of those, I suppose," I said. "So all things considered, the best thing to do is put the whole thing out of my mind, unless she comes back for a second go at me."

"He or she. Yes, I think so."

"He or she, of course. I don't know why I said she. Perhaps it was the handwriting, or because the nutters you mentioned must have all been women."

"They come in all shapes and sizes and sexes, I assure you. The difficulty is to sort out the difficult and dangerous ones."

"Of course. I suppose the truth is all that the others call for is a thick skin."

Patrick raised his eyebrows.

"Surely you've got that already."

"I suppose so. I'm a Yorkshireman, and a Yorkshire MP. I've had to get used to bluntness. Somehow personal things are different."

"I'm not sure that they are," Patrick said, finishing his pint. "The political slides quite easily into the personal. You'd be well advised to get an all-purpose thick skin pretty damned quick. This government will have a honeymoon period, but after that, if there are any peccadillos, political or personal, to make capital out of, the opposition and the tabloids will make sure the shit starts flying—pardon my off-duty language—the same as with the last government. Are there any skeletons in your cupboard?"

I shook my head with more confidence than I felt.

"I haven't even got a girlfriend at the moment. We split up last year. We'd lived together for two years."

"That counts as respectability these days."

"But I've had no illegitimate children, never molested minors, haven't even had a boyfriend."

"That's starting to count as respectability with your lot."

"Looking back, I feel almost ashamed at the dullness of my personal life."

"You should be grateful for it. But it's a pity you

and your girlfriend split up."

I shrugged.

"Politicians are a bit like policemen: they need a stable home base more than most, but the conditions of the job make it very unlikely they'll have one. I think for the moment loneliness is the lesser of two evils. The thought of having a relationship that I had no time to give anything to is not attractive."

And, symbolically, off he went home to family and Sunday lunch, and off I went back to the Ministry.

It was not this talk of a stable family base that decided me to go and see my father the next weekend. My father was not in a condition to provide me with any sort of base. I had decided, whether I got a job in the government or not, to be as good a constituency MP as I had been in the last Parliament. Many of the MPs who were joyfully thrown out at the election were men (usually men) who had treated their constituencies as a sort of fief-dom: they gave voters the impression that they believed they held their seats as a right. The voters had taken pleasure in showing them that they were mistaken. Arrogance is not a preserve of any one political party, and I was resolved not to fall into that trap.

So on Friday night, at the end of a week of stimulus and discovery such as I had never had in my life before—I was, I think, drunk with delight in power, experiencing all its aphrodisiac qualities—I took the train to my constituency, to my home.

That is not quite true: my constituency is Milton in South Yorkshire, and my home—the home where I grew up—is in the nearby village of Bardsley, which has become over the years a sort of dormitory suburb of Milton, but which lies in a neighboring constituency. However, I represented the place where I had gone to school, where all my oldest friends were, where I had seen my first films and plays and concerts, where all my early memories were. It is a matter of pride that they chose me.

It was natural that in the train I should think about that, and about my early years. I hadn't been born in Bardsley, but my parents had moved there when I was only a few weeks old. My father had had a job in local government in Milton, in the planning office. He had retired ten years before, and he and my mother had had a happy time pottering, doing charity work, and watching my political ambitions bearing fruit. This last made them very happy. I know neither of them sympathized with my views, but nevertheless the day I was elected to Westminster was the proudest of their lives, and the village joked about the fact that they could only with difficulty be persuaded to talk on any other subject.

Then, two years ago, my mother had been diagnosed as suffering from cancer, which had been mercifully fast in its progress. After her death my father had been a lost man, and had declined mentally so badly that six months before he had had to go into a nursing home. It was there I would go to visit him the next afternoon, tell him my news, and know that he would nod and understand almost nothing. Seventy-five is too young to be in that state. I asked myself if, had I been living at home, the decline would have come more slowly.

I slept in my old bed, in the house I grew up in, then I held a "surgery" at my party headquarters (half the people seemed to come along not with a problem, but to tell me how delighted they were with the change of government). Then the local party chairman drove me to the Ivies.

I did the best I could for my father, and the

Ivies was it, granted that he wanted (in so far as he could formulate a preference) to stay in the area that had been his home for thirty-five years. The street frontage was a modest-sized Victorian home, the windows of which peered through trailing stems of ivy and other climbing creepers. Behind it, at the end of a long, well-stocked garden, was a modern annex, with big windows, better central heating, and every sort of provision for the disabled. I opted for the annex, for comfort rather than style. My father was not in a condition to care for style.

My instinct was always to walk straight through the place to my father's room. There is altogether too much of memento mori about these homes, however well run—or rather, not reminders of the horrors of death, but of the horrors of the approach of death. But I am an MP—and there were plenty of very spry people there, people with a lively interest in the great world around them. People with a vote, who would use it if possible. I'd got to know many of them, and they wanted to stop me, congratulate me, ask what it felt like to be in government, and so on. "I won't keep you," they all said, as they launched into stories of what it felt like when the election results of 1945 came through, or how they'd once met Harold Wilson. It was half an hour before I could get to my father.

The sun was shining into his room, which was cheerful if inevitably slightly hospital in feel. He was half awake and half asleep, as he is for much of the time.

"Hello…Colin," he said.

He always dredges up my name, eventually. It will be horrible when he finally fails to do so.

"Hello, Dad."

"Still…*there?*"

By now I knew what he wanted to ask me.

"That's right," I said, sitting down by his bed. "Still MP for Milton. We had an election last week. I got in with a much bigger majority. We're the government now."

That was too much for him. His eyes glazed over and he just murmured, "Good, good."

My father's face has always been rather gaunt— and his body, too. I've always thought of him as a rather splendid old Viking leader, though not a ravaging and pillaging one. When I was small he was keen to join in whatever game I wanted to play: he went at it with a will, but he was a little short on fun. He was just, he was dependable, he was undemonstrably loving, but I was always conscious that he was old. Older, at any rate, than other children's fathers. My mother was softer and sweeter, and it wasn't so noticeable with her.

"How's…Susan?"

Oddly enough he always remembered Susan's name. I'd told him a year ago that we had split up, but if it registered then it had been eradicated since. He'd liked Susan, and perhaps to him she represented the continuation of the line. Absurd that ordinary people should think in those terms, but they still do.

"Susan's fine, Dad."

"You haven't…?"

"No, Dad. No wedding plans yet."

I'd toyed with the idea of lying to him about that, of inventing wedding plans to string him along. But it seemed to strip him of still more of his dignity (he'd been, in his later years, a very dignified old man). And in any case in his mental state he couldn't be said to *worry* about that or anything else—not, anyway, for more than a few seconds.

He nodded regretfully and then seemed to sink back toward slumber, or at any rate toward that twilight state that is neither consciousness nor unconsciousness. I took his hand, which was lying on the counterpane, and a tiny smile from him registered my having done so.

I stayed there for a long time, his hand in my hand. A lot of my visits were like this—just my being there with him. I could have thought about all my departmental concerns, but oddly enough that day I could think only of the past: of cricket games on the beach at Bridlington, with Dad's splendidly gangling overarm bowling; all of us round the table at one of my mother's Sunday teas; coming home from school to tell them I'd won a scholarship to St. John's College. The light in their eyes was one of the things I could always bank on when I brought them good news of myself.

I was suddenly conscious that my father had opened his eyes. He was looking at me—his eyes bleary still, as they always were now, but in the back of them something of that same light, that irrepressible pride.

"We were so happy when you came," he said.

Then, after a moment, the old eyes closed again, and I sat there pondering over that word "came."

CHAPTER THREE

Best Friend

I stayed with my dad for ten minutes, holding his hand, making sure he had left that no-man's-land where he was neither "here" nor "there" and was soundly asleep.

My first thoughts were that I was foolish to make anything at all of my father's words. It was all a matter of generations. To people of his age babies "arrived," or more rarely "came." It was, I supposed, a late survival of Victorian propriety. "I had to give up work when my son arrived," a woman would say. Or "naturally things changed when my daughter came." It neatly sidestepped all consideration of the messy process of conception and childbirth. Silly, maybe, but not something to put any weight on.

On the other hand I never remembered my father using any such genteelism before, and he used direct words. Babies were "born." Though on consideration I never remember him or my mother saying anything about my birth—whether it had been easy or difficult, whether they had been frightened at the prospect of such a late first delivery (my mother was forty), whether my father had been in the maternity ward with my mother at the time of the birth (probably not in 1962), whether there were any amusing or terrifying moments during labor.

Nothing.

That had never struck me as odd before. I had, so to speak, taken myself and my birth for granted. Surely most people do. And the average parent doesn't embarrass a child by stories of how he came into the world. Yet somehow that phrase still had a ring to me of something—what?—something that my father and my mother often discussed together when I was not there. "We were so happy when he came," I could imagine them saying, and I could imagine too a look of complicity passing between them, as I sometimes saw it do when I had done something that pleased them—got into Cambridge, got the nomination for the Milton seat, got elected in the by-election. And in this case I imagined that look of complicity as meaning: "when he *came*. When he was delivered to us. When someone handed him over to us and our hearts soared with joy because at last we had a baby."

I was getting fanciful. I had no evidence they ever did anything of the sort. Nevertheless I walked back to my old home in Bardsley, a matter of two miles, and in between greeting people and swapping the odd word about my new eminence I thought about it, about the implications of my vague suspicions if they were right, about what it meant to me—whether in fact it meant anything at all.

When I got home to Connaught Avenue I made myself two monster sandwiches with a tin of corned beef I found in the pantry and sat considering. My first and firmest conclusion was that I didn't give a damn if I was adopted. My dad was my dad. My mother, still vivid in my mind in spite of the two years since her death, was my mother and always would be. And my certainty was not just because no one could wish for better parents, but because they were the ones who had always been *there*. No suddenly discovered natural parent could trump that, or wipe out the love and gratitude it aroused in me.

And if that natural parent turned out to be some kind of wrong-un (was that what the postcard had implied?) it wouldn't faze me one iota. I didn't believe in "bad blood." Still, on consideration, over a cup of strong tea, I had to admit it would interest me no end.

I shook myself. I was jumping the gun with a vengeance—jumping several guns, in fact. I decided I would go and have a talk with George Eakin, my father's best friend—the only friend he had who was still alive. It was George who had alerted me to my father's increasing vagueness and inability to cope, George who had made sure he was connected to my father by an accessible bell which could summon him at any time. I would have paid him a visit in any case, but the conversation would probably have taken a different turn if I hadn't been preoccupied with the postcard and its stark question.

George lived just around the corner, coping well on his own after ten years of widowerhood. The first years, I knew, had been rocky, because he had been born into, and accepted, a traditional working-class pattern of the man as breadwinner and the woman as homemaker. But George was nothing if not capable, and he solved problems of cooking, washing, and cleaning for himself with the same clear-eyed practicality as he had brought to problems at the mine where he'd worked. When he saw me on the doorstep his eyes lit up with pleasure, though not surprise.

"Colin! Thought you might come round. Have you got time for a cup of tea, lad?"

"I'm relying on you for one."

"Don't give me that. Your mother wasn't so daft that she brought you up to be helpless."

He was walking, slowly but firmly, down the hall to the kitchen. I remembered George throughout my childhood as a well-set-up man: he'd made his way up the local ladder from working at the pit face to an administrative job in the mining industry, and at weekends he was a keen walker and an enthusiastic cricketer—something of a slogger, but a match-winner at his best. Now his frame had shrunk, but his spirit was still determined. He had made it to middle-class respectability, but he had never lost his humanity or his enthusiasm for experience. He was as traveled as any workingman of his generation, and he'd failed only by a whisker on his one attempt to get into Parliament, at the

1966 election.

"Won't take a minute," he said, bustling round the square, family-sized kitchen. "Got a few biscuits here. Chocolate you like, don't you? Pretty poor celebration, but I don't keep whiskey in the house now I'm not allowed it. How's your dad?"

"Pretty much the same. All there is to hope now is that it doesn't go on too long."

"Aye," he said ruminatively, his sharp eye on me. "That's a hard thing to have to say."

"It's wanting what's best for him, and what he would want for himself. He would hate not being in control, if he could realize it."

"He would. And 'appen he does realize it, now and then, when the haze clears a bit. We both know your dad, don't we, Colin? But what I was meaning was that it's a hard thing for you. 'Specially at this time."

"It is." I nodded.

"But I'm forgetting my manners. I ought to have congratulated you properly." He turned and shook my hand, making it something heartfelt rather than absurd, which it could have been. "I didn't write because writing's hard these days, and I knew you'd be round as soon as you could. Eh, lad, it's a right good opportunity for you, though, isn't it?"

"It is, George. I couldn't ask for better."

"And getting opportunities for folk who've never had even the opportunities we had, which wasn't all that much. Tell me about how it feels to be a minister, Colin. And tell me what you're planning on doing."

Those two questions were typical of George: the human side and the political side—they existed on a twin track in his mind. The conversation lasted us into the living room and through the first cup and several biscuits.

"Have you been to see Dad?" I asked, in a pause.

"Oh aye. Went a week ago—our Ray took me and waited. Always fond of your dad, was Ray. I told your father about you getting into the government, but he couldn't take it in—you know how it is."

"I know. I tried to tell him too, but it didn't get through. He'd have been so chuffed!"

"He would. He and your mum were so proud of you always. Every other step has meant so much to them, and now this last, the best one of all comes along and your mother's gone and your dad's beyond rejoicing. *That* must be hard, too."

"It is."

"You're right, you know. There's nothing to hope for. It's a pity the Good Lord if He exists didn't make the physical decay go along with the mental one, so the agony wasn't prolonged. But there you are—He didn't."

George always spoke respectfully of God, in case He existed.

"I hate seeing him there. It's as if he was stranded and unhappy in a foreign country," I said. "Dad was such a home person—always there, either in the house or pottering around the garden. It's like a ghost house now."

"It's the same for me when I walk past and see the garden," said George. "That's where I saw him first."

"I know. You brought him a cutting."

"That were a day or two later. I first saw him the day you all moved here, with the Pickford van in the street and your dad supervising the men. I didn't guess what mates we were going to be. But the next day I spoke to him in the garden. It was a bit overgrown, like it is now, and your dad never liked mess. So I leaned on the fence and we had a bit of a natter. I liked him at once, but with your dad—and your mam, too—you only got close step by step."

"Mum and I were up here by then?"

"Oh yes. We'd only been talking for a few minutes and you started crying in the house. Your dad excused himself and ran inside. I thought to myself: 'You're a new father, for all you look middle-aged and older than I am meself.'"

"Did you see me then?"

"No, I didn't catch sight of the mighty morsel that you were till some days later. That's when I first met your mam. I called with a cutting from my garden for their garden—I used to like to do that with new people in the area, as you know, Colin: it gave us a link, a talking-point. Of course with your dad and mam it grew into something much more than that. Anyway, your father was out, and your mother was rather shy, as she always was, but welcoming for all that. You were in your pram in the hall, and as soon as you decided to have a bellow she was there, and taking you up in her arms, and behaving as if she thought your last minutes were come."

"Mum always was overprotective."

"Terribly. I gave her advice—our Ray was five

by then, and we'd been through it all before him with the two elder ones, as you know, so we were quite relaxed about it all. Over the years she improved, gave you plenty of freedom, though it went against the grain as I'm sure you grew to realize. If she could have had you within sight for twenty-four hours of the day that's what Elizabeth would have liked. But there—she was a sensible woman, and she saw it wouldn't do. And of course when I first saw you, you were no age. It's natural to be overprotective of a new baby."

"How old was I?"

"They said three weeks, but I'd have guessed less."

At that point he looked up, and saw something in my face.

"Sorry for all these questions," I said hurriedly. "I suppose it's natural, seeing Dad in his present state, wanting to go back to the beginning."

He digested this while pouring us both second cups of tea.

"Nay, lad, don't treat me like a goobie," he said at last. "You've been coming to see your dad at the Ivies these last six months, and dropping in on me afterward as often as not, but we haven't had any of these trips down Memory Lane. Come clean,

Colin. What is it has sparked all this off?"

So I swore him to secrecy (which was unnecessary) and told him. George took his time before he responded.

"I always like the simple explanation, at least until it becomes impossible to hold it any longer. I think somebody's got the idea you're getting too big for your boots—not that you *are*, Colin, don't get me wrong. Or maybe this someone thinks there's a danger of it, and you ought to be warned."

"In that case they should have sent messages to all the new ministers. We're all facing the same moral dangers, and some of us are outgrowing our boots at double-quick speed. But I've not heard of any other cards."

"Mebbe them as receive them kept quiet about them because they're too sensible to take it as seriously as you do, lad—have you thought of that?"

"I'll keep it in mind as a possibility," I said, grinning. He grinned back. We understood each other perfectly, George and I—in some ways better than my father and me, because we were on the same political wavelength. When I was in my teens we would often go off on long tramps around the hills and moors of West and North Yorkshire, sometimes talking, sometimes companionably silent. My father had shown no jealousy about this. George Eakin was one person he trusted absolutely.

"You said I looked less than three weeks old," I said—and George sighed, because he'd have preferred to let the thing drop entirely. "It seems odd to move with a baby that young."

"Probably they had no choice. Your dad was moving to a new job, remember."

I pursed my lips skeptically.

"He was high up in the Milton Council planning offices. Surely they'd have given him a few weeks' leeway?"

"He could have wanted to make a new start: new baby, new job, new part of the country to live in…I'd have to admit there was a bit of comment at the time: the neighbors wondered why she didn't stay behind with friends or relatives, then come up when the baby—you—was a little bit older."

"I never heard of any relatives or friends back in the Southampton area. It was as if they made a clean break."

"I admit they never talked about anyone close,

or had anyone to stay. There again, even if there was anyone your mam could have stayed with, a middle-aged couple with a longed-for new baby—and you were that, lad, that I do know—would probably want to share the first few weeks of his life, be together for it."

"I'm sure they did. But I bet they could have shared it back in Southampton if they'd really wanted to." Something he had said earlier had struck me, and I went back to it. "I think you hit the nail on the head when you said new baby, new job, new part of the country. The question is why? If—"

"Aye, lad, you don't have to spell it out. I'm not so failing in my mind that I don't get your drift."

"If," I went on, remorseless in the face of his disgust, "I hadn't been born to them, if I had been acquired by them in some unofficial, even illegal, form of adoption, then they would have *needed* to make a completely clean break."

George Eakin nodded.

"And would it make any difference to your feelings for them if that's what did happen?"

"No, I've thought about that. No difference at all."

"Then why are you mithering and worriting about it?" he said, not concealing his exasperation. "Let sleeping dogs lie—sleeping demons, more like."

"If I'm right about the postcard the demons are not lying anyway. They're rearing up and making their presence felt."

George considered this in his habitual measured way.

"Colin, you've had your photo in the papers, been on telly when the poll at Milton was announced, before long you'll be interviewed about this and that, and your face will go into houses up and down the country. You have a pretty individual face—not the standard article. What if the poor girl who gave you up as a baby, maybe for money, sees you, recognizes herself or your father in you, and says, 'That's my child, grown up.' Do you think it would add to her happiness? Do you think if she made herself known to you that you would take the time or trouble to form any kind of relationship with her that would mean anything to her or to you?"

That I did have to think about.

"At the moment probably no."

"Then forget about it, lad. The way you're going

can't possibly lead to happiness, and most likely would lead to pain. Pain probably for you, almost certainly for her."

I thought about that for a time, and was forced to agree.

"You're right, George. I'll forget about it."

So we talked about other things, and eventually I went home, back to the semidetached I grew up in, back to sleep in my own bedroom, with the Roald Dahl books on the book-shelves, along with my old school textbooks, and the classic novels I'd studied for exams with all my scrawled notes in the margins, and the old exercise books with the essays I'd written in them. The detritus of a life that had seemed crowned with hope and success, but which suddenly seemed empty. Who was I? Where had I come from? Why was I now, with my father senile, left without relatives, without anybody with links to the past who could tell me how I had come into the world?

I would forget about it, I had said to George. But I now made the mental proviso: if I am allowed to forget about it. And something in me hoped I would not be.

∽∽∽

It was early afternoon when I got back to my

Pimlico flat, and I settled into a session at my ministerial papers. It was about seven o'clock when I had a surprising phone call.

"Colin Pinnock speaking."

"Hello, Colin."

"Susan!"

Suddenly she was there before me, the wide-spaced eyes, the thick auburn hair forming a flaming halo, the mouth set in a slightly skeptical expression. I knew from just the two words that she would be skeptical that night.

"I'm just ringing to congratulate you on your new greatness."

"Don't give me that line. I'm as lowly a drudge as any government could employ."

"Hmm. You sound pretty pleased with yourself. I thought of ringing last week, but I knew you'd be busy and...well, somehow it seemed to look bad."

"It wouldn't have. We're still friends, aren't we?"

"I suppose so. It's just that we're friends who haven't seen each other or exchanged a word since we split up."

"No, I suppose we haven't." I was unable to keep the surprise out of my voice, because I really hadn't realized. She obviously had. "I suppose as usual it's really a matter of me getting totally caught up politically."

"I wouldn't be surprised," said Susan dryly.

"By the way, my dad thinks we're still together. Asks about you every time I go to see him."

"Really? I suppose that means he's getting worse."

"Yes. Quite quickly. He's in a nursing home, and just about knows me. It seems better not to try to tell him about us. Not that he'd take it in if I did."

"Sad. I always liked him."

"I know. And he you….To me he'll always be my dad."

There was a silence at the other end of the line.

"What on earth do you mean?"

"Sorry, I was thinking aloud. It's…something that's come up. It's been suggested I was adopted, maybe illegally."

Susan practically brayed at me.

"For God's sake! 'It's been suggested!' You sound like a government minister already."

"I am a government minister already. All right, then: I got a postcard saying 'WHO DO YOU THINK YOU ARE?'"

"Good question. Obviously from someone who thinks you're beginning to sound like a pompous prat. I thought the same a moment or two ago."

"I got it on the day I got the Education job."

"Oh…still, they could have been following you during the election. Was likely victory and possible government position making you swell like a bullfrog? All right, don't answer that. Maybe it was one of the people standing against you wrote the card, wanting to get a dig in. Everyone knew it was going to be a landslide, but if it hadn't been the Tories and the Liberal Democrats would both have been in with a chance in the Milton seat."

"Hmmm. I'll keep the possibility in mind."

"Though actually, when I come to think about it…"

"Yes?"

"It always struck me that physically you had not the slightest resemblance to your father or your mother."

"That's not unusual."

"No. But you have such a strongly marked face: thick eyebrows, strong chin, somehow *assertive* in the effect you make. Whereas your father's was a quiet, retiring type of face, in spite of the cragginess. And your mother, even in old age, was sweetly pretty."

"I never thought I resembled them as a person either."

"No. Too hail-fellow, too assured and emphatic."

"I love your command of English, but I can think of nicer adjectives for myself."

I could hear Susan thinking. We really know each other very well by now.

"Colin, if you ever want any digging done about yourself, just say the word. Either I can do it myself, or I could find someone who would do it for you without charging the earth. You know I'm interested in demographic change in the postwar period, particularly relocation."

"You mean people moving. Now who's sounding like a pompous prat? At least you're not telling me to let it alone."

"When did that ever stop you doing what you want to do?"

"Thanks anyway, Susan. I may well get in touch."

"I could tell you were worried, and wanted to talk. Otherwise you'd never have said that about he'd always be your dad."

She knew me quite as well as I knew her, or

better. She knew I hadn't been thinking aloud, but had dropped it into the conversation deliberately. Susan is a historian specializing in the postwar period, with a bias in favor of the view that changes of government generally made no difference at all to ordinary people's lives. That hadn't helped when I spent on political matters most of the time I should have spent with her. I stood for a moment when I'd put the phone down, wondering whether I welcomed her reappearance in my life, and deciding that on this semiprofessional level I did welcome it, but it didn't change the fact that I was not interested in getting into a relationship that was a sort of spare-time recreation, coming a bad second to my job.

I often think I have a lot of rather old-fashioned Puritan attitudes, probably inherited or acquired from my father.

The next morning I got a postcard in my mail. It read:

NOT WHO YOU THOUGHT YOU WERE,
ARE YOU?

At least now I could discount the idea that somebody thought I was getting too big for my boots.

CHAPTER FOUR

A Figure from the Past

Spring wore on into summer—a chilly, unfriendly one it was, in June and July. The infatuation of the country with its new government should have been wearing off, but to everyone's surprise, including our own, it wasn't. Polls put our approval rating at an impossible high. Could a honeymoon last forever? Reason told us it could not, but, basking in what seemed like universal affection, reason's voice was often ignored. We were like children who imagine that they will live forever.

As the session wound down toward the summer recess, I was asked to dinner by the formidable Margaret Stevens, the permanent secretary at the Ministry, and the person whom, quite wrongly, I regarded as my boss.

"Nothing formal," she said. "I'm asking Chris Cunningham and his wife as well. You don't have a partner, do you?"

"Not at the moment," I said. Margaret and I were getting on rather well by now, more relaxed and appreciative in each other's company, so I added: "I asked one of my constituents recently if he had a partner, and he said: 'My brother George—you know that, Mr. Pinnock. We're plumbers.' And when I said that I meant did he live with anyone he said, 'Mind your own fucking business, Mr. Pinnock.'"

She laughed.

"Well, so long as you're happy to come on your own. When you're Prime Minister you'll have to ask your sister or someone like that to act as the Downing Street hostess."

I shook my head, smiling.

"No sister. No relatives of any kind or of either sex. Didn't Mr. Heath do without a hostess when he was Prime Minister?"

"Perhaps that was Mr. Heath's problem," she said tartly.

So Margaret and I were now on the sort of terms where comment of a personal nature could be made on politicians of the past. Nevertheless I was careful over dinner about what I said, and I saw no evidence that she was on similar terms with Chris Cunningham—but his wife's presence may have made Margaret more careful than she otherwise would have been. Chris's wife, Mary, was heavily pregnant with what the pair called their Party Conference baby, and soon after dinner they had to leave rather precipitately. It certainly wasn't anything they ate. Margaret was a good cook of a very traditional kind. There were no exotic dishes or ingredients, and the results made clear that she would have no truck even with the crunchy vegetables nonsense.

"You'll stay, won't you?" she said, as Chris and Mary retreated to the lift and out to the official car. "It'll make them feel worse if they hear they brought the whole evening to an end."

"I'd like to," I said, coming back into the beige and blue living room of her Earl's Court flat. "I bet Chris and his wife would have planned things differently if they'd known he would get a ministerial post."

"If they planned at all," she said lightly. "Sex and politics—the two great imponderables."

She sat down and began pouring the coffee, which had been sitting stewing during the minor panic of Mary's bad turn.

"I think I handle the political hazards more confidently than the sexual ones," I said, keeping the tone of the conversation light.

"But then you've been in the political thick of things for a long time, haven't you?"

"Oh yes—I've been 'politically active' since my teens," I said, leaving well to one side the question of my sexual activity. "First locally, then nationally. But of course government is another matter."

"Naturally. More exacting, and more dangerous. But you've proceeded very cautiously, I think."

"Oh, I make mistakes. Making little jokes about my predecessors to civil servants, for example. Second nature to me, that kind of joke."

"Oh, everyone with a sense of humor makes that kind of mistake. It's very minor. But you do see the problem, don't you?"

"I think so."

"We've all served lots of masters and mistresses, we who work in the Civil Service. Some we've liked, some we've loathed. The liking or loathing has little or nothing to do with their performance as ministers. You can have a minister who's totally incompetent, a one-man disaster area, someone who drives you to distraction professionally, yet personally you may be very fond of him. I've even been fond of one who was…let's say corrupt. So as far as recent ministers are concerned, it's on the whole best to keep off the subject."

"Point taken. But you go way back, of course, so a little idle banter about figures of the past is not out of order?"

"Oh yes, I go way, way back," she said cheerfully. "Isn't it awful? I've been married to the Civil Service. And even before I went up to university I'd been a typist-cum-dogsbody in a government department. What a life! most people would think. Some would say hardly a life at all. Yet something in me right from the start said: 'This is what you want to do.' You could say that was me recognizing my own mediocrity."

"No one who knew you would think that," I said, gallantly but truthfully.

"I'm not so sure. But I admit that there have been times when I have looked at the minister or the Secretary of State I've been working for and I've said to myself: 'I've got a damned sight better brain than you have, you pillock.' No names, no pack drill."

"You've worked for practically everyone who's

been anything in politics," I said guilelessly.

"Oh no, that's an exaggeration," she said, in that downright, factual way of hers I found endearing. "But lots."

I had, I must admit, been leading this conversation in a certain direction.

"On my first day at the Ministry you came into my office, you saw me at my desk, and you were startled."

She looked embarrassed.

"Did you really see that? You are a deep one! I could have sworn you hadn't noticed."

"Why?"

"Why was I startled?" Her elderly face, framed by gray, undyed, and little-cared-for hair, became rapt in thought. "Something in you," she said at last, "your looks—not your face but your stance, your way of sitting at your desk—reminded me of someone."

"Who?"

She shook her head.

"Oh, it went as soon as it came. As you say I've had an infinite number of men set over me in my time."

"I expect if you went back over your career in your mind you could pinpoint who it was."

I said it easily, but she shot me a glance.

"Who said it was one of the ministers I've served that you reminded me of?" she asked.

"I'd have thought it quite likely. I was sitting there at my new desk, the new boy, but I reminded you of someone in the past, sitting at that or a similar desk, and you started."

She nodded, reluctantly.

"Yes, I suppose it's quite likely."

"I'd be interested who it was."

"Good heavens, it could be anyone."

"Going through them would be good preparation for writing your memoirs."

"That's something civil servants never do."

"Never?"

"Not usually, except in private and for posterity. It's mainly the more self-important ones who do that. This is getting a bit like a parlor game.... Though I said it could be anyone, I think we can be a bit more selective than that, because it must have been one of the *memorable* ministers you reminded me of. That rules out sixty or seventy percent of them—the ones who sort of coalesce in my mind into an undifferentiated lump." She paused, swallowed, then began. "Well, I started in 1962, and that was in what was then the

Commonwealth Office…"

And so she started through the thirty-five years of her career in Whitehall and her bosses: names that had gone on to distinguished political careers, names that had meant something at the time but had fallen by the wayside through election defeat or sheer ennui, names that were just names.

"Now," Margaret said, getting to the seventies, "we can rule out the women—"

"Why?" I asked. "I've no objection to reminding you of a woman."

She shot me another quick glance.

"Well, I don't think it's likely, but if you insist. Much of the time in the seventies it was either Margaret Thatcher or Shirley Williams. That was in my first spell at the Department of Education."

"What were they like?"

"About as far apart as you could get in ideology, behavior, treatment of people, likes and dislikes. Funnily enough, what they actually *did* was strangely similar."

"The power of the Civil Service machine winning out over political standpoints?"

"I don't think so. Force of events, a case of the prevailing orthodoxies swamping the personal ideologies.…Anyway, you certainly don't remind me of either of them."

And so she went on, covering her transfer to one of the big economic ministries, then back to the Department of Education in the late eighties.

"Ken Clarke, John Patten, emphatic *no* in both cases, Gillian Shepherd the same…" She pulled her hand through her wiry gray hair. "No, I'm sorry, Colin. I've failed you entirely."

"No point in going over the less remarkable people?"

"No, there's not. As I say, you reminded me—momentarily, be it said—of someone who for one reason or another is etched on my consciousness. Unremarkable ministers are not."

I stood up regretfully.

"Sorry I involved you in a fruitless trip down Memory Lane, Margaret."

"I've quite enjoyed it as a memory-retrieval exercise."

"It was certainly a lesson to me on how short political reputations can be." I was just about to give her the conventional thanks and assurances that I'd had a lovely evening when an idea struck me. "You said you worked as a typist in Whitehall even before you went up to university."

"Yes."

Her brow furrowed again, and I struck in with: "What about the people you worked for then?"

Suddenly she sat down on the sofa.

"Oh."

"You've remembered something?"

But I knew she had, and I sat down again, too. This was going to repay some going into.

"You won't like this," Margaret said after a moment, probably one spent wondering if she could avoid saying anything, and deciding she couldn't. "This is actually more serious than you've been pretending, isn't it?"

"Yes."

"You're—I don't want to pry—in some way trying to find out who you are."

"Yes."

"I'm sure this has nothing to do with who you are, but—"

"Margaret, I'm not looking for a cozy ending," I said. She swallowed.

"It was Lord John Revill."

I blinked. That was someone I had heard of.

"The man who—what?—murdered his children's nanny?"

"Murdered his wife, and was sleeping with his

children's nanny."

"You worked for him?"

"As a typist. He had a very junior post at the Home Office....You could say he was the most disturbing man I ever worked for...in retrospect."

"Why in retrospect?"

"Because at the time he had seemed so ordinary, so conventional, so *nice*."

❧❧❧

Without asking, she poured me more black coffee, and I drank down half a cup without sugar. Watching me do this decided her to pour me another glass of brandy, and a stiff one.

"The man who disappeared," I said at last.

"Without trace," she said. "The most successful vanishing act in criminal history. Usually they surface in the heart of South America, or in some African state riddled with disease and corruption. Even the Nazi war criminals eventually seem to be traced to places like that, and with half your mind you say, 'Well, that's *some* punishment for them.' Lord John has never given a hint of where he might be if he is still alive. The tabloids are always haring off on false scents of course, but there's never been anything that the police thought worth a second glance."

"Did the police *want* to find him?"

"What are you suggesting? The usual Masonic conspiracy notions? I never heard rumors of that, or even that Revill was one. I think it genuinely has been a case of 'The police are baffled.'"

I was racking my brains to remember the little I had ever heard about the case, which was before my time of political or any other kind of awareness.

"Was there a suggestion that his rich friends had sheltered him and arranged for his escape from this country?"

Margaret nodded.

"Suggestions, but no evidence. And if they found him a safe haven he's still had to *live* there for years, decades. And yet there's been no solid evidence."

"What do you remember about the murder?"

She shook her head, troubled.

"Very little, beyond the bare facts, I'm afraid. I was out of the country on a trade mission to Eastern Europe with the then-Minister of Trade. My first trip abroad it was, though in a very junior capacity. Any news about it I learned from the BBC World Service, and it wasn't the kind of thing they dealt with at any great length—not the sort of image of Britain they were interested in projecting. When I got home it was still hot news, but the papers assumed you knew the basic facts.…I think I tended to black the whole thing out."

"Why?"

She gave a self-deprecating grimace.

"Because I'd liked the man, I suppose. That's what made it so terrifying. That a man you thought 'a nice bloke' could suddenly become a murderer, the most sought-after criminal in the country."

"When was this?"

"The first half of 1962. Before long the Profumo case swamped it as a political scandal. But talk has gone on."

"And to you he was just 'a nice bloke'?"

"Yes.…Remember I was very young. He was good-looking, or moderately so, he was a minister, a Lord." She was serious, absorbed. She had gone back forty years, and was wrestling with her feelings as an adolescent girl. "But to be honest I don't think that really clouded my judgment."

Somehow I was sure it hadn't. Like Miss Buss and Miss Beale, the young Margaret hadn't felt

Cupid's darts. Then, as now, she looked, she considered, she judged.

"What did? I wonder."

"Cloud my judgment? I can only suppose inexperience."

"Tell me what sort of person you *thought* he was."

"Ah." She was typically unwilling to be rushed. "Not altogether easy, that. On the surface, and on paper, a very conventional figure. He'd done all the usual things a man of his class does, or did at that time. He'd been in the Brigade of Guards, he'd been a deb's delight, he'd married a wife from the landed gentry, and produced the necessary son—and a daughter, incidentally."

"Why should a son matter? His was a courtesy title, surely, so it would die with him."

"So it would. But his elder brother, the heir to the Marquis of Aylesbury, was…unlikely to marry."

"So, on the surface, a typical upper-class scion without a rebellious bone in his body?"

"That's right. And distantly related to Harold Macmillan, like a lot of the members of his government."

My eyebrows shot up.

"I didn't know that."

"Either to him or to Lady Dorothy, his wife. It was said that, as Prime Minister, Macmillan liked to surround himself with people he knew. That was the polite way of putting it."

"Well before my time, all this. It seems like another age."

"Not so different from all those Kennedys in America," Margaret pointed out. "Anyway the appearances in Lord John's case were a bit misleading, or so I felt anyway, with all the confidence in my judgment of a teenage secretary who had just left school!"

"What went against the stereotype?"

She drew her fingers through her hair again.

"Let me get my thoughts in order. It's ages since I've thought about him....He was very considerate. Not just to me—which was remarkable enough, remembering that I was what today we would call a temp, and in no way good-looking—but all the way down the line: civil servants, office workers, cleaners, doormen. They were all fond of him—and some of the women dewy-eyed about him. He never, to my knowledge, took advantage of this."

"Was he happily married at this point?"

"So far as anyone knew. I wondered, though. I only saw the wife once. A very English type: flawless complexion, rosebud mouth, impeccably dressed and jeweled. I thought she was cold and hard and manipulative, but it's a type I don't usually take to."

"It's not like you to make sweeping judgments."

She smiled—a rather sweet smile that I'd never seen before.

"I'm being Margaret Stevens tonight, not the permanent secretary. Another thing: his class never showed. He was very open in his relationships. Class, nationality, color, never made any difference. That was very rare then."

"Still is."

"It is much, much more common, young man," she said, leaning forward to speak forcefully, so I knew it was something she felt strongly about. "Dinosaurs like Alan Clarke abounded then; now they stand out…There's one more thing, but it's not something I *know*."

"Yes?"

"I *think* he was a very passionate man. None of the modern words—sexy, oversexed—seems to cover it. I think he felt deeply, loved intensely, even if not wisely. I think it was the strength of his feelings gave meaning to his life."

I wondered, not for the first time in that conversation, whether a small part of her had been in love with him.

"Have you any reason for thinking that?" I asked.

She grinned.

"None whatsoever. The intuition of a teenager—and one who had already half decided that love, sex, or whatever was not going to get in the way of a career. And it never has."

"By the way, it's irrelevant, but what was Lord John like as a minister?"

"I was much too junior to really know. I just put typing in front of him from time to time. But going by comments in the Ministry I'd guess middling. Did his job, got things done on a limited front, not so good on wider issues, matters of principle, raising his eyes to the horizon."

"One of those people who are better as constituency MPs rather than in government?"

"Probably so. Certainly the shock when the murder took place was very intense in his constituency. I knew someone living there, and he said that they had *loved* him. Still, in those days

Conservative activists did dearly love a Lord. Now they love a successful used-car salesman more."

"What was the constituency?"

"One of the South Coast ones, I can't remember which."

At last I got up, really intending to go. When I had made my thanks for the meal and the evening in general, I said:

"I hope the crash course in memoir-writing hasn't been too painful. You've been a lot of help."

She had got up, and was standing close, looking at me quizzically.

"Can I get something clear in my mind, Colin—just in my mind, where it will stay. You're looking for your natural parents?"

"Yes."

"Having found out—what?—that you were adopted?"

"Well, that's been suggested."

"By whom has it been suggested?"

She was definitely permanent secretary again, and with her steely eyes on me I had to come not just clean but totally clean.

"In an anonymous note. And it was a bit ambiguous."

Her eyebrows ascended to the ceiling.

"And on the basis of that, and on my reaction to you on your first day at the Ministry, you are now building a castle in the air that your father may have been Lord John Revill?"

I shook my head vigorously and I hope convincingly.

"I'm building nothing at the moment. I'd only vaguely heard of the man before this evening. I'm going to go away, think about what you've said, maybe try to find out more about him, and what he did, but that is all."

"That," said Margaret briskly, "is a hell of a lot. If you're going to do that, you know, you will need to have your government minister hat on, not your human being hat. Cool, judgmental, all that kind of thing, is what you will need to be."

"And it's what I will be." I kissed her. "I'll be everything you're teaching me to be."

"Kissed by a minister! That's a first!" She laughed. "Perhaps the world really is changing for the better."

It had been a kiss of the most genuine gratitude. But she would not have approved of the fact that as I went down her stairs, preferring to avoid the lift, I was feeling a whole new sensation. I was on

a trail, and I suddenly felt it was the most important trail of my life. I hoped it was no disloyalty
to my parents, but all the way home I was saying:
was that the man who made me? Did a murderer
help make me what I am? Was he the cause of my
lifelong interest in politics? Was Lord John Revill
bone of my bone, flesh of my flesh?

CHAPTER FIVE

Old Blood

The summer recess came upon us within the week, as welcome as tall waves for surfers. Well, not welcome to all of us. There were ministers and rank-and-file MPs who were so intoxicated by power after eighteen years in the wilderness that they would have been happy if Parliament had sat indefinitely to enact a rackful of legislation which their ingenious minds had been contemplating over the long barren years of opposition. But the sensible ones, after three months of delicious political activity, took themselves off on relaxing holidays in Tuscany or the Dordogne, hill-walking in Khatmandu or coastal cruises round Scandinavia. Even those who made a rather puritanical virtue of holidaying in Great Britain found the weather had mightily improved.

I had no plans for a holiday of any sort.

This was not because I was intoxicated by power, or because I am one of those for whom a holiday is a passport to boredom. I was a huntsman, with a quarry in sight—the difference being this was not a game or sport, but something intensely, perhaps embarrassingly personal. Parliament being in recess meant that I had nobody to report to, no terriers tugging at my trouser seat—it meant in short that I had more time, even though I regularly toiled away at the Ministry. I could never have lain on a beach, or even walked Yorkshire with George Eakin—my mind would have been wondering without the means of acting on my speculations. I remembered my promise to George to forget the whole matter, and felt the odd twinge of guilt. But I am a politician: I am used to breaking promises.

There is always awkwardness involved in calling up an old girlfriend. It's like inviting a guest to a warmed-up meal. I expect Susan felt the same, and that was why she had left plenty of time before she rang to congratulate me on my appointment to government. So I stewed over the matter, got quite clear in my mind how far I wanted to involve her, before I steeled myself, picked up the phone, and rang her at her flat in Greenwich.

"Susan?"

"Oh, Colin."

Cool, very cool. Well, that was how I wanted it.

"Susan, were you serious about being willing to help me in the matter of how I came into the world?"

I took the ironic, flippant tone because it was the one I felt safest with, though I knew it sometimes irritated Susan when I used it in talking about serious topics.

"Of course I was. It's just up my street."

"Well," I had to admit, "this may not be quite what you were expecting."

"Oh? Why? Have you made progress?"

"I *may* have. All *very* speculative, and probably not something a historian should be looking at yet."

She immediately became the academic she was.

"I don't like the sound of that. Is this whole business robbing you of your common sense and your analytical brain, Colin?"

"No, it is not, Susan," I said sharply. "I have good reason for what I'm asking, believe me. What

I want is the best—that is the most authentic and detailed—account you can put together of the Lord John Revill affair."

There was silence at the other end.

"You mean the murder."

"Yes."

Susan's voice when she had taken this in was less dampening.

"Well, well. That shouldn't be difficult. It's nicely in my period, and it did contribute to the fall of the Macmillan government. It was part of the crumbling process. Actually, going into it could be quite fascinating."

"Good. I don't suppose there are any books on the case?"

"Not so far as I know. People may have been put off by the possibility of libel."

"Libel? Lord John was hardly likely to return from the dead or the South American jungle to bring an action, surely."

"No. But since there had been no criminal action, no one had been found guilty. Remember there was the nanny, with whom he was supposed to be having an affair. And of course there were the children. No question of libel there, but people may have felt compunction on their account about raking over an old affair like the Revill case."

Now she was in fantasy land.

"Compunction? Don't make me laugh, Susan. We're talking about hacks and muckrakers. They don't feel compunction."

"Hmmm. I suppose you could be right. It probably just hasn't attracted a serious historian. Politically it was no more than a warm-up to the Profumo affair. There were attempts to portray it as symptomatic of the moral corruption of the aristocratic circle Macmillan surrounded himself with."

"I gather he was nepotistic."

"Very much so, though he loved newspapers to point out he was a Scottish crofter's grandson. It made a good story, and was a case of choosing the ancestor that was most politically useful."

"Did the Revill affair damage him politically?"

There was silence. Sue didn't give historical judgments lightly.

"Not greatly, so far as I'm aware. The public probably realized it was just a case of people who had got their lives into an emotional mess, and the whole thing had become a powder keg. It was a private matter, even though one of those involved was a politician. If there was political fallout it probably sprang from the disappearance, and the feeling that the aristocracy had closed ranks to frustrate justice taking its course."

"There could be later newspaper stories on that angle, I suppose?"

"Could be. It sounds like a good topic for one of the color supplements. I'll look into that."

"So you'll help me, Sue?"

"Raring to go. Do you want me to do anything on the Pinnocks as well?"

I had almost forgotten my own family.

"Only if you can do it easily. No harm in making a few preliminary moves, I suppose. But now I've got the bit between my teeth I'm fascinated by the Revill angle."

I could almost hear Susan's mind ticking.

"You must wise me up on that when we meet," she said carefully. "Odd how the aristocracy always gets people in, isn't it? You sound as if you're becoming obsessed with having a second identity. I'm guessing you could probably quote Iago's words: 'I am not what I am.'"

"Thanks, Sue," I said, to ring off—dismissively, but feeling I had been warned. "I can't say he's ever been a hero of mine."

To give Susan her due, she got on with the work at once. It was no more than five or six days later that she rang me to say that she'd got enough material for me to make a start on.

"I've been collecting it up here," she said. "Is it convenient for you to come round?"

"Of course."

"I'm a bit diffident, seeing that I'm talking to a government minister," she said slyly.

"It will wear off quickly when we meet, I imagine. Actually I've still got the key to the flat. Pure forgetfulness. I'll give it to you when I see you."

"Oh, eventually. It could be useful to you while I'm doing this for you. Shall we say Friday at eleven? Let yourself in if I'm not there."

I felt oddly pleased Susan didn't seem anxious to have her key back. She was not out when I got to her Greenwich flat, which was part of an early-nineteenth-century house, but she was under the shower. As I rang the bell I could hear the water cascading, as I often had in the past. Susan was a country girl who believed that London was so disgustingly dirty and polluted that you needed to shower often. She was right, of course, but fighting the most hopeless of losing battles. I let myself in, went through to the living room, and stood contemplating the piles of newspapers and photocopies that she had stacked up on the floor.

"Those are the initial reactions," said Susan, coming through from the bathroom with a towel around her, and pointing at two piles, "the coverage of the first two or three days. *Those* are the more measured treatments of two or three weeks after that, and *those* are the later things, so far as I've gone, and many of them are more concerned with the disappearance rather than the murder, as I suspected. I'll be adding to that pile, but the first piles are more or less complete."

She disappeared into the bedroom we had shared, and I heard her getting clothes out of the wardrobe and brushing her thick auburn hair. I felt my stomach churning with—with I know not what: old love returning, old love remembered, lust, regret. I could no more sort it out than I could ignore it.

"Well, there's plenty to be going on with," I shouted, in what was not quite my normal voice.

"Should be," she said, appearing at the door in a simple red dress that contrived to be striking and intriguing on her. "I've got a lunch date, but

I'll be back about two or half past if you want to talk over what I've collected."

I felt what was definitely a stab of jealousy toward whomever she had the lunch date with.

"I will want to talk it over," I said.

She nodded, gesturing toward the piles, and went back into the bedroom. When she returned immediately with a light coat on she just raised her hand and said, "Bye." I stood for a moment, somehow dissatisfied. Then I shook myself. What had I wanted? Had I hoped to go back, pick up the pieces of the relationship? Of course not. I settled down to the first two piles, one of actual newspapers, one of photocopies. All of them were dated March 1962.

They wrote good, sharp headlines even then. All of them were a variation on a simple theme: MURDER IN MAYFAIR. MINISTER SOUGHT. Those with more space tended to say GOVERNMENT MINISTER SOUGHT, to avoid giving the idea that it was a mere fashionable cleric who was involved. This story had a political dimension, and was all the better for it. Those were the initial, morning-after reactions, and they all realized it had a class dimension as well as a political one: MAY-FAIR SLAYING; WEST END SLAUGHTER, and so on. All got the crime-in-fashionable-circles angle through. Not bad, considering that the police had not been called till toward midnight. By the second day after the murder they had latched on to another aspect: the sex angle. Friends of the couple had mentioned the nanny.

I sat back at this point and reviewed my impression of the instant coverage of the affair. One thing that had been lacking had been photographs. Of course no one had expected the Minister for Overseas Trade as he then was to emerge distraught from his house and disappear into the night, so no one had been there to record it. As a consequence most of the photographs of Lord John Revill were posed, respectable, formal affairs. They could have been, and very likely were, put on his election addresses. The best the popular papers could achieve was some blurred ones taken at a party, where he appeared raffish, slightly drunk, and with a high color. At first glance there appeared nothing worse to these photographs than the fact that he was holding a glass, but when I looked more closely at the one in the *Daily Sketch* I felt that the eyes looked desperate.

I saw no resemblance in that face to myself.

What were the facts, so far as they had been

gathered by the reporters covering the initial breaking of the story? The bare outline of events was that Lady John Revill—christened Veronica Martindale—had been murdered in her bed by her husband, who had then left the family home in Upper Brook Street. Police had been called to the house, and the photographic coverage was of a massive, floodlit presence there. Those were in the evening papers of March 5, a Wednesday. The Thursday papers had pictures of Lady Veronica's parents driving away from the town house, very much in mourning, with the two children, Caroline and Matthew. Reporters had chased the car, but its destination was predictable. Hadleigh Grange in Northamptonshire, the home of Sir George and Lady Martindale, the grandparents. A substantial police presence there kept the posse of reporters at the high, wrought-iron gates half a mile from the house. Little more was heard of the people inside. The children, obviously, had been very efficiently protected, with the cooperation of the police.

That same day mention had been made of the nanny. Reporters asserted confidently that the only people in the house apart from Lord John and his immediate family had been the nanny and the housekeeper in her basement flat. By the Friday the usual "friends of," sometimes varied to "sources close to," the family had told the newspapers that Lord John and the nanny had been having an affair. Several papers printed a fuzzy photograph of a window in the house in Upper Brook Street, behind which there seemed discernible a female face. By Friday the police were saying that the nanny had helped them with their inquiries and had left the house. They were also saying that reports that fingerprints on the murder weapon, a kitchen knife, had been identified as those of Lord John were "speculative." On Saturday they revealed just how speculative they were. Lady John had been strangled. By Saturday Lord John's post at the Department of Trade had been filled by an obscure backbencher. Sources close to the government emphasized that the Prime Minister was making no judgments on the case, but had come to the conclusion that government had to be carried on. Ho-hum, I thought. I knew political flimflam when I read it. Government could survive the absence of a junior minister for a few days. Mr. Macmillan was engaged in damage limitation.

By then attention had begun to switch to the

whereabouts of Lord John. Here the reporters had even less to go on. Literally speaking they had nothing to go on. He had left the house and had never been seen again. Oh, of course there were "sightings," but even newspapers desperate for something, *any*thing, on the subject had to admit that the sightings were always vague and unconvincing, sometimes absurd. It didn't take them long to decide that someone must have seen him, someone must have talked to him, someone must have shielded him, and taken him in. By Monday, always a lean day for news, several had decided that one or some of Lord John's aristocratic friends had arranged for his disappearance.

There was never, as Margaret Stevens had said, any convincing indication that that was the case, let alone proof of any kind. Yes, the Revills had mixed in an upper-crust circle, had—in a fairly modest way—partied, nightclubbed, crush-barred in places where they were likely to meet and mingle with people of their own kind. But there was little indication from the newspapers that Lord John was part of a tight-knit group who were so devoted that they would feel they had to sacrifice reputation and even liberty by spiriting him out of the reach of the law.

"How are you getting on?"

I had been so absorbed that I hadn't heard Susan's key in the door of the flat. She swung in, still looking as fresh as a morning meadow in a butter ad, carrying an interesting-looking plastic bag stuffed with paper.

"Not too bad," I said, still having to make an effort to keep my voice normal. "I've got through the first two categories, and I've still got the longer-term coverage to go."

"And what are your impressions?"

I followed her academic example and pondered long before answering.

"I've got a stronger sense of the *situation*, the ménage à trois, than of the people."

"Was it a ménage à trois?" Susan asked, something that it hadn't occurred to me to question. "To me that means a willing threesome. But I haven't seen any evidence that the wife was complaisant."

"Well, she'd chucked him out of the marital bed, according to one or two of these reports. How on earth would they know?"

"Could be the housekeeper. Could be the police. They tend to leak little droplets of information to keep a story alive. I think it's on the principle of using a sprat to catch a mackerel. The more alive a story is the more likely they are to get further information."

"Well, it doesn't seem to have worked in this case."

"Not so far as we know. So you got no sense of the main players in all this from the early reports?"

"Actually I'd got some sense of Lord John and of his wife from the permanent secretary at the Department—very much an outsider's view, but strongly held. It needs to be checked and modified, to say the least. But I didn't get any idea from these reports of the character of the nanny."

"No," Susan agreed, nodding vigorously. "I had the feeling that the police very much kept her under wraps, and eventually spirited her away."

"There seems to be a lot of spiriting away in this case. Why would the police do that?"

"Maybe they thought that as the main witness she was in danger. Maybe they thought she'd sign up for a 'Nanny Tells All' exclusive in one of the papers."

That was a new angle. I'd grown up in the era when any such stories before a trial were inconceivable.

"Could she do that? Could they print it?"

"I'm pretty sure they could at that date. And it could have prejudiced any trial—given a handle to the defense."

"Of course. That's presumably why the rules were changed….And yet the nanny must have been crucial in all this."

"Maybe. Or maybe it was the wife who was crucial and that's why she got murdered….I rather wish I hadn't set you on to reading the early reports first."

"Why?"

"Early reports in popular newspapers are very misleading."

"The reports in the posh papers convey pretty much the same information in a different way. The *Telegraph* has always been very hot on sensational cases—murder, sex, or whatever. And particularly combinations of the two, as here."

"You hadn't got to the third category, you say, Colin?"

"Not yet."

"A bit more came out later on, about the nanny. She was Australian, by the way."

"Yes—one paper picked that up in the piles I have read."

"A graduate—Sydney University. She and the Revills went around to plays, opera, and so on."

"Was that in the early days, before Lord John seduced her, or vice versa?"

"What an old-fashioned word! You have no evidence who seduced who, or if anything that could be called a seduction took place. It was probably mutual attraction and shared enthusiasm. I don't think it was only before the affair began. There's mention in one of the gossip columns of their having been seen at *Turandot*, and *Chips with Everything* and *All's Well* as a threesome. That was in the month leading up to the murder."

"Could still be before the affair began, or before it was found out by the wife....Presumably someone baby-sat the children."

"What do you mean? Someone who could have known or got to know what was going on? It could be the housekeeper. She's another shadowy figure."

"Yes, she is," I agreed. "So, with the nanny, it wasn't just a matter of having a typical upper-class servant. The formidable dragon, passed on from one aristocratic family to another. It was more in the nature of an au-pair arrangement, with her doing the cultural sights in return for housework and child-minding."

"That's right. Lucy Mariotti was her name—christened, presumably Lucia. English graduate, but no English relatives to get hospitality from when she came over to do the cultural scene. There was a big Italian migration to Australia just after the war. In fact the Mafia took over a lot of the markets and raised the crime profile no end. Not that that's relevant in this case. As far as the reports went there was nothing to suggest that her background was anything other than respectable."

"Did the Revills advertise for a nanny in Australia?"

"No, in *The Times*. She was already over here, and replied."

"Well, that starts filling in the picture…" I cast my mind back, lighting up a cigarette to Susan's predictable annoyance. I went over and puffed smoke out of the open window. "What were you looking so pleased about when you came back?"

She smiled her slow smile.

"I'd been lunching with someone who's doing a thesis on the color supplements."

Oddly enough I felt a sudden spurt of joy: she hadn't been lunching with a boyfriend. Oddly, and stupidly, too—because she could have been doing that on any or every of the four hundred or so days since we had split up. I tried to keep my voice low and natural when I spoke, though I guessed she had observed my reaction. Susan was a first-rate observer.

"What a very silly thing to do a thesis on."

"Not at all. The color supplements have molded middle-class tastes in the last thirty or forty years. They say you ought to want it, and in no time at all you do. They also contain articles of general interest…"

"Such as the Revill affair."

"Such as indeed. My informant came up with three, all in the last twenty years."

"'Where are they now?' stuff?"

"To some extent. Pictures of the children grown up, but never anything more than that. Caroline and Matthew their names are. They've never cooperated with any of the muckrakers, or any of the serious investigators, come to that."

"There are some serious investigators?"

"Well, one. Someone who seems to have done his homework." She rummaged in the plastic bag and pulled out a color supplement with an anorexic and slightly stoned-looking model on the cover.

"He didn't make the front page," I commented.

"Articles like this are essentially fill-ups to the ads and the fashion and furniture features. You know that, Colin. Still, the man who wrote this got five pages, and he really used them. Mind you, he makes mistakes."

"What sorts of mistakes?"

"About English titles. Says that Lord John could sit in the House of Commons because his father, the Marquis of Aylesbury, was still alive—that sort of thing. I think the author may be American."

"That sort of thing confuses us as well."

"His name is Elmore Hasselbank."

"Well, you could be right. But remember we're a global village, and we get some pretty way-out names here too these days."

"Anyway, he's got a very good picture of the wife—something not posed or prettified." She flipped through the magazine and found the page. "Does your heart warm to her?"

I looked at the picture.

"No," I said at once.

The photograph was an off-guard one, like the earlier ones of Lord John snapped at a party, probably a fashionable one. Lady John was talking to another woman, of whom only the bare shoulder was visible. Lord John's wife was clearly retailing and relishing scandal: her mouth was twisted, her eyes had an icy sparkle, and one had a sense of a corrupt nature under a glossy exterior.

"You know," I said, "I'm almost getting a very ideologically incorrect view of this case, with Lord John as this woman's victim instead of vice versa."

"Oh, these days feminism doesn't demand that female monsters have to be explained away as a reaction to the prevailing male dominance. Women have to be given the freedom to choose to be monsters. Still, that is rather a ridiculous view of things."

"Of course it is. He did kill her, after all."

"Is it the permanent secretary's view of the man that is influencing you?"

"You know, I rather think it is."

"Was she in love with him?"

"A little, I'd guess. But love is not really her line, and I don't think that affected her judgment."

"Hmm. It usually does."

"Anything else in the article?"

"One or two suggestive things. Read it for yourself—you'll probably pick up more. And there's certainly one thing that will interest you."

"What's that?"

"At the time of the murder, the nanny was pregnant."

CHAPTER SIX

Joker

It was about ten days after this that a disturbing thing happened.

It was a hot Wednesday, and I'd been working on new initiatives for autistic children all morning and into the early afternoon in the Department in Great Smith Street. I left my office in my shirt-sleeves and walked toward Victoria in the nourishing sunlight, registering the brown or peeling red office workers coming from the direction of St. James's Park after their lunch hour. I meditated getting into my car—my little-used car as it was, these days—and driving out into the country for a pint and something to eat. I wondered if Susan would come with me. In case neither thing happened—and things did crop up with increasing frequency now that I was a minister that stopped me doing what I wanted—I dropped into Marks & Spencer for a prepared meal.

Once in the middle of the lazy person's cuisine I avoided the slimmer's meals and even the meals for one. I like a hearty-sized main course, and can do without any of the other courses. Anyway it was not beyond the possible that I would be feeding Susan as well as myself. I chose something called Chicken Fiorentina, then went round the food section picking up things I'd made a mental note I needed: marmalade, fresh peas, and a packet of frozen whole prawns. I went to the check-out, paid with a ten-pound note, then put all my bits and pieces into a plastic carrier bag. This is one of those Markses where you have to go back through the food section to get to the door, and I did this and tripped up some steps to the door out to the street.

Suddenly an electronic bleep sounded, and before I realized what had happened a man in brown was at my elbow.

"Could I look at your purchases, sir?"

I suppose this or something like it is a common nightmare. For a politician it comes below being caught soliciting in a public lavatory, but it nevertheless ranks pretty high. I was led through to a little room with frosted glass and no connecting window to the main store. The security man pressed a button on the little table there, then began going through my bag. Luckily I had dropped the till slip in with my purchases, but it didn't save me.

"You don't seem to have put this through the till, sir."

He proffered toward me a packet of sticky toffee pudding.

The whole thing began to take on the air of black farce. The young man, with his subuniform of brown trousers and epauletted shirt, seemed in his youthful solemnity like something out of Gilbert and Sullivan. At any moment he might be expected to burst into a patter song in which Gilbert would discover outrageous rhymes for sticky toffee pudding.

"That's certainly not mine," I spluttered, acutely aware of sounding pompous and unconvincing. "I'm not fond of sweet things, and I certainly wouldn't eat anything as sickly as that."

The young man gave a dubious shake of the head, to show he wasn't interested in my tastes, only my actions.

"Look I'm an MP," I said unwisely, "a government minister. We're sometimes targets for people…"

A righteous light came into his eyes.

"You're not suggesting we should apply different rules because you're a government minister, are you, sir?"

"No, of course not," I said, aware that my voice was rising in timbre and volume. "But I am suggesting that people have a vested interest in embarrassing us or trying to bring us down, even."

More people had come into the little room, summoned by the buzzer. Two of them were in uniform, but one was a middle-aged woman with a sensible face, in street clothes.

"If I could say a word."

I looked at her with ridiculous apprehension, as if she was about to say she had seen me slip something into my bag. That sort of situation makes one unsure even of things one should be most certain of. She nodded toward the package of sticky toffee pudding.

"I don't know anything about that, but I was watching a woman in the food section. She was shabbily dressed, and had a large, floppy hat on.

In any case I was watching her from behind, so I couldn't see her face. I didn't see her take anything, but I realize now she was following this gentleman fairly closely. He went to definite sections—the fresh vegetables, the jams, the frozen section. She went behind him. I saw him go through the cash desk, and while he waited in the queue I saw her leave off trailing him and going in the direction of this door. I didn't see him or her after that—I was called away to look at a suspected young addict who was pocketing stuff."

And that, effectively, was that. She was quite convinced that I couldn't have concealed anything so large in my trousers or my shirt pockets before going through the cash desk. The fact that the woman had been following me suggested a doubt as to whether I or she might have slipped it into my bag on my way out. Marks & Spencer is vigilant, but it doesn't like unnecessary public fuss. The young man, still solemn, said he was sure there was no wrongdoing on my part, and he hoped I would be careful in the future. That was ambiguous if you like, but I didn't feel I was in a position to argue or protest.

There was no trip to the country that evening. I walked the mile or so back to my flat pondering, and I lay on the sofa for some time afterward, still pondering. It was lucky that the matter had come up so immediately, because such memories as I had of the trivialities of my shopping trip were still very fresh. I tried first of all to recollect other shoppers in the food section, but could manage no more than one or two: a smart, bejeweled old lady with ravenous eyes, a hungry-looking young student. I could put no face or form to the person described by the store detective: a shabby woman with a hat. But then she had been following me, so probably I wouldn't have seen her. Where, I wondered, had she followed me *from?* The Ministry? Or had she encountered me by accident in the street?

Was it in fact a woman, or a man dressed as a woman, aided by a large floppy hat? If I could get no handle on the person I tried to be more definite about the moment. The crucial time was between the cash desk and the door to the street. I could remember tearing a carrier from a small stack of them, loading in my four purchases, then setting off for the door. After that...after that I could remember only one tiny thing—one moment when I thought the bag had bumped against the side of one of the stands of sandwiches. That could have been when she slipped it in—though if she was an expert shoplifter and exceptionally light-fingered it could have been at any time. But *very* deft she must have been, because two sticky toffee puddings in a carton are not light.

Sticky toffee pudding! I thought disgustedly.

Whoever chose that to plant on me knew nothing about me. I do not have a sweet tooth: I have no taste for puddings, trifles, ice creams, sorbets—whatever. If I am out to dinner I either refuse them, or I toy with them. Any sugar I get comes from fruit and nut chocolate, which for some reason I relish. So maybe it was the slightly ridiculous nature of the pudding that made her choose it. If so perhaps I didn't have too much to fear. If all this woman wanted was to make me into a figure of fun, then there was no reason to get worked up about her and her intentions.

Then another thought struck me: what wonderful headlines the papers would have come up with if the matter had gone any further: THE STICKY-FINGERED MINISTER; MINISTER CAUGHT STICKY-HANDED. They would have had a field day in the popular press, left or right wing. I wouldn't be the first politician whose career had foundered on a public guffaw. What kind of mind was it, what kind of twisted sense of humor, that could think up such a scheme?

I shook myself. I was getting paranoia—the occupational disease of the politician.

Nevertheless, the next day I told my driver to take me first to the Palace of Westminster. I know a lot of policemen there to talk to, but as luck would have it the first one I saw, taking a rest from dealing with the tourists on the pavement outside, was Geoff Marrit, whom I had spoken to on my first day in office as a minister.

"'Ullo, 'ullo," he said, in parody-policeman style. "It is you today, is it? What can I do for you?"

"It's a silly little matter," I said, "but I thought it best to register it with the police here."

So I gave him a potted version of what had happened since we had last talked, omitting my fascination with my own origins. That, of course, was the only thing that gave the story any interest, and the thing that really suggested someone was directing my attention to those origins in some kind of spirit of derision or revenge. I could tell from his expression as my narrative proceeded that he was not impressed.

"Nothing in it for us, is there, sir?"

"Oh no."

"There's no definite connection between the postcards and what happened yesterday, is there?"

"Nothing demonstrable. I quite realize I'm sounding paranoid. But I do get a definite sense of someone taking a malicious interest in me, wanting to do me some harm. After all, the woman was definitely following me."

"Do you expect us to look into that aspect, sir?"

"No, I don't. But I would like you to take note of it. The possibility exists that the jokes or whatever they are could become more serious. Then I'd like to be able to refer to the police here as witnesses that some kind of malicious campaign had been registered as a possibility."

PC Marrit's face showed he realized I hadn't taken leave of my senses.

"Fair enough, sir. That's often a useful precaution. I'll write a brief report, give it to the appropriate person, and you'll know it's on the files."

"I'm very grateful." I had been storing something up in my mind while we'd been talking. "By the way, when you saw me coming up to you, you said, 'It is you today, is it?' What on earth did you mean?"

He looked a mite embarrassed.

"Oh, more talking to myself than talking to you, sir. There was a bloke through here yesterday—well, I won't say he was the spitting image of you, but there was a definite resemblance. I tell you, I started toward him, thinking to swap a few words, being convinced it was you—had to fall back when I found it wasn't."

"I see. What told you it wasn't?"

"Oh, he was a bit older, more wrinkles around the eyes, losing a bit of hair on either side of the temples, fuller face altogether. As I said, he wasn't a spitting image, so I knew when I got closer it wasn't you."

"You didn't get his name, I suppose?"

"I did. I looked in the register just out of interest, to see if it could be your brother. His name was Matthew Martindale."

That stopped me in my tracks.

"That really *is* interesting."

I paused, irresolute, in the lobby, conscious that PC Marrit was watching me. What was I to do, and who could I get to do it for me? Finally I went along to the Commons Library, and talked to a young woman called Sarah Sharp, who had done work for me in the past.

"Could you turn up for me any material—obituaries, say, at least to start with—on the Marquis of Aylesbury?"

A brief expression of surprise wafted over her face, to be replaced at once by professional impassivity.

"Easily, I should think. Which one?"

"Eh?"

"Well, it's bound to be an old title. Is it a specific Marquis, with a number?"

"I haven't the faintest idea. Sorry to be so dim. Could we say any Marquis of Aylesbury who has died in the last twenty or thirty years?"

"No problem. When would you like it?"

"On my way back from the Ministry—say three-or four-ish?"

"I'll have it put out for you."

I can't say my mind was on my work at the Ministry that day. Until then I had been able to compartmentalize, to keep my private wonderings and my public actions quite separate. Now the one kept intruding on the other. Matthew Martindale. The Christian name of the son of Lord John Revill, the surname of his mother's family who had taken him from the Upper Brook

Street home after she was murdered. It needed no great exercise of the imagination to see that they could have decided to hide the children's identities under their own name: not just the murder but the hue and cry about their father's disappearance would mean that their own name would have been a perpetual embarrassment, even a torment, to the children. Public schools, I am told, can be the cruelest places in the world.

So Matthew Martindale had come the day before on business to the Palace of Westminster. What could that business be? Anything, of course. I knew nothing about his life. He could be a stately home owner—perhaps of that manor house Hadleigh Grange, to which he and his sister had been taken—particularly if his grandparents had had no sons. He could have been lobbying the government or his MP. Stately home owners were always in the news, especially so at the moment, for grandees had been doing a cunning little dodge of getting tax concessions for themselves by claiming to open their piles to the public, but in fact doing it for one afternoon a year, keeping very quiet even about that, and at all other times keeping the Great Unwashed strictly at bay.

Speculation was useless. It was also inevitable. I

was wasting my time at the Ministry, and the civil servants' time, too. At three I packed my papers into my official box and left.

When I got to the House of Commons Library Sarah Sharp was waiting for me. She gestured toward a place at which yellowing copies of newspapers were piled. I nodded my thanks to Sarah and went over. There were copies of *The Times, The Daily Telegraph*, and *The Guardian*. The Marquis of Aylesbury, then, was not one of those grandees of interest mainly to the tabloid press—not, in other words, a man of scandalous life or ludicrous opinions. Lord John had been, at least in that one terrible action of his life, the black sheep, the rotten apple.

I took up *The Times* from the top of the pile. I looked at the guide on the front page—features were placed differently then. The date on the masthead was April 29, 1967. During the Wilson government, then, that had taken over—after the brief interregnum of Lord Home, that deceptively vague but crafty aristocrat—from Macmillan's government. I turned to the obituary page.

There, looking out at me, was myself.

No, not myself. Myself when much older. Hair gray, face lined, chin and neck becoming scrawny.

But thick, strongly defined eyebrows, jutting chin, prominent straight nose with flaring nostrils, high forehead. This was the Seventh Marquis of Aylesbury, father of Lord John Revill.

I raised my head, thoroughly unnerved, and wiped my sweating face. I saw, looking at me, Sarah Sharp, my librarian friend who had collected the material. She was clearly fascinated by my reaction, showing she had been before me looking at the obituaries. I had an uneasy sense that my secret was no longer contained in the little world of my friends and acquaintances.

CHAPTER SEVEN

Some Kind of Relative

"Jim," I said, coming up behind a man hunched over a computer in the Labor Party headquarters in Walworth Road and putting my hand on his shoulder.

That "Jim" was a piece of politician's fake mateyness, I'm afraid. You adopt all the techniques Americans use for remembering people's names. It goes down awfully well with constituents, less well, perhaps, with toilers at the political coal-face. Jim was perfectly aware that I hardly knew him, had met him no more than once or twice, and would not expect him to be on first-name terms with me. He looked up at me, hardly bothering to hide his surprise.

"Good Lord," he said. "Shouldn't you be in Tuscany?"

"No, I hate crowds," I said. "Jim, you've got all the candidates of all the parties over the last few years on that computer of yours, haven't you? Local as well as national?"

"Sure."

"Could you do something for me?" He nodded. He had realized I wanted something from him. "I'd like you to check whether someone called Matthew Martindale has ever been involved in politics at any level."

"No problem." He fiddled with boxes of discs and within a couple of minutes came up with the name on his screen.

"Ah, so he has been," I said with satisfaction. Jim peered at a meager line or two of information under the name.

"Hmmm. Not really what you'd call politically active," he said, with a professional's contempt for dilettante politicians. "He stood as a Tory for Wellingborough Council in 1988. The beginning of the turnaround—turndown, rather—in Tory fortunes. He didn't get elected. And that's about it. Not exactly a heavyweight political figure."

"No, hardly," I said thoughtfully. "What was he doing visiting the Houses of Parliament? I wonder. He's been here recently." Understandably Jim shrugged.

"Could be anything, surely. What's the inter-est?"

"Political-cum-personal," I said gnomically. "Is that absolutely all you've got on him?"

"All except his address. He hasn't stood for anything again."

"And what's the address?"

"The Dower House, Chatstock St. Mary, near Welling-borough, Northants." He considered. "A nice address that. The sort of address people write to *The Times* from."

I noted it down, thanked him, and turned away.

"Oh, and by the way, it's Jack," he said to my departing and mortified back.

"House of Commons first, then the Ministry," I told my driver.

In the Commons Library I managed for myself rather than seeking help. I had wondered in the car whether I was creating too many hostages to fortune by roping in so many people to answer my queries. If they didn't get my drift at once, as the librarian had done, they would certainly be puzzled. Anyway, it was easy enough to find the *Landed Gentry*. It was probably required reading for Tory MPs twenty or thirty years ago, in the days before the composition of the party had changed and it had become *arriviste* rather than vested.

I found what I wanted easily enough. Sir George Martindale of Hadleigh Grange had died in 1980, and the baronetcy had passed to his son Edward. Sir Edward's seat was still Hadleigh Grange. He was married with two children, both sons. His sister Veronica was recorded as having married Lord John Revill. "D. 1962," it said tactfully but bleakly. Her children were recorded as Matthew and Caroline, with no mention of a change of surname.

I resolutely put the matter from my mind during work. I had spoken sternly to myself, made it clear to the conscious part of my brain that I was a (junior) minister first, a person second. Any investigation of my origins was strictly for my free time. Nevertheless as soon as I was home and listening to music on the CD player or watching television with half my attention, the subject insisted on taking over.

I knew I was going to have to talk to Matthew Martindale.

But what sort of meeting was it going to be?

Was it going to be "structured," even confrontational? I knew of course what I wanted to ask him about, at least the basic things, but had no right to confront him, no grievance to lay at his door, no reason to demand answers as a sort of compensation for wrongs. He, like me, was someone who at an early stage of his life had been caught up in events beyond his influence or comprehension.

I decided that the meeting should be improvisational—an encounter of two men who surprisingly find they might be related, might have interests in common. That way, I thought, I could pay him a visit without any heavy burden of preparation.

I drove up to Northamptonshire the following Saturday. There was only one pub in the village of Chatstock St. Mary, and it was doing a nice little trade when I dropped in there at lunchtime. I ordered a ham sandwich, and as I waited for it I remained with my pint at the bar.

"Is the big house I came past on the road from Welling-borough the Dower House?" I asked the landlord.

He was big and slow, and he nodded his head ponderously.

"That's right. Fine old place. Built long ago—before the Martindales took over at Hadleigh

Grange."

"And how long ago was that?"

That puzzled him. He'd been retailing local lore not personal knowledge.

"Don't rightly know. History's not my strong point. But well over a hundred year, folk say. They're big people around here, the Martindales."

"And it's Matthew Martindale in the Dower House now, isn't it? I think I knew him at school."

"Could be. He went away to boarding school, like they do, but I don't mind where. I wondered whether you might be related. You favor him."

"Could be, I suppose. We might have a common great-grandparent or something."

"Oh aye. Nobody knows their own relatives these days, do they? Now then, I saw Mrs. Martindale with the children an hour or so ago. They were off to Northampton to see one of those films kids always think they have to see in the school holidays. Brainwashed, that's what they are. So you could find Matthew up at the House, or maybe up at the Grange. He's estate manager for Sir Edward, and he's not a nine-to-five sort of chap."

So he'd understood what I wanted without my asking. I rather regretted my lie about being at school with Matthew. The landlord was obviously sharper than he looked. Lying is something you can all too easily slip into, allow to become a habit, assuming that practice makes perfect.

Slightly abashed I took the sandwich which had been put on the bar and my drink to a table by a window. To cover my aloneness I took out of my pocket some of the photocopies I'd taken in the library of the obituaries of the Marquises of Aylesbury.

The ones of the old Marquis I had studied several times. The ones of his son I'd barely looked at. They were almost derisorily short, and even so they seemed to be searching around for anything to say. He had been born in 1924, had succeeded to the title in 1967, was elder brother to Lord John Revill, who had disappeared in 1962 after the murder of his wife. He had, one gathered, been a collector of nineteenth-century paintings. And that, essentially, was that. Two of the obituaries contained the classic sentence "He never married." None speculated about the future of the Marquisate. If events had followed their natural course it would have gone to Lord John. He would probably have seemed, by comparison with his brother, a figure of towering stature.

I downed the rest of my pint and walked out into the sun. I decided to leave my car in the pub car park and walk. There were no long distances in Chatstock St. Mary. Five minutes later I found myself standing on the doorstep of the Dower House. It was redbrick, early nineteenth century, covered in Virginia creeper, and altogether a desirable residence that was also warm and welcoming. I suspected the garden was full of interesting plants, but I was too ignorant to be certain—I only knew they were not things I was familiar with.

I rang the bell.

The house was substantially built and I heard no footsteps from inside. The door opened without warning and I was looking straight at a high forehead, near-black hair, jutting chin, and flashing nostrils. He had been starting to ask my business but his jaw dropped and no sound came out. It was a couple of seconds before he began to regain his poise.

"Ah. This is a bit of a stunner. I won't pretend I don't know who you are. How did you find me?" I was about to reply when he stood aside. "You'd better come in. The family's at the cinema, so this is a good time. I suppose you want to talk?"

He led the way down a broad, elegant hallway to a long and airy sitting room furnished in traditional style—some stylish eighteenth-century small tables and bulky, enveloping armchairs and sofa. The pictures, without being valuable, looked as if they had been around in one or other of his families for some time. He went straight to the sideboard.

"I think I need a slug of whiskey. Could you use the same?"

"A small slug."

There passed a glance of understanding, almost of complicity, between the two of us. He handed me a glass, then downed his own small measure, set his glass back on the sideboard, and sat down. I did the same, and sat waiting for him to begin.

"I don't usually drink during the day," he said. "Exceptional circumstances…"

"I realize it has come as a surprise. But you say you know who I am."

"Saw you in the paper the day you got your government job. And your age—they were highlighting the young ones, with pictures. I expect you saw it. Wouldn't normally see the *Evening*

Standard, but I was in London to meet my sister back from New Zealand. I'm afraid I hadn't registered you before."

"There was a fair bit of TV coverage when I won the by-election in '93."

"Not that interested in politics these days. Sometimes don't see the news on television for days at a time or a newspaper either." He looked at me. "But I'm more interested in how *you* got on to *me*. I'm a person of the utmost obscurity."

"Except for your parentage," I ventured. His expression told me he had expected this, and was almost relieved it had come out into the open.

"Except for that," he said, nodding. "Of course people around here know who I am. I can't pretend they don't talk about it, because I suspect they do. That's just human nature. But not to me. They don't talk about it to me. So it isn't a factor of any importance in my life."

"What about when you stood for Wellingborough Council?"

He grimaced.

"My childish peccadillo. Why on earth did I bother? If people knew about my father they made nothing of it during the election, and it never got into the local paper. It's a very old scandal now."

"That's true. People had to jog my memory as to what actually happened," I conceded.

"People?" He raised his eyebrow. "You haven't told me how you got on to me. Somehow I assume it's recent, otherwise you would have tried to make contact before."

"It's recent. The day I got my job at the Education Department I had a postcard pushed through my door. It said: 'Who do you think you are?' I may have been wrong, but I read it, took it as a challenge. I've had another one since that suggests I was right. And the permanent secretary at the Department had once worked for your father. She saw the resemblance—not in the face, but in the stance, the shape, intangibles like that. Sitting at my desk I reminded her of your father sitting at his desk."

"Neither of us is much like my father facially. But we are very like my grandfather."

"I know. I looked up obituaries for him a few days ago."

He raised his eyebrows.

"You *have* been doing your homework. What's it all about?"

I settled into my chair. Something I hadn't

expected was happening: I was beginning to feel comfortable in his company.

"In the first instance it's about satisfying my curiosity. I had always assumed that the parents I knew were my natural parents. Suddenly it seemed they weren't."

"So they'd never told you that you were adopted? That's unusual these days....And in the second instance?"

I was silent for a moment, thinking how to put this. Most people were pretty unimpressed by my feelings that, for reasons unknown, someone had me in their frame.

"There were the postcards for a start. Someone wants me to get wise about my origins. Why? How can that matter to anyone but myself? Then something distinctly odd happened the other day. Someone slipped something into my bag at Marks & Spencer, so that I was accused of shoplifting."

If he was skeptical he hid it well.

"Ah....Of course that could have been just any crank wanting to discredit a member of the new government in a minor way."

"Yes, it could. And the fact that it was of all things a package of sticky toffee pudding would suggest that. And also the fact that at this stage the whole thing doesn't seem terribly serious."

"But you cling to the idea that one brain is behind all this, and it could get serious later on?"

"Yes, I do. That said, I should add that I've reported these things to the Palace of Westminster police, who have aeons of experience of what people get up to in relation to politicians, and they're not terribly impressed."

"You reported it as a sort of insurance?"

"Exactly," I said, impressed by his understanding. His face was thoughtful and also sympathetic.

"All this is interesting, but we're rather skirting round the major issue, aren't we?" he said.

"And what do you see that as?"

"Who do you think you are?"

I sat back, thinking not so much about the question as about him. I was in no doubt that I liked what I saw—even if what I saw was a version of me, so it seemed like vanity. This version of me, in his early forties, was by the look of him a serious farmer, a man of the soil, even if on the managerial level. He was strong, capable, he would be willing to get his hands dirty—in fact he frequently did so by the look of them: they were chapped, lined with soil, and hard. I also thought he was honest: there was a warmth about him, an interest in me and my predicament, that was very congenial to me. It struck me suddenly that I was rather lonely, and that this man was my brother. I had to pay him the compliment of being honest back.

"I could be your father's son by the nanny," I said.

He nodded without surprise or consternation. He had considered this already.

"Yes. Of course you could be my father's son by any number of women, but I have never had the impression that he was a promiscuous man. And she was pregnant at the time of the murder."

"How do you know that?"

"My sister is two years older than me. It was one of the things we whispered about in the days, weeks, after the murder, in bed at the Grange. Then at school it was spoken of. My grandparents chose an exceptionally good and concerned school for me—it's something I will always be grateful to them for. They also had my name changed, adopted us officially—eased our passage in every way they could. Still, schoolboys will be schoolboys. One or two little shits made sure I knew that they knew who I was: that my father was a murderer, and that he'd been having it off with the nanny, and that she was going to have his child."

"I suppose by then she'd had it—*me*."

"You're making assumptions. Yes, I suppose she had, though. I never heard anything concrete about her after the day of the murder. She was a taboo subject at the Grange."

"But the taboos must have broken down when you and your sister were alone."

"That's true. We did talk about Nanny, as I said, but she hadn't been there long, we didn't particularly like her, and of course we were more interested in our mother and what had happened to her."

"You knew she was dead?"

"Oh yes, we knew that. That was the reason given for taking us from London to the Grange."

"But not that she was murdered."

"That idea got through to us very gradually."

"How?"

"Probably by overhearing the servants talking, or my grand-parents when they thought they were alone."

"And the fact that it was your father who had done it?"

"The two ideas made their way simultaneously into our minds. People talking about one thing inevitably talked about the other."

"You say you were more interested in your mother than the nanny, which is only natural. You must have been fond of her."

He pondered, not wanting to make a snap answer, perhaps because he was talking to a virtual stranger, perhaps because he didn't lightly embark on any act of disloyalty.

"I think not. Of course one had the conventional notions of a mother and what one ought to feel toward her—those had been dinned into us by earlier nannies. But I don't think we really *felt* them. And I don't think we had any reason to. She was…a distant figure. Emotionally reserved—no, *cold* is the right word. She kissed us now and then, but as if that was one of the things one was expected to do. She never held us. No, I don't think we felt a great deal for her."

"That must have left the nanny to supply her place, then."

He shook his head vigorously.

"Oh no. Not just Lucy—the two before her didn't try to be stand-in mothers either. They were massive elderly dragons, rather quick to use the hairbrush, but at the wrong end. They were very traditional nanny figures. The upper class entrust their children to extraordinary types: first a nanny, then public school teachers. They tried a different type with Lucy, but one always thought she was interested in other things than us."

"This must have left a big gap in your lives," I said. I hazarded a guess: "Did your father supply the missing affection?"

"*Yes.*" It was said with great love and enthusiasm. "It was our father who was at the center of our lives. He wasn't always there, of course—not by any means, since he had his political career, as MP and as minister. Still, one always felt that that was a bit of a hobby, that he was at best a dabbler in matters of state. He *was* there a lot for us—in the house, taking us to the park, to circuses, and pantomimes. Oh, Mother would sometimes come along, but it was father who *took* us."

"I see."

"He was loving, involved, interested, charming, and funny."

There was a break in his voice as he went through the catalog.

"And suddenly you lost him."

"Yes.…I don't like talking about that. And it

couldn't be relevant to the question of who you are."

"Maybe not. Unless just possibly after he disappeared he resumed the connection with Lucy Mariotti."

"I doubt that, though of course I *know* nothing. I do know she was in Britain for some time after the murder. Caroline heard people say the police wouldn't let her leave, had confiscated her passport."

"Do you think he lived for some time after the murder?"

He shook his head, disclaiming knowledge again.

"I just don't know. I was too young to follow things at the time, and I've preferred to leave him in peace since I've been an adult." I was covertly watching his face. It was blank, almost ingenuous. I think he knew I was watching him. "They want me to have him declared dead."

I pricked up my ears.

"Oh? Who does? Your family?"

"No, no. It's never discussed in the family. But the Conservative leader in the House of Lords does, for one."

"But why?" In a second, though, I had worked

it out. "Of course. You are by rights the Marquis of Aylesbury."

"If my father is dead," he said firmly. "The last Marquis, his brother, died four years ago."

"Yes, I've just been reading his obituaries, such as they were. He was not the marrying type, they all said or implied. I'd gathered that already."

Matthew laughed.

"The archetypal sad gay."

"Not a distinguished holder of the title, I guessed from what I read."

"Far from it. Almost invisible. He had a life of sorts, I suppose. A sex life with vigorous Australian and South African visitors whom he paid or boarded. Intellectually his one interest was early Victorian genre painters. He had enough money to live as he wanted, but not enough to do anything good with it, or splash it effectively on anything."

"You weren't close, I take it?"

"Barely knew him. He threw a party on my twenty-first—the sort of occasion he wished he didn't have to hold and I wished I didn't have to go to. I suspected he was trying to discover my sexual orientation, and that of my friends. He was, by and large, disappointed. But I shouldn't slang off at him. He left me the house in Upper Brook Street, which was a family one, and a lot of bad pictures. I sold the house sight unseen, but I was silly enough to look at the pictures. Anyway, they fetched a tidy sum: I could stop working tomorrow, or work for myself, but I'm happy as I am."

"Happier than you would be as a working peer?"

"Good heavens, yes! To be fair I don't think anyone is suggesting I be that. They'd just like my vote against your lot's plans to reform the House of Lords, and also against things like the ban on hunting. I'm afraid I don't give a damn about hunting either way, though I'd rather die than turn out myself—I don't fancy poncing around in a red coat with a collection of prats who most of them work in the City or in Canary Wharf or places like that."

"So I take it you're not ready to become Marquis of Aylesbury?"

"No. I went up a week or two ago to talk to the Tory leader in the House of Lords. I told him it wasn't on."

"Because you don't want to be Marquis? Or for some other reason?"

He left a pause before he replied.

"Because I don't want to be the one who has my father declared dead." He leaned forward and looked at me. "Think of it. At the time of the murder my father was thirty-five. Now, if he's alive, he'll be about seventy. That's no age. Who am I, of all people, his son, to assume that he's dead?"

"What do you really think?"

"I tell you I don't know. Any number of people have asked, but I always say the same: I don't know. I suppose I hope he's dead, because he can't have had much of a life. But then, what if he's in a Greek monastery or something, happy and at peace? I don't know, and I see no reason to take action. The Marquises of Aylesbury have been pretty undistinguished figures for generations, apart from my grandfather, who held something or other at the coronation of George VI and became ambassador to Russia when Khrushchev was in power. The country as a whole can jog along quite happily without a Marquis of Aylesbury. The estate went long ago, and most of the family wealth with it. Good riddance. Anyway, I'm not even sure I'm a Tory anymore. And before you start trying to sign me up for your mob I should say I genuinely don't think I'm *any*thing politically."

"I'm not in this as a recruitment officer for the Labor Party," I said.

"That brings us back to the question: What *are* you in it for?"

"To find out whether I am the son of your father and Lucy Mariotti," I said promptly. "And to find out how I came to be brought up by my mother and father—by Claud and Elizabeth Pinnock."

"You haven't got a quixotic subagenda to prove that my father wasn't a murderer?"

"No. The idea hadn't crossed my mind."

"Because I think it's quite certain that he killed my mother. Nothing I've ever heard has suggested that there's any doubt about that whatsoever. Nothing."

"I'm interested in myself only," I said, "proving where I come from. I just want to talk to people who might help me. Your sister, for example."

He waved his hand dismissively.

"Oh, Caroline comes and goes a lot. She's a fashion buyer, often out of the country. If she's ever stationary long enough to see you I'll let you know. But Caroline doesn't know anything that I don't know."

"The housekeeper too—I'd like to talk to her."

"Mrs. Gould. Mrs. Selena Gould."

"You remember her?"

"Just the name. Nothing at all about her. She didn't figure much in our lives, I suppose."

"I'm wondering about the American who did the color supplement piece on the case—wondering if he had any information that he didn't use, or which was cut by a subeditor."

Matthew nodded. He knew about all the coverage.

"Elmore Hasselbank. We didn't cooperate, of course."

"Naturally."

"But he did a very thorough job. He had several of these razor-sharp researchers behind him."

"Interesting. Maybe that's what I need." We were interrupted by the sound of a large estate car drawing up at the back of the house. "I'd better go."

"No—don't scuttle away. At least stay and say hello to the children and Janet."

There wasn't much option anyway. In a matter of seconds three big and boisterous children, ranging from about nine to fourteen in age, had burst in and taken over the room, shouting things like "Daddy, it was absolutely awful!" "Daddy, that was the *worst* film I've ever seen" and "They wouldn't even show that film on Channel Five," and so on. They were followed by a substantial lady, big-boned and getting plump, with a tolerant smile.

"Well, our children may not be the brightest in the world but at least they seem to be developing a critical sense. Oh!—"

She had caught sight of me. I think she wanted to look back inquiringly at her husband but was too polite to. Instead she came over and shook hands.

"Hello. We haven't met."

"Colin Pinnock."

"I rather thought so. I am glad you and Matthew have made contact. I think in his heart he wanted that. You will stay to dinner, won't you? We eat early because of the children."

And stay to dinner I did, had a very happy time at the heart of a family, got to know the children and their mother, and felt safe and settled—more so than I had in years. The children, much to my surprise, noticed no resemblance between their father and me: he was Dad—known, accepted, loved, hardly noticed. I was someone else. Janet Martindale on the other hand was fascinated, looked surreptitiously from one of us to the other, as if making an inventory of similarities and differences, then smiling in embarrassment and forcing herself to look away. The dinner was splendid: pork chops with taste, vegetables with taste. I suspected part at least of the Hadleigh Grange estate was farmed organically. We talked about me, my upbringing, my work, the political situation. Nothing of interest came up about my particular preoccupation until the children had noisily got up and gone out to visit their friends in the village. Then Matthew said:

"You know, I've remembered a scrap of information about Lucy."

"Oh?"

"I told you Caroline used to say Lucy wasn't really interested in us. What she often said after the murder was: 'She was only interested in her professors.'"

"Her professors? Who on earth were they?"

"I think Lucy was only filling in with us before doing more work at university. What do they call it—postgraduate research, is it? Caroline used to say she never had any friends round to visit her in Upper Brook Street—no fellow Australians in Britain, no other young people. When she talked about herself what she mainly went on about was 'her professors,' and the work she was going to do with them."

"I see," I said carefully. "Do you think this is relevant?"

"Probably not. But if she didn't have any friends much here, wasn't too bothered about making any, and wasn't in with any expatriate Aussie set of people of her own age, then I did wonder what she did when she was forced to stay on here, without a job—she wouldn't have found it easy to get one, after what had happened—without money probably. It seemed to me possible that the people she might have turned to for help might have been 'her professors.'"

CHAPTER EIGHT

An Inspector Calls

I am beginning to understand how people in Eastern Europe felt, in the days before glasnost, about the knock on the door in the middle of the night.

I am being neurotic. Actually it was about half past nine, because I'd just watched the BBC news. By now all the politicians were returning from their summer vacations and we were entering the run-up to the autumn party conference season. Politics was rearing its ugly but unavoidable head once more. And the conference season has become over the last few years the time when the newspaper moguls delight in embarrassing politicians—not, as a rule, about their politics, but about their private lives.

I jumped when the knock came. I was rereading *Great Expectations* and had got to the return of Magwitch. I would not have been surprised by the telephone ringing, because it had rung all the time since I became an MP, but I *was* surprised that anyone should call on me in person at that hour. I left the door on its chain and peered through the crack.

The man in the corridor outside was in plain clothes, but everything about him shouted policeman. He was approaching fifty, heavily built, with cold eyes and a set mouth. There is a particular sort of policeman—a small but appreciable minority—who entered the force because they have rigid certainties, overtidy minds, and an idea that they have the right to force other people into a mold of their making. Over the years their blinkered confidence in themselves makes them cut corners, and subsequently in some cases slide toward the absolutely illegal. This one was tightly encased in a brown suit with a nondescript tie and brightly polished shoes. In the background, shadowed by the dim lighting in the corridor, was another, younger man. Nothing particular about him shouted policeman, but everything shouted stooge.

They flashed their cards at me in a way that was menacing rather than reassuring.

"Mr. Colin Pinnock? I'm DI Rawson and this is DC Miller. Could we come in?"

"Please" would clearly have been a sign of weakness. My stomach churned over in anticipation. This was the next stage.

"Please do. Come through." My voice played no tricks because I consciously forced it not to. I was becoming experienced.

I unhooked the chain and opened the door wide. They both wiped their shoes on the mat, and then I led them through into the bright light, in which they looked no more comforting than in the dimness. I waved them to the sofa. DI Rawson sat with his knees neatly together, then took out a notebook and spoke by rote.

"Mr. Pinnock, we have reason to believe, based on information received—"

"From whom?"

"That need not concern you, sir. Based on information received, that you may have in your possession a collection of pornographic material of an illegal nature. Our information—"

"Your informant, did she tell you that I was a government minister?" I asked, trying not to sound pompous or bullying.

"As I said before, the source of the information is immaterial. We are aware that you are a member of the present government, and we are anxious to keep this whole thing low-key."

I refrained with an effort from shifting uneasily in my chair. His tone belied his words. He said "the present government" in a way that announced that he wasn't one of those who thought New Labor betokened a new heaven and a new earth. And his stated anxiety to keep things low-key contained an undercurrent of threat that he could raise the key at the first opportunity.

"So you have no search warrant, but you'd like to go through my flat with my consent?" I hazarded.

"Well, sir, that would—"

"And do you know what, Inspector?" He was beginning to lose his bully's confidence, and said nothing. "I'd be willing to bet that you find something. I don't know where it will be, or what it will consist of, but I'd bet you'll find something."

"You're not suggesting we've planted something, I hope?"

Guilty conscience that, I thought. Planting evidence was a horticultural activity he was not unused to.

"No, I'm not. But I am suggesting someone has."

"Would you mind explaining yourself, sir?"

"Willingly." I felt I was beginning to get on top of him. "I've already informed the House of Commons police that I believe I'm becoming the victim of some kind of campaign. A campaign of persecution designed at the very least to bring me ridicule, unfavorable publicity, maybe bring about my resignation. Goods have been planted on me so that I was suspected of shoplifting. Postcards have been sent with certain…insinuations."

His expression was dubious, and he seemed to regain confidence.

"I see, sir. Is that all?"

"Obviously not, since you are here on this wild-goose chase."

His skepticism mirrored that of the Commons policemen.

"You do realize that your story to the police at Westminster could be something in the nature of a preemptive strike, don't you, sir? I'm implying nothing, merely suggesting a possibility. You could have a collection of pornography, you could have the itch to shoplift—all sorts of people do—and you want to get this story, this pretty cock-and-bull story, in first, to protect yourself."

And of course, from a policeman's point of view, he was right. Still, for someone who was merely suggesting a possibility, his mind seemed pretty made up.

"You seem to have come to your own conclusions already, Inspector," I said sweetly. "When you've found this collection of pornography I'd like you—or your constable here, who may have a more open mind—to examine my front door for signs of illegal entry. Now I suggest you go about your business."

Inspector Rawson didn't seem to like my telling him what to do, but he got up and his stooge followed his lead. Then they looked around them. Rawson made for the sideboard and began rummaging, but Miller seemed more uncertain.

"I suggest you try the guest bedroom," I said, gesturing. "It's a room I hardly ever go into."

It was a lucky guess. Within a couple of minutes Miller was shouting to his superior. I went along and stood in the doorway. The constable had yanked a large and ragged envelope from the top of the wardrobe and was laying it on the unmade bed. A collection of glossy magazines was spilling out of it. Rawson went over, his compact body showing every sign of excitement, and he began going through the assorted items, flicking through them and laying them out on the bed. I went over.

"A pretty miscellaneous lot," I commented. "I seem to have varied tastes."

And that was a truth he could not deny. From the covers alone it was clear that there was straight porn, gay porn, pedophilic porn, porn for leather fetishists, and so on. Some of the magazines were crumpled and grubby, as if retrieved from litter bins on the streets. The covers suggested that as porn most of the magazines were at the soft end of the spectrum, and as Rawson flicked through them his obvious disappointment told me the covers didn't lie. He was changing gear, and was now intent on damage limitation.

"Well, Inspector?" I said.

Rawson went round the bed and had a whispered conversation with Miller—or rather told him what he had decided. He turned back to me, his face a mask.

"I don't think we need to trouble you further, sir," he said.

"But *I* need to trouble *you*," I insisted. "I would

like these magazines tested for fingerprints."

"That won't be necessary, sir. And it wouldn't prove anything."

"It will prove that, if I've had any contact with them at all, I will have been wearing gloves. I think any court or any further investigation of me concerning other matters will find that pretty hard to imagine. It might also show who planted them here. Do you have the fingerprints of your informant? Can you get them? I want my door investigated, as I've suggested, and I demand to know the name of the person who lodged this information against me."

Well, we argued it back and forth. Rawson conceded the door, and Miller was dispatched to look at it, coming back to agree that there were scratches that could suggest illegal entry. That led Rawson to concede the fingerprinting, and we all went down to the Pimlico station where I obligingly stuck my hand on the black pad. On the final point Rawson would concede not an inch: it was against all procedures to tell me the name of the false informant. Realizing that in this he was telling the truth, I had to give way.

Later, back in my flat with a celebratory drink, and flicking through the Yellow Pages to find someone who could change the lock on my door, I had a feeling of euphoria, almost of triumph: I had bested the inspector, whom I thought of as well over toward the fascist pig end of the police spectrum. And in the process I had also had the better of "her"—whoever she was. The police wouldn't be in a hurry to act on her information in future.

I phoned a twenty-four-hour locksmith service and arranged for someone to come early next morning. I put a dining chair up against the door and piled it with silver and cutlery: if anyone tried it again I wanted to be woken up. Then I had another drink, going over the details of my duel with the inspector with a view to profiting from my experience in future encounters. I went to bed feeling pretty good.

But when sleep came the shadow side took over. I was running down dark, narrow streets at night, fleeing from something which took no shape except a black coat or cloak, with no human features visible. The more I ran, the narrower and darker the streets became, until they were little more than alleyways, foul and litter-strewn. It was like being trapped in a Soho that was continually contracting until it seemed the very streets would crush me.

When I awoke I got up at once, unrefreshed. I showered and made myself some black coffee. As I waited for the locksmith I realized that I had never felt exhilarated by London, as some do, never felt a sense of limitless possibilities, of an exciting world that would open up for me. Instead I had felt *shut in*. My dream, as well as a reaction to the policemen's visit, was also a reflection of this.

Perhaps I should have had a summer holiday walking in Yorkshire with George Eakin.

～～～

Three or four days later I was having a drink with Susan in a Greenwich pub. We had gone over the visit of Inspector Rawson and its implications, and it led me back to my usual preoccupation.

"Would there be some kind of directory of American journalists?" I asked her.

"Sure to be. They go in for that kind of thing. And there'd be some kind of professional association as well. Do you want to contact Elmore Hasselbank?"

"Spot on as usual."

"What other American journalist has come up in this matter, and what else do you think about?"

"My work for a start."

"Well, what else do you think about in your spare time?"

"I would like to talk to him if it's practicable," I said, trying to ignore her implication. "Matthew Martindale said he was very sharp, and agreed he did a good job."

I'd told her briefly on the phone about my visit to the Martindales. Now she pressed me for more.

"What was your overall impression of him?"

"I liked him, as I said, very much. Straight, strong-minded, and remarkably unscathed by it all. After all, it's not everyone whose father has killed his mother."

"He was the younger, wasn't he?"

"Yes. I wondered—"

"What?"

I shifted in my seat, trying to sort out vague impressions, niggling discrepancies.

"Well, in general, he took my arrival on the scene surprisingly well. As if he had half expected it—as possibly he did. Perhaps all his life he'd wondered about his half-brother or sister by the Australian nanny. That news had filtered through to the children. So he accepted me, there was no edginess—you could say we got on famously. But when I mentioned his sister—"

"Yes?"

"It's difficult to pin down, but thinking back I feel there was a sort of oddity, an inconsistency. On the one hand he said his sister was hardly ever around—was always off here, there, and everywhere, and he gave the vaguest of promises that if she was ever settled for any length of time he'd arrange for me to see her."

"What does she do?"

"Something in the fashion world."

"Figures."

"Oh yes. But on the other hand he talked about being in London on the day I got my government job—the day my picture was in the paper, where he saw it—in order to meet his sister off the plane from New Zealand."

"I see," said Susan, chewing over this. "Slightly odd, but no more than that. Flights from that part of the world are horrendous—a lot different from a quick flip from Milan or Paris."

"Fair enough. Maybe I'm seeing evasions where there were none."

"Did you talk about his father?"

"Our father. Yes. *Apparently* he showed no sign

of wanting to trace him. Took the view that if he's had a life on the run then he rather hoped it was over, and on the other hand, if he's found peace somewhere or other, then that's great, but he doesn't want to disturb it. He certainly doesn't want to be the one to have him declared dead, which the whips in the Lords have been pressing him to do. I don't know how I'd feel in the circumstances."

"On present evidence you'd want to trace him, or at least find out what happened to him."

"But I haven't had the trauma of losing him in that terrible way. Anyway Matthew and I only *look* alike. We're probably very different characters, and we were brought up in very different backgrounds. He's happy to get on with his own life—or that's the impression he tries to give."

"What about his mother?"

"Cold bitch. He realizes it now, if not then."

"And the nanny?"

"Hardly remembered, except that the children didn't much like her. It was the father who gave them love."

I went up to get us another round of drinks, and when I came back to our bench seat I put my arm around Susan's shoulder. I tried to make it look as if unconsciously I was slipping back into old routines, but in fact I'd thought over whether I should while I was at the bar. Susan removed it.

"Colin, I'm not getting into that again. Starting up a second time with an old boyfriend is something you shouldn't do unless you've really thought through why it didn't work in the first place and why it will be different now. We split up because your whole life was politics and I was just a fringe interest. That's still true—and in spades, now you're a government minister. Let's have it that we're good friends, shall we?"

"I've no choice, if that's what you want," I grumbled. "Still—"

"By the way, do you know there's a Pinnock still living in Southampton?" she said briskly.

"I realize you're changing the subject, but no, I didn't. You think it might be a relative?"

"Seems quite likely, the name not being particularly common. Would you like me to take it further—try to set something up? I got the name and address from the telephone directory. I could ring her up."

"On what pretext?"

"Oh, research into family history—something like that. It's not far from the truth. I could inquire whether she is any relation to the Claud and Elizabeth Pinnock who lived in Southampton in the 1950s. If she was I could arrange to visit her."

That definitely attracted me as an idea.

"Sounds interesting."

"You could come along, as my husband or boyfriend or something."

"That seems to be as close as I'm ever likely to get to being either," I grouched.

But the truth was I had no clear desire even to resume the relationship, let alone become Susan's or anybody else's husband. My life seemed to go on independently of any emotional drives—or at least of any other than sexual ones. Educating the disabled and the underprivileged, investigating my origins and the identity of my persecutor—these were my twin preoccupations. Putting my arm around Susan meant little more than that I wanted to go to bed with her. Putting it away meant she wasn't having that, thank you very much. And of course she was quite right. I was beginning to fear too that she was right when she implied I was becoming obsessed.

She was also extremely effective as a research assistant. The next day she was on the phone to me with Elmore Hasselbank's current job, though she warned me the directory of journalists she had consulted could well be out-of-date. The day after that, home in the evening, I discovered by ringing the paper named that he had gone from a high-sounding job on the *Seattle Star* to another high-sounding job on the *Chicago Observer*. These high-sounding jobs either mean you're very important or that you've been shuffled to one side. With Elmore Hasselbank I suspected it was the former. I used my status as a government minister to get him on the line in person. He sounded very important and very interested.

"Well, well, Mr. Pinnock—one of the New Labor ministers! I'm afraid I didn't recognize your name, I apologize for that, but I'm very pleased to talk to you. There's a lot of interest in your government over here."

"Yes, we seem to have been taken as a straw in the wind."

"You're rather more than that, with the majority you gained. The question here is how left wing you are, and how right wing. Left on what, right on what? At least it means there's a *political* content to the discussion over there. Here nobody talks about anything but the President's penis."

So we swapped ten minutes of political talk

before I got on to my own matters.

"What I was ringing about—"

"I didn't think you were going to appoint me your American contact for disseminating leaks and rumors."

"Perish the thought we should ever use such tactics! It's the matter of Lord John Revill."

There was a moment's silence on the other end.

"Good Lord! That old business? You won't get any political capital out of raking that up again, will you?"

"Of course not. Three quarters of the electorate either won't have heard of it or won't remember it. And in fact there was never much political capital in it, even back in 1962. It's the mystery and the human interest that has kept the story alive, as you must know. I'm afraid it was a bit naughty of me to use my government title when I rang you. This is a personal matter."

"I see." I could hear all sorts of journalistic questions buzzing around in his agile brain. "New Labor meets Old Tory. There could be a story in this somewhere. In the past I understood you were born 'either a little Liberal—substitute Laborite—or else a little Conservative.'"

"There's been a meltdown since then. As in your country. Pretty much the same could have been said of your people till the late sixties. And *no*—there won't be any story if I can help it."

"That's a shame. I'll restrain my curiosity for the moment. What can I do for you?"

"Well, for a start, I thought your coverage of the story brilliant—much the best I've seen so far."

He was obviously pleased. Americans are so often accused of getting things British ever so subtly wrong.

"Thanks a bunch. I enjoyed covering it: it had everything except religion, and it gave spice to my time in London. I had two brilliant researchers. If you set researchers on with the right questions, they'll do three quarters of the work for you. Then the rest is interviewing the key people yourself—particularly if they're bigwigs—and writing the thing up."

"Did you interview many bigwigs?"

"Some. The family clammed up, of course. We knew they would. I talked to his closest political friend, Sir Donald Fairbanks, but I didn't get a great deal out of him. Never got the feeling that politics was close to Revill's heart."

"I get the same feeling."

"The housekeeper refused to speak to us."

I perked up.

"You located her then?"

"Oh yes—in a nursing home in one of your seaside places. Bournemouth—that was it. Went there to try to change her mind, but I never got within a whisper. The nanny I never located, as you'll have gathered from the article. So most of the people I talked to were friends, real or so-called."

"What about friends of Lucy Mariotti?"

"We didn't get the impression she had any, at least in Britain. We talked to some in Australia—never very satisfactory, interviewing by telephone. They said the usual things: bright, fun-loving, ambitious. She'd been very interested in furthering her academic career."

"So I gathered."

"We talked to a couple of contacts in universities, but of course she hadn't actually started her work, so they didn't have a great deal to contribute."

"Do I take it she didn't start on her research after the murder, when the fuss had died down?"

"Oh no. Unless she went elsewhere."

"Do you remember who the academics were?"

"Oh dear…Frieda will know—Frieda Brewer,

the main research assistant I had. I can give you her phone number, because I still use her on British things. Wait a minute…It's one-eight-one, six-nine-two-seven-six-eight-seven. She's a poppet…Warnock was one of the names. Shakespearean wallah. Can't recall the other name."

Well, that felt like getting somewhere, at least.

"Can you tell me anything about the people involved, or anything—just an impression maybe—that didn't get into the article?"

He thought, but quickly, like any good journalist.

"Lucy Mariotti: sexually adventurous, and when they said ambitious her friends were putting it mildly. A brainy go-getter with enormous drive and nervous energy. Wife cold and ruthless, and I have the impression there was a new man in her life. Husband nice guy, funnily enough. Everybody seemed to feel that."

"That's my reading of him too. Did you form any idea of whether he was alive or dead?"

"No. I'd have put it in if I had."

"Nor whether he actually did the murder?"

"Oh, he did it all right! Nobody doubted it. I think the marriage had been on the rocks for some time."

"That's a reason for divorce, not murder."

"You'd be surprised, young man! You'd be surprised!"

Yet there were explanations needed here. Nobody doubted he'd done it, but they all thought he was a nice bloke. And in ninety-nine point nine percent of cases, breakdown does lead to divorce, not murder.

"Have you got any suggestions of further avenues to explore, or ones that might bear going over again?" I finally asked.

"Obvious ones: family, if you can get them unawares. The housekeeper. Any surviving policeman, the higher up the better. We got no joy there.… Then there's the child of the nanny. You knew she was pregnant? But perhaps you don't need to contact him.…" He was playing with me. I left a silence. "Beyond that, I'd talk to Frieda. She's got a ferret's brain. If there's anything we left undone she'll want to get back to it."

I ended the phone call with a good feeling of a job well done and possible areas of exploration identified. I pushed to the back of my mind the obvious fact that I had alerted a first-rate journalist to the existence of a story.

CHAPTER NINE

Second Cousin

Primrose Avenue was a cul-de-sac in one of the pleasanter parts of Southampton. The nearest busy road was a quarter of a mile away, and the stillness was only occasionally broken by the sound of a car. One had the impression that any outbreak of pop music through an open window would have brought a firm and instant response.

"Rather a nice place to grow old in," I said to Susan, as we walked along from the wider Plymouth Road, where we had left the car.

"Which is what I suspect most of the people here are doing," she replied.

The houses were prewar detached and semi-detached ones, slightly larger than average, with neat squares of front garden sporting chrysanthemums and late roses, and doubtless good space out the back. The usual halfhearted bits of timber were stuck onto stonedash, and the windows had colored lead-lighting, usually of flowers: tulips, crocuses, and irises reared their stylized heads in the small top panes of the living rooms and in the front doors. The door of number fourteen was beginning to peel, suggesting times were harder than of yore.

The woman who came at my ring was in her sixties, and had a sweet face lined with care. She was dressed in pale blue with a string of pearls. It occurred to me, and it was a slightly guilty feeling, that she had decided our visit justified putting on her best. But then perhaps it was an all-too-infrequent pleasure these days.

"Miss Towler?" she asked, peering at us. "Is it Mrs. or Miss?"

"It's Miss—Susan please. It's very good of you to see us, Mrs. Pinnock. This is my boyfriend Colin. He'll just sit quiet while we talk. He's only here as my driver."

"It's very nice of him to do that. Things have changed so much since my young days. Come through, won't you?" She led the way down the hall and opened the door to the sitting room, bright and lived-in, with tea things and biscuits

set out on a coffee table. "Make yourselves comfortable. Tea won't take a moment."

We sat down and took in the room. It too spoke
of things that could have been replaced, but were
pressed into service for a few years more. The
walls had prints of old Southampton, and a musty
nineteenth-century landscape. The delicate brown
of the ceiling spoke of a smoker in the house, as
well as financial stringency.

"It's a bit of an event, your coming," Mrs. Pinnock said, confirming my guess as she bustled
back with a tray. "As you get older friends find
getting about more difficult. And frankly some of
them don't like calling when there's serious illness
in the house."

Susan looked up, also feeling guilty.

"Oh, you said your husband was ill. I didn't
realize—"

"Nothing catching. And don't feel bad about
coming, because it's a treat for me. My husband
had a stroke three years ago, then another just as
he was recovering. People find it awkward—they
don't know what to say, because there's not really
any hope of things getting much better. And
he's a sort of reminder: we're all going to go."
She suddenly smiled. "But I'm not going to be

morbid, not today, and not with young people in the house. *That* doesn't do anyone any good. How do you like it?"

When we had got our tea as we liked it, and chosen a biscuit to nibble at, Mrs. Pinnock sat back, her duty done, and Susan poised herself over her notebook, a serious expression on her face.

"Now, let's get the basic details down. First of all your husband's name."

"John Claydon Pinnock."

"And yours?"

"Mabel, just plain Mabel. You don't get Mabels these days, do you? My maiden name was Marshall, and I was called for an aunt, who came good and left me a thousand pounds—that was a lot of money in those days."

"Called for," I put in. "You must be from the North."

"That's right. I was born in Shipley."

"What about your husband's parents?" Susan asked crisply, the pencil still busy making notes.

"John's the son of Wilfred Arthur Pinnock, and his wife, Victoria, née Claydon. Farther back than that I can't go. We met, by the way, John and I, soon after the war when he was doing his National Service and was stationed at Catterick."

"What was his job after he left the Army?"

"Well, eventually he was one of the managers at the dockyard here—before things got really difficult and shipping and shipbuilding became almost a thing of the past."

Susan circled round the subject for a bit, asking about children and grandchildren. We already had what we wanted. I had the vaguest recollections of grandparents. Only one of either side was living by the time I came into the Pinnock household, and the one I have some recollections of was my mother's mother, who died when I was about six. But I had done some homework, and I did know that my paternal grandfather, Lionel Pinnock, had had a brother called Wilfred. In fact I remembered my father mentioning him now and then. So the John who was lying upstairs was my father's cousin, and they had lived in the same town. Eventually Susan got round to the subject.

"Now, you say your husband's father was Wilfred Pinnock. I'm going to guess that he had a brother called Lionel."

"Oh, you have been clever!" A smile lighted up Mabel's face. It was pure pleasure that something about herself had a more general interest. "You're quite right. Uncle Lionel. He was retired by the time I married John, and living in Southsea. But we were quite friendly with his son Claud and his wife."

"Oh yes. I think of them as the Milton Pinnocks," said Susan brightly.

"That's where they moved to. But Claud was born and brought up here in Southampton. His wife was a secretary at the university, the English Department, and Claud was in the town planning section in the local government offices—I forget his actual title, but quite high up. They only moved because he got a better job up North."

"He was ambitious, was he?"

She took the question as criticism.

"Oh, I wouldn't say that. But it's only natural to want to better yourself, isn't it? As I say he'd done very well down here, because he was a conscientious type of man, and very thorough. Deputy Planning Officer—that was his title, I remember now. Anyway he felt he'd gone as far as he could go down here, and he didn't like the idea of sitting around waiting for dead men's shoes."

I was pretty sure that for the first eight or nine years of my life my father was Deputy Planning Officer for Milton, and Milton is in no way a more prestigious or larger town than Southampton. Another piece of confirmation slipping into place.

"I'd like to hear anything more you can tell me about Claud and Elizabeth," said Susan, pressing on. "You say you were friends with them."

"That's right. Not exactly friends, but relatives living in the same town, and always keeping in touch. We'd drop by each other's houses now and then, go to the theater or the cinema together. Elizabeth loved a play, and I was mad about films. There were a lot of good British films around that time: *Room at the Top, Saturday Night and Sunday Morning, Two Way Stretch.* You still see them on the telly now and then."

"I see. You went around together."

"Yes—not regularly, but when we thought the other pair would really enjoy what was on. And we were both newly married, you see, at least when it started."

Susan looked up from her pad.

"Oh, were you? But they would have been older, wouldn't they?"

"Several years older. They didn't marry till they were both in their thirties." She smiled, remembering her own youth. "It was quite sweet really:

they were so much in love. Not teenagers by any means, but a real Romeo and Juliet pair. Just seeing them take each other's hand when they thought no one was watching, in the theater or the cinema for example—they were a picture. But we had to be careful, John and I."

"Careful?"

She looked a touch embarrassed.

"Well, we had Jan and Derek quite quickly after we were married. Jan was…a mistake, but we soon wanted another as company for her. Claud and Elizabeth hoped and hoped, but no child came. It was very important for them—being older, you see. We decided that two was enough, but any little jokes about…you know, making sure we didn't have any more caused awkwardness, red faces. We knew they didn't like it. My John's not the most sensitive of men, but even he realized it. Even so I had to give him a real talking to about *not* going on about the kiddies the whole time, because it made them so sore about what they were missing."

"So it was a real grief to them."

"Oh, it was. A tragedy you could say. Elizabeth couldn't wait to give up her job, become a real housewife, bring up the babies. And the babies never came."

"Still, she did eventually have one, didn't she?"

"Oh yes, they had a boy. That was after they had moved. The move may have helped. Sometimes new excitements do, so they say, and getting away from all the people who are waiting and watching and making little remarks."

"Did you see a lot of them after they moved?"

Mrs. Pinnock stiffened.

"Hardly anything. We saw Claud at his father's funeral. He'd come down to Southsea and organized everything there. He said the little boy—Colin his name was, and of course he'll be well grown up by now—had a cold, and Elizabeth had had to stay at home to nurse him. I suppose being a late mother she was overprotective."

"Often they are."

"But it meant I never saw her after they moved away."

"Oh dear. That was sad when you'd been quite close."

"We had a card at Christmas, that was all." There was an undertone not of resentment so much as of slight bewilderment.

"That seems odd," commented Susan.

"I don't know about odd, but we expected more. You'd have thought they'd have written telling us how they were settling down in the North. And when Elizabeth got pregnant."

"Maybe with such a late pregnancy that would have seemed like tempting fortune."

"Yes, I suppose that could have been it…"

"But they told you when Colin was born?"

"Oh yes. That was two Christmases after they moved. Just said they'd got a lovely baby named Colin. Didn't give his birthday so we could send a card and a little something, which we'd like to have done. We were sad, to tell you the truth, John as much as me, because it was his cousin. It was as if they wanted to have the least possible contact."

"I'm sure that wasn't so. Didn't you write yourselves?"

"A letter? Well no. We're not great writers, John and I. And it was them that moved, them that had all the news. We waited, and nothing came, so it was just cards we sent, same as them. After Elizabeth died a couple of years ago even the cards stopped."

"I believe Claud is in a nursing home," said Susan. The woman's sympathy was immediate.

"Oh, poor old boy. So he's got his troubles, just like John."

"It was two Christmases after they moved when you heard about the birth of Colin, was it?" asked Susan casually.

"Oh yes. They moved in the September, and I'd have known if Elizabeth had been pregnant when she left—that pregnant, anyway."

"I've got a note Colin must have been born some time after the move, most likely between the two Christmases. Almost certainly in 1963."

But I wasn't. I was born—I was always told I had been born—in September 1962.

"Oh, you already knew when Claud moved, then?" said Mabel Pinnock, who was sharp as well as sweet.

"I've done a bit of work on that side of the family, though not much," said Susan briskly. "I haven't chased up birth certificates yet. Do you remember exactly what they said on the card about the birth of Colin?"

"Oh, it was nothing very much. Just that Elizabeth had had a boy, and that he was doing well."

"You don't think," said Susan carefully, "that he could have been adopted?"

"Adopted!"

"That would make a difference genealogically," she hurried to explain. "To the family tree. We'd note that he wasn't of the bloodline."

"But…but Elizabeth was late having him, but still of childbearing age," said Mrs. Pinnock, having trouble coping with a new idea. "About forty-two, I'd guess. It had never occurred to me…"

"But it's a possibility?"

A thought struck her.

"No. No, I don't think it is. You see, they'd already been rejected as candidates to adopt. It was partly their age, partly because Claud had a mild form of epilepsy. That was one of the things that wasn't talked about between us, but it went around the family—the talk, I mean."

"Ah, so definitely their son," said Susan, in neutral tones, and making a note in her pad.

We had really got all we could expect, and all we had come for. The rest was top-dressing for Mabel Pinnock's benefit, and we went into that gladly, asking questions about Southampton in the fifties and early sixties, her husband's job in the dockyards, and often getting back to her grandchildren, two of whom still lived in the area and were obviously the light of her life, which otherwise centered itself on the sickroom upstairs.

"I'd ask you up to say hello to John," she said apologetically, as we got up to leave, "but to tell you the truth it's more of a trial and an embarrassment to him than a pleasure. He was such a strong man, you know, and such a jolly one, and knowing he's reduced to this—well, it upsets him."

"You should get an interest for yourself," I said, for a moment donning my ministerial hat. "Do a course or something—maybe start one of the Open University units you could do entirely from home."

She laughed openly.

"University? Me? Oh dear, that wouldn't suit me at all. I'm not at all bright like that."

"Colin is right," insisted Susan. "To be frank, you'll need some interest when—"

"When he's gone. Don't mind saying it. To tell you the truth I've thought about that. I dread not having him here to nurse. It gives me something to occupy myself with, sad though it is."

"But you'll need something," I insisted. "And something you could start now, here at home, would be ideal."

"It's nice of you to be so concerned," Mabel said, perhaps a bit surprised. "I'll think about it. But you know to me it's as if my life is almost over. Doesn't seem any point in taking courses or things like that."

I sensed it was her generation speaking, as well as her particular situation. It was a sad leave-taking, imbued with a sense of a life prematurely ended—not her husband's, but her own. She was an outgoing woman, but her life had been reduced to four walls.

As we walked to the car I said:

"Bingo!"

"Modified bingo," Susan corrected me.

"In what sense modified?"

"You're jumping to conclusions as usual. There's nothing to prove you weren't adopted in Milton—nothing to prove they didn't move to South Yorkshire *precisely* because adoption rules were less rigorous there. They do vary from area to area, you know. Or practice does, at any rate."

"They arrived there with me," I pointed out. "Can you imagine them being told a baby would be handed over to them the moment they crossed the boundaries of Milton?"

"Now you're being facetious."

"No I'm not. And can you imagine anyone being allowed to adopt who had epilepsy? That's quite true, by the way. Dad did have a very mild form of it, though it was never a problem, so I hadn't thought of it before."

"It's possible. You could have been fostered out first, and then adopted later when it was clear the fostering was going well."

"You are a cold water merchant."

"Cold water? Colin, are you somehow drunk with the notoriety of being the child of a noble murderer? It's not a background everyone would want for themselves."

"I'm drunk with the fascination of finding out who I am. I'm just wondering what the next step ought to be."

But it was some time before I could work out what that step should be, and how it should be taken. Because that evening I received the first of the phone calls.

CHAPTER TEN

Getting the Call

We separated after getting back from Southampton because Susan said she had something on that evening. I wanted to ask her what it was, but that would have been to court a rebuff. When I dropped her off at her flat we said we'd be in touch in the next few days, and I drove off with a slightly bruised feeling which I knew had no basis in reason.

There is a Chinese takeaway close to my flat, and I collected a chicken and cashews and a fried rice, and I kept it warm in the oven while I had a long bath. Mature reflection in the glorious water convinced me that I should be feeling grateful to Susan for finding Mrs. Pinnock and for undertaking the questioning of her. But somehow mature reflection never really gets the better of bruised feelings. I had to make a conscious effort to simply block the silly hurt feelings from my mind and think about something else. It was with some satisfaction that I could review the conversation with Mrs. Pinnock, because it was now clear that my parents had been declared—ridiculously—unsuitable candidates to adopt a child. It was also obvious that they'd kept my existence a secret from their cousins until the second Christmas after their move so that there could be no awkward questions made about my mother's pregnancy, or lack of one. And they'd made doubly sure they need answer no questions by virtually cutting off all connections with the Southampton Pinnocks—a most uncharacteristic proceeding.

The call came after ten o'clock, when I had finished my Chinese and the glass of wine I had had with it, and was drinking coffee. The compact disc I was playing was Bryn Terfel doing numbers from the great American musicals—I was in a period of preferring relaxing music at night. I silenced the great, rich voice and went to the phone without a twinge of foreboding.

"Colin Pinnock here."

There was a click, and then:

"Who do you think you're—" the well-known ridiculous little ditty, followed by raucous laughter which formed a rhythm and a tune but one quite different from the ditty. I kept the receiver to my ear, in the hope that something would be said. Instead there was just another click, and then silence.

Was someone waiting at the other end for me to say something? I decided that, if so, it was best to disappoint them. I poured myself another cup of coffee, then on reflection awarded myself a stiff brandy to go with it.

The call, I have to admit, unnerved me and more so on reflection than at the time. You answer the phone expecting to hear a voice—cheery, questioning, angry, whatever. Instead of which I'd been played to, and played to in a way that was clearly meant to get at me. The ridiculousness of the recordings only added to the unnerving quality of the call. What kind of person was it whose idea of tormenting someone demanded that it include such a strong vein of the ridiculous?

I thought I recognized not just the first but also the second part of the tape. The first was the signature tune of *Dad's Army*, sung by Bud Flannigan:

Who do you think you're kidding, Mr. Hitler, *When you say Old England's through?*

The old sixties comedy series was currently being rerun on Saturday nights, and the tune could simply have been taped from the television. "Who do you think you're" was not quite the same thing as "Who do you think you are?" but it was doubtless the nearest my persecutor could get. The laughter was more difficult, but I suspected it came from an old twenties or thirties record called *The Laughing Policeman*, which my father sometimes mentioned and imitated—it was a popular joke of the time. Who on earth would have a copy today? A collector of old 78s?

The next day, just before my car called for me, I was rung up again, and the same tape was played. This time I was ready. I had by the phone my own little recording apparatus—one I use if I get an idea or a memory of something that needs doing when I don't have a pencil or paper handy. I switched it on before taking up the receiver and I recorded the ridiculous little song and the laughter. Armed with the tape I told my driver to take me first to the Houses of Parliament and I lodged the tape with the police office there. Whether they were impressed or faintly contemptuous I did not wait to find out.

But as I settled into my chauffeur-driven car one answer did occur to me as to why all the little persecutions had such a strong vein of the ridiculous. It was precisely so that no one other than the person they were aimed at would take them seriously. Did that, I wondered, tell me something about what they were leading up to?

That evening I rang Frieda Brewer, the research assistant whose name and number Elmore Hasselbank had given me. The voice that answered was rich, mature, and intelligent. A woman of strong opinions, I surmised, and a rack of arguments to support them.

"Oh, Mr. Pinnock. Yes, Mr. Hasselbank said you might be ringing, and in fact I rather hoped that you would. I've had my file out on the case, and been through it."

"Did anything occur to you, going back to it?"

There was a second's hesitation.

"To be honest I've been through it several times since we did the original article, so I wasn't coming fresh to it and there weren't likely to be any surprises, or things that we'd missed. So I can't say anything new struck me."

"Do I take it the case interests you, apart from being employed on it?"

"Yes." The voice was definite, unembarrassed. "Decidedly so. A whole series of questions occur to one: why he did it, where he went, if he's still alive. They say everyone has a book in him or her—which usually means some dreary autobiography, I imagine. I do sometimes wonder if the Revill case isn't my book."

"If you were starting to write it now, what would you want to do again, or what would you try to do that you didn't manage to do for the article?"

She thought. A careful, thorough woman.

"The housekeeper, if she's still alive. Hasselbank insisted on approaching her himself, but I always thought that was a mistake. She could be the sort of stiff person who automatically distrusts an American voice—she's the right generation. Then the family, of course, though I wouldn't expect any joy from them. I in their shoes wouldn't want the thing raked up again every few years....But would you mind telling me what you've done yourself?"

I felt I would rather not tell her, because I didn't altogether like the sound of that book she thought she had in her. But it would have been absurd to employ her as researcher yet to leave her in the dark about what I'd found out. She would not be able to ask herself the right questions or set herself on the right path if she had only a partial knowledge. So I told her in strict confidence about the postcard, about my suspicions concerning my own birth, about my parents' move from Southampton to Milton, about the nanny's pregnancy, about my visit to Matthew Martindale. Though she questioned me very closely about that, she agreed that the memories of a five-year-old child were not likely to be very germane.

"So you think I should start with Mrs. Selena Gould?" I asked, when I had brought her up to date.

"Yes." The rich and confident voice hesitated. "I wonder—just slap me down if I'm putting myself forward too much—but I *wonder* if she wouldn't be more likely to talk to a woman."

That immediately struck me as a possibility, if she was old and maybe straightlaced.

"You'd be willing to do it yourself?" I asked her.

"Yes, I would. There'd be another advantage in that, because I could use any story I liked as an excuse for talking to her and there would be no damaging fallout for you. I do hope we can meet sometime, but officially there's no connection between us. That would leave me freer."

"That sounds like altogether a good idea," I said.

"By the way, Mr. Pinnock, I cost." There was no trace of apology in her voice—more, in fact, a touch of pride. "I'll certainly keep the bill down, due to my own interest in the matter, but, nevertheless, I cost. It's how I make my living."

"Understood."

"When—if—I've talked to the woman I'll prepare a written report. That's always best, though I try not to make them too dry. Then when you've gone through it and thought about it, that's when perhaps we should meet."

She obviously knew her job and was experienced enough to know the best procedures so I said that was a perfectly satisfactory arrangement. When I heard about Mrs. Selena Gould, about ten days later when I returned from the party conference, it was in the form of a written report, which was waiting for me on my doormat.

REPORT OF A MEETING WITH SELENA

GOULD AT THE CHALFONT NURSING HOME
BOURNEMOUTH, SEPTEMBER 14, 1997

I thought the best plan was to make my
visit to the home a general one, rather than a
visit to one particular inmate (or guest as they
are called there). That way a refusal to talk
at all was much less likely. I, therefore, rang
the owner/manageress in advance, claiming
to be head of a team from the Department
of Social Security in London, investigating
nursing home care for the elderly. I said that
somebody—it could be me, it could be one
of my team—would be calling on September
14 to interview all their residents. My manner was very Civil Service, and the owner
accepted my story completely. I knew from
my earlier research with Mr. Hasselbank
that this was a nursing home with only
eight patients, and I guessed some would
be virtually uninterviewable, which turned
out to be the case. Mrs. Walden, the owner
and matron-figure, insisted on introducing
me to everyone herself, so that they were
not confused or frightened by a new face.
When I had finished with my fourth patient,
from whom no intelligible word could be

got, Mrs. Walden came to get me and take me to the fifth interviewee.

"I'll take you to Mrs. Gould next. She'll be a real treat after poor Clarrie. She's eighty-three, but she's got all her wits about her and she's had an interesting life."

"Oh, that's good. Has she been here long?"

"Eight years. Bad arthritis. But she's had her moments, has Selena: housekeeper to the rich and the aristocratic. She's *quite* a lady herself. Knows what she wants and insists on getting it. Oh yes, everything has to be just so for her, and she'll instruct you how it's to be done. But she's a sweet person…Mrs. Gould, this is the visitor I told you about."

My first impression of Mrs. Gould was that "sweet" was not the word I would have used—but then it was probably an all-purpose word used in the home for all its female inmates, a desperately dated hangover from the days when "sweet" was exactly what a woman was expected to be. Reserved, dignified, serene, were some of the terms that came to my mind first to describe her. She was beautifully and suitably dressed—probably *not* for my visit, I decided, but as a habit—and she sat in her upright armchair in a posture as straight as her arthritis would permit.

Mrs. Walden slid out of the room, to await a call on the buzzer that was set close to the hand of all the patients. I won't go into the first part of my talk with Selena Gould, the talk that was the necessary pretext for what I had really come for. I don't think that if I had really come for the facts about this nursing home Mrs. Gould would have been the one to give them to me. "These people are my friends, I've been here so long," she said. She was a model of tact and diplomacy, of the ambiguous or unrevealing answer. I realized this was going to present difficulties when—if—we moved on to the meaty part of the interview, and I determined if possible to have a conversation with her rather than a question and answer session, which might have put her back up. I was sure that if there had arisen any sense of conflict, I would have been the one who would have been worsened. She, after all, was the one who could simply declare the conversation at an end. I report this to explain the fact that to stimulate natural conversation I had to tell one or two lies, which in the normal course of events I try to avoid.

I found out that for the last ten years of her working life she had been in partnership with a friend running a catering service that threw high-class parties for well-heeled clients.

"We did very well," she said, in her cool and careful way, "but I sometimes think I was *too* particular. I had to have everything just as I was used to at the best places, and it was thrown away on some of our clients. But then, that was my training..."

"Your training?" I asked. By the way, the rest of this conversation is taken verbatim from my tape, which I had switched on without, so far as I could see, Mrs. Gould noticing.

"Not training in the modern sense, but it *was* training, and the best possible sort. I went into service as a girl—at Chatsworth, just before the war. Of course the war virtually put an end to domestic service as a way of life, so that after it was over I was much in demand, getting high salaries and great responsibilities, even though I was still quite young. I *should* have joined up, or joined the Land Army, done my patriotic duty. But I loved what I did so much, and strings were pulled, and I got out of it."

"I suppose you worked for some very influential families?" I asked, trying not to vary my manner from the earlier interview.

"Oh, I did. The Wriothesleys, the Herberts, the Revills—"

"Oh really?" I said brightly. "My mother used to work at a high-class couturier's in London" (truth) "and Lady Revill was one of their customers" (lie, or so far as I know it was).

"Lady *John* was her real title."

"Of course," I said hastily. "That's what my mother said they all had to call her. It's rather confusing, isn't it, in spite of Princess Michael of Kent."

"Lord John always referred to her as Veronica, so it was definitely confusing for us at first. But I've always liked to get things right."

"I do, too. There's so much slovenliness around. So you were actually housekeeper to *that* part of the family?"

"Oh yes. The old Earl had moved abroad for tax reasons, and the eldest son…had an unusual lifestyle. Lord and Lady John were the only ones who could be said to have a household to run. Since he was in politics that was almost a necessity."

"That must have made an interesting life for you. And of course when the murder took place"—I caught myself up, since I'd been about to link that in as one of the interesting things about the job—"that must have meant things turned very unpleasant."

"Very." Her lips set in disapproval, which was clearly something one went to great lengths not to encounter. "It was partly because of that that I later set up the party business with my friend. Subsequent employers always knew about what they called the Revill affair, and were curious. It was unpleasant—a distasteful intrusion into what didn't concern them. I told them nothing, of course, beyond that the whole thing had been totally unexpected."

"That's what my mother said. She'd talked to Lord John sometimes in the showrooms when he came to collect his wife after a fitting, and she thought he was such a lovely man."

"Everyone did. I think he was the best employer I ever had. I always felt guilty I couldn't help the police more, but you see when I got to be able to pick and choose my jobs, I always insisted on a flat to myself—somewhere where I was completely independent and could lead my own life."

I nodded sagely at this, and I really did sympathize with her point of view.

"Otherwise I suppose, if you became part of the family, you might never have had a moment to yourself."

"That's exactly it. Especially as the children of the aristocracy often have…difficult upbringings. Or unusual ones, at any rate. I'm not criticizing, of course—"

"Of course not."

"—but the parents are often so busy they have very little time for them, so someone else has to step in—nanny, housekeeper, scullery maid, whatever. If I'd wanted a family I would have married."

"I thought—"

"*Mrs.* Gould is a courtesy title." The old woman's eyes sparkled. "I was very young when I got my first job as housekeeper, so I made believe I'd been widowed in the war, to give myself a bit of dignity and experience."

"How clever."

"It served its purpose. What I really wanted was not a husband and children but my independence. That would have been impossible in the big houses in the old days, but it wasn't after the war. I wanted to be alone, even lonely if necessary. I've always found loneliness rather a positive thing. But it meant I knew very little about what happened above stairs. Caroline and Matthew were terribly cut off from children of their own age, but they had their nanny. I might arrange special treats for them now and then, but that would be all I'd do."

"I think you were wise. If you got attached to children in the households you worked for and then went on to a new job, it would be an awful wrench. And you might have continued in a job you didn't like for their sakes."

She nodded, impressed by my sagacity.

"I've known domestic staff who did. As it was I simply ran the household, cooked when necessary, and retreated to my basement flat at night. That was my sanctuary, and I didn't even have to hang a DO NOT DISTURB notice on the door. It was understood: whatever went on in the rest of the house after my hours was nothing to do with me."

I ventured on a new tack.

"My mother was always convinced Lady John had a new man in her life at the time she…when it all happened." Mrs. Gould had blushed, and I went on hurriedly. "Of course she had nothing to base that on—just a sparkle in the eye, I expect, or a new taste for glamorous clothes."

"No…no, I'm sure nothing like that was going on."

"Obviously my mother got it wrong. You'd know, being in the house most of the day."

Her face took on the pursed, disapproving look again.

"Inevitably people talked. Of course it wasn't my job to make beds, unless the maid failed to turn up, but she would have talked, and I would have seen signs....We all knew about the problems in the marriage. It wasn't a happy household toward the end, though that doesn't make it any less surprising."

"So of course you knew about Lord John and the nanny."

She paused before replying, as if wondering whether to cut the conversation short. I think it was the "fact" that my mother knew Lord John that made her talk more openly, perhaps, than she had in years about the case.

"Oh yes, I knew. If I didn't know from any other signs, she would have insisted on telling me herself. She often tried to talk about it. She'd come down into the kitchen or wherever I was, and she'd sit down and start skirting round the subject, and of course I could see through *her*, hardly more than a chit, and I'd say: 'I'm very busy, so if you'll excuse me...' And she'd take herself off, smiling her catlike smile."

"She sounds like a very unlikable young woman."

"Oh, she was—not on the surface, but

not very far underneath. Clever and cunning. Whatever happened, the only thing that mattered to her was that she got what she wanted—whatever it was at the time. Other people were only there for her benefit and convenience. I say she was clever, but she wasn't clever enough to hide the fact that she knew she was clever. Full of herself she was—and that's like a cat too, isn't it?"

"It is. And so is cunning."

She nodded vigorously.

"That's right. Lovely creatures—I always had one as soon as I was independent—but I never trusted them. I got Lucy's measure as soon as she came. She went on and on about the research she was going to do—though she might have known that was of no interest to an ill-educated woman like myself. 'Professor Marryott thinks I ought to look at Arcadian themes in Shakespearean comedy,' she would say, or 'Professor Frere thinks the Shakespeare Apocrypha is ripe for a new consideration.' Such nonsense, talk like that to me! Anyway there was less of that sort of thing once the...bed arrangements changed."

My eyebrows raised.

"I didn't know it went as far as that. My mother always guessed they probably snatched opportunities when Lady John was busy with her social round."

She hesitated, but eventually went on.

"Actually he'd moved out of the double bedroom and into the guest room even before Lucy Mariotti was given the nanny's job. Things weren't going well."

"Obviously."

"There was always a pretense made later on that the guest bed had been slept in, but we knew who was sleeping with whom....It was a very tense household by the end."

I shook my head wisely.

"It was surely asking for trouble to appoint a beautiful young girl on a live-in basis when they needed a new nanny."

"I suppose it was, but it was only for a short time. She came in November, and she was intending to leave in June to travel round Europe."

"Frankly, in sexual matters that is not a short time."

Mrs. Gould shook herself. My words,

I think, had been too explicit and too modern.

"I mustn't keep you. I've taken up a lot of your time."

"Not at all," I said, pressing the bell to summon Mrs. Walden. "I've taken up an awful lot of *yours*."

"I have an awful lot of time begging to be taken up," she said, but without bitterness. She stood by her choices.

"Do you think that Lord John is still alive?" I asked her, as I stood waiting.

"I haven't the faintest idea, nor who might have helped him get away. It's as much a mystery to me as to other people and the police. It's what my later employers always asked, but I had no basis for an opinion, even if I'd cared to give them one. But I would have a guess on one thing."

"What's that?"

"If he's still alive, the children will know. He loved them, and they loved him. If anyone in the house gave them time, it was Lord John. Once they grew up he will have made contact."

"Even though he killed their mother?"

"Even though. I told you, it was only a guess. But the children felt nothing for their mother."

"Well, you *have* had a long conversation!" said Mrs. Walden, bustling in and shepherding me into the corridor toward my next patient.

"Not about what we were supposed to be discussing," I admitted. "She's a very interesting woman. She did make clear what a very high opinion she has of the arrangements and the staff here."

"We're the family she never had," said Mrs. Walden. "Mind you she's no more lonely than some of those that *did* have family."

To sum up: my impressions of Mrs. Gould after our long talk were that she is truthful, clearheaded, and disinterested. I would trust anything she said, because her memory seemed remarkable. Lack of personal and emotional involvements for herself have meant, I suspect, that her memories of other people's lives are more vivid than most people's would be. It's possible that, in spite of her apparent frankness (granted that that frankness was often expressed in a roundabout way, part of the discretion that went with her job), there were some things concealed—I couldn't make up my mind about this, but I think it's possible. Whether this was from discretion, unwillingness to indulge in conjecture, or simply embarrassment about some subjects I wouldn't like to guess.

Frieda Brewer

She had got far more out of her than I could have done, that was clear. Never in a million years, I was sure, would Mrs. Gould have talked in that unbuttoned way with a man. There were some interesting facts—the names of the academics, for example, and confirmation of the fact that the marriage was on the rocks even before Lucy arrived. But what was most valuable of all was that she had been the first to give me some idea of the atmosphere in the house, the feel and the mechanics of the household. And one could see that the arrival of Lucy served to light the fuse that slowly spluttered its way along to the dynamite. I was beginning to get the idea that Lucy was a young lady who relished blowups.

CHAPTER ELEVEN

Followed

How does one get the eerie sensation of being watched? Followed? I suppose the followed bit is easy. But in my case I got that sensation after a day or two in which I had a much more amorphous feeling of uneasiness, which crystallized itself into the idea that eyes were on me. It's difficult to explain that without recourse to the supernatural, but even at the time I tried to keep my feet on the ground, and resisted notions that would have the police at the Palace of Westminster grinning behind their hands. It is just possible that in a crowded street one registers a face, then registers it again, quite unconsciously of course, and eventually that eerie sensation starts building up. It's not at all a pleasant feeling, and it takes you over.

And that's the reason, I imagine, why I noticed

the footsteps. I make a habit of getting out of the Ministry, either at lunchtime or for an hour or two at some point in the day. A minister who gets himself immersed in his meetings and his routine for the whole of the working day and beyond eventually gets swamped by it. Sometimes I go to Vitello d'Oro for a quick lunch of pasta or gnocchi, but mostly, if the weather is anything better than foul, I prefer to stay outside. Just the fresh air, the uncaring faces, the feeling of being part of a big city, an ant in an anthill, is healthy—psychologically speaking.

It was a Tuesday in early October, an unusually bright day for that time of year. I'd worked through lunchtime because I'd had a long meeting during the morning with a delegation concerned about education for the blind. But while I'd worked I'd stolen glances out of the window. About two o'clock I decided to take my hour off. I left the Department, crossed Victoria Street, and made for St. James's Park, pausing at the entrance to light a cigarette. That's when I became conscious—or *thought* I became conscious—of footsteps behind me, stopping when I stopped. I was in no hurry to light my cigarette, thinking what I should do. When I did start walking again the footsteps also started up again behind me.

I had decided to find a seat with a good general view around the park. I walked some way in, watching the squirrels, unnaturally tame and skittish, until toward the lake I found a seat, facing the way I had come, that seemed ideal. Casually I wheeled round, sat down, and took a drag at my cigarette. Casual, be completely casual, I said to myself. So I cast my eye slowly, lazily, barely interestedly, at the people coming in my direction.

Tourists, office workers, young lovers, civil servants, clandestine hand-holders, businessmen discussing share options and takeover bids. All as expected. But one figure did catch my eye, cause me to focus more sharply. He had swerved aside from the tarmacked path as soon as he saw me sit down, and was now walking across the grass in the other direction. Clearly he did not want to pass me, did not want me to see his face.

I could make little from his back. Sports jacket, rather illfitting, perhaps shabby or just shoddy; gray flannel trousers, again not in first-rate condition, longish hair, uncut rather than styled. A meager haul of impressions. He walked, not turning, until he was several hundred yards away. Then he stopped under a tree, turning round slowly and pretending, like me a minute or two before, to survey the scene casually. His face was in the shade and I could not clearly discern any particular feature. A front view reinforced the impression the back view had given me of someone poorly dressed—not someone who didn't care what he looked like, but somebody who wore cheap clothes because he was poor.

I finished my cigarette, and put my head back to drink in the sun. When I brought it back upright he was still there, fishing in his pocket. He brought out what I took to be a tube of sucky sweets, and put one in his mouth. I took out my packet in my turn, and lit another cigarette. I told people I was down to four a day, but not that day. I smoked, he sucked, neither of us looking directly at each other, but catching glimpses as we each nonchalantly surveyed the passing scene.

Eventually I decided to return to the Department. I took the same route I had come by through the little streets around St. James's Underground station and across Victoria Street. This time I could not distinguish the footsteps behind me—there were no more people around to muffle his, so presumably he was keeping a greater distance between us. At the entrance to the

Department I paused to have a word with Sam Baldry, the doorman. I contrived to turn back to face the street quite suddenly. I saw the calf of a gray-flanneled leg disappearing into a doorway.

I used my official car to get home that evening.

❧❧❧

Frieda Brewer and I agreed on the phone that the only place we could discuss her report and the way forward from it was in one or other of our flats. Anywhere more public and we'd be continually looking over our shoulders for eavesdroppers. In the end we decided on mine. When she arrived she seemed to be concealing surprise at the humble nature of my flat and its location. She looked around the living room briskly, as if wanting to memorize its salient features for a paragraph in her book.

"You haven't let being in the government go to your head," she said. It could have been one of my more downright Yorkshire constituents speaking.

"Only the very top cabinet ministers get assigned fine homes for their exclusive use," I explained dryly. "This one is very convenient for Westminster."

"Of course. Still, I imagine as the sleaze factor shifts from the other side to your lot, expectations will rise and you'll start moving upmarket."

"You're very cynical," I said. "We are dedicated to stamping out sleaze. I'm certainly not planning to accept wodges of banknotes in brown envelopes."

"I'm sure you're not. Still, in politics the offers can come in forms a lot more subtle than that, especially as your lot is obviously intending to stay in power for yonks, barring accidents." She sniffed. "Smells good."

I was cooking a vaguely Arab dish of leg of lamb roasted at a fierce temperature on a bed of scalloped potatoes. I got her a gin and tonic and myself a beer, and we sat down with her report. She was much as I imagined her: a full figure, handsome if unsubtle face, in manner direct and exuding efficiency. If she'd been a singer she would have been a mezzo, singing roles such as Amneris and Eboli. I have to admit, though, that her no-nonsense manner put me off—not just from nonsense, but generally. I couldn't quite work out whether this was a traditional male reaction, or simply a personal one.

"Anything strike you?" she asked. I looked at

my notes.

"I was interested in what she said about Lord John, and how he would have made contact with the children if he was still alive. If so, Matthew Martindale put on a good performance."

Frieda shrugged.

"That's hardly surprising. He would have had immense practice in stonewalling curiosity about his father's fate by now."

I considered the general situation.

"I wonder if Mrs. Gould is right. Lord John could feel that he's done enough harm to his children's lives, and that the best thing he could do would be to keep away from them."

"That could work the other way," she said, her analytical mind working overtime. "He could want to make things up to them. Have you thought about the question of whether he *is* still alive—or let's say whether he lived on after the murder?"

"A little. As a sort of side issue. This is not a quest to find my father, though. To me the lack of a body is crucial. We're talking about suicide here, aren't we? There's no question of any revenge killing or any sort of melodramatic thing. Of course it's possible to kill yourself so your body is never found, but why should he want to? On the contrary, if he decided to end it all, he'd want the thing known, cut and dried, so that his children could put him in the past and get on with their lives."

"Maybe," she said, neither agreeing nor disagreeing. "If he survived, was it with the connivance of anyone?"

I shrugged. "Impossible to say. No doubt it would be easier with someone else's help but all that talk there was in the tabloids about society pals closing ranks and making sure one of their number didn't have to face the consequences seems to me so much balderdash. Lord John gives me the impression of rather a lonely figure, someone with few close friends. I did wonder about the Conservative Party—"

She frowned.

"How do you mean?"

"Spiriting him away to avoid embarrassment for themselves."

"Isn't *that* rather melodramatic?"

"Oh, I don't mean it was done by them as a *party*. That's never the way political parties do things. I mean Macmillan drawls a word or two to a colleague—'Isn't there someone who could

get him out of the country? Get him a new identity?'—and hey, presto, someone has a word with
someone, who has a word with someone else, and
in a trice the job is done."

"Possible," she said, but she made it obvious she
was skeptical. I could see she was a Conservative
supporter. But what she said made sense. "How do
you think it happened? Did Lord John ring Tory
Party HQ the next day and say: 'This is Lord John
Revill here. Look, I'm frightfully sorry but I seem
to have murdered my wife. Do you think there's
anyone who could get me out of the country to
somewhere safe?'"

"No, of course not."

"The truth is, there's not been sight or sound—
recorded sight or sound—of him since he left the
house in Upper Brook Street. *If* he had help, he
must have contacted someone. We don't know
who it was, or even who it was likely to be."

"True. Anyway, it's a side issue." I went into the
kitchen, carved the lamb into great chunks, served
it on warm plates on top of the potatoes, and we
sat down at the table. I opened a bottle of cheap
red wine, which she looked at suspiciously, but
we drank and ate companionably enough. "It was
interesting to get the names of the professors," I

said, to get the discussion going again.

"Right." She nodded. "I had one name, but not the other. Now, I've checked up on them both—"

"So have I," I said. "So far as I can see from *Who's Who* Marryott is dead and Frere is still alive."

"That's right. Which suits us nicely, because Marryott is the one Hasselbank has already talked to, while we never got on to Frere. I've rung Frere and checked, by the way, pretending to be a scholar wanting permission to quote him in a book. He is still alive, sounds hale and hearty, and lives in Sussex."

"You're a dab hand at a cover story, aren't you?" I said admiringly. She raised her eyebrows.

"A lie, you mean. If I was working for a newspaper, or a politician in his official capacity, my ethical standards would be a notch or two higher. The fact is, this is so unofficial and personal that it…liberates me somewhat. I regard myself as working partly for myself."

In a niggling way that last remark did not please me, but I brushed it aside.

"So I can go along and talk to Frere? Did you get any impression of him, beyond his being hale and hearty?"

"Not really. Straightforward, still very clear in his mind, so we'll hope in his memory, too. By the way, I think honesty about your reasons for asking him about Lucy would be the best way, and the least dangerous for you."

"Dangerous?"

"A government minister who goes around getting information out of people by telling lies is asking for trouble."

"Hmmm. Fair enough, I suppose. What about Marryott? Did you talk to him seven years ago for the color supplement article, or did Hasselbank?"

"Elmore did the questioning, but I went along… I didn't greatly like Marryott. Neither of us did. He talked only about Lucy's academic ambitions, but there was something—I don't know—sleazy about him. A leering, smirking kind of man, and one wondered whether a combination of that outlook on life and Lucy's sexual go-getting might have been pretty poisonous, destructive."

"I see. You're wondering whether there might have been a more personal connection between the two, either before or after the murder."

"Well, yes. But *just* wondering."

"You know, one thing puzzles me from your report."

"What's that?"

"The Revill marriage was in a pretty rocky state, right?"

"Right."

"And yet they engage as their nanny *not* one of the traditional dragons that the upper crust normally plump for, probably passing them on from one family to another, but a beautiful, sexy young Australian girl on the loose in Europe. I should have thought that anybody could have seen that was a recipe for disaster, and Lord John was no fool."

Frieda Brewer paused in her eating.

"I get the impression that an upper-class marriage then—perhaps now, too—was very different from the average middle-class marriage today. Though heaven knows that's hardly the dull, stable thing it once was. One reason why I'll never, but *never*, think of getting married is the fact that it's almost meaningless. Imagine going into it with the sort of dim hopes and expectations people have of it today! But I wonder with the Revill marriage being in such a poor state of repair whether they didn't go into the engaging of

Lucy Mariotti with their eyes open—deliberately, with an end in view."

I tried to get her drift, and failed.

"I must be naive. I can't imagine what that end could be."

"Stimulus for a marriage that had gone stale? To provide sex for him to relieve her of something she found distasteful? To leave her freer to go with other men?"

I considered the suggestions, but without finding them convincing as they stood.

"Well, I'll say one thing: if that was the intention, it certainly went disastrously wrong."

As we drank our coffees we talked of other things. She was very frank about herself, said she was looking for a father for a child she wanted: someone who would make no demands, leave her entirely free to bring up the child in her own way, in return for which she would make no financial demands.

"You have a relationship and, however much he may seem to be unbroody, unpaternal, there's a danger that when the baby comes he'll want to muscle in and have his say."

"Anything wrong with that?"

"Yes, from my point of view. I go through the

pain and danger of having a baby, so it's going to be my child. I'll do all the business of juggling baby and career, and I'd rather not even have him around as a baby-sitter."

"And how are you going to manage this?"

"There's various ways, but if I pick on a man and engage him for the purpose he's going to sign a deed disclaiming not just responsibility but rights."

"Perhaps you could advertise in a legal journal," I said wryly. "You might find a dry-as-dust solicitor who's just what you need."

"Could be," she agreed. "Anyway it will have to be someone very unlike you."

"Oh?"

"You wouldn't be any good at all," she said briskly. "Much too much into the families' business."

I tried to understand her, to respect her motives, but somehow the conversation left me with a feeling of dissatisfaction. It's the old argument about whether you have a child for the child's sake, or as an appendage to yourself. My own parents had quite obviously adopted me for my sake, and had put themselves last through all the years of my growing up, and beyond. Frieda Brewer's future child I felt rather sorry for.

I began to feel I wanted as little as possible to do with Frieda, and nothing at all to do with any book she might write about the Revill case. She would ride roughshod if it suited her over any personal susceptibilities or squeamishness. About her abilities as a researcher I had no doubts, and she showed her worth at the end of the evening as she got her things together with her usual brisk-ness and prepared to go out to her car.

"By the way, you said you checked up on Frere. Did you notice the details of his academic career?"

"Just the main outlines that were in *Who's Who* or *People of Today*. They don't give much space to academics. Professor at Leicester, then at Man-chester, wasn't it?"

"That's right. Went to Leicester in 1965. But from 1962 to 1964 he was temporary Professor of English, replacing someone who was sick, at the University of Southampton. Makes you think, doesn't it?"

❧❧❧

The very next day I was followed again. I was conscious of the sound of those footsteps by now: waiting for them, tensing up when I heard them.

I had deliberately left Great Smith Street and Whitehall for the quieter streets leading first to Northumberland Avenue, then to Charing Cross and the Strand. There they were: some way back, tentative, but indubitably following me.

I took care not to look round. I waited at the lights to cross the avenue, then proceeded forward toward the station. The temptation to try to snatch a glimpse, even to let him know I knew I was being followed, was almost irresistible. But this time I wanted to get a good look at him. Who was he, this dogger of my footsteps, and what was his connection with the joker who rang me with silly ditties, and the one who dropped shoplifted items into my carrier bag in Marks & Spencer? Was one male, the other female, or were they in fact one and the same person?

Around Charing Cross Station the scurry of people made listening impossible. I had to rely on guesswork to tell me he was still following me. I got to the traffic lights to cross the Strand, and again had to resist the impulse to look back toward Trafalgar Square to see if I recognized any shabby figure coming along from the same direction as myself.

Once on the north side of the Strand I turned

away from King William IV Street, walked past Coutts's Bank, and, shielded by a knot of people, slipped into the Music Discount Center. I immediately made for the bargain disc section to my left, commanding an excellent view through the large plateglass window. Taking up the nearest CD and inspecting the details on the back I watched the lunch-hour crowd swelling, hurrying in the direction of the Aldwych.

Within seconds he was outside the window, looking ahead uncertainly, then around him, wondering how he'd lost the trail. He was shabbily dressed as before, the jacket, poor quality to begin with, looking as if it had been slept in, the trousers crumpled and dirty, the shoes going in the direction of disintegration. Without suggesting he was sleeping rough, he did seem only a step or two away from it—though whether going toward it or going away from it, I couldn't judge.

Then he looked at the shop door. My eyes were intent on the disc, but I could judge the face. He must have been thirty or so, I estimated, but the face was unformed, even pathetic. There was no strength to the chin, and the jaw generally was slack. The eyes were watery, the nose overprominent. His hair was long and greasy, and his skin had that unhealthy paleness that people who have been in jail get. Phrases like "born loser" or "born victim" occurred to me, though I'm sure one can't be *born* either thing.

His eyes swiveled from the door toward the window I was standing in. I raised mine as I casually put the disc back on the rack. For a second, two seconds, we looked into each other's eyes. Then he turned and hurried on in the direction of Aldwych. I dashed back out into the street. I was sorely tempted to reverse roles and follow him, but I thought I was unlikely to find out anything to the purpose about him. As I watched he swerved off into one of the little streets heading up toward Covent Garden.

I turned toward the square and the National Gallery, had twenty minutes with the Spanish paintings, and coffee and a sandwich in the cafeteria. Then I went back to work, and this time there were no footsteps dogging mine.

CHAPTER TWELVE

More Problems Than One

The footsteps ceased from that time on. I felt free now to look behind me, scan the crowds following in my wake, but I never saw the slack-jawed, slightly pathetic creature who had so ineffectually dogged my course for a time.

One evening in the next week I was sitting in my flat working on my red boxes (soon, it was said, to be computerized) and listening to a little-known Donizetti opera in one of those pirate recordings made at performances long ago—recordings that made one feel slightly guilty that someone was being swindled. This one, made in the sixties, had a soprano called Margherita Roberti. I had a fantasy about her. This was that

Margaret Thatcher, née Roberts, having too little to use her energy on in the years of the Wilson government, formed an opera company during the long summer recesses with herself as star, and toured the Italian provinces with the local version of her name. The fact that Margherita Roberti had a confident, slightly shrill voice added credence to the fantasy. Dennis would of course manage the enterprise, and the company would be formed on the nineteenth-century principle of "My wife and four puppets." That, with an increase in numbers, was pretty much the principle adopted when the lady formed her cabinets.

I was meditating on Mrs. Thatcher's emasculation of her male colleagues and how the process of turning prime ministerial government into presidential government seemed to have been adopted by our side once in power, when the phone rang.

I picked it up with no forebodings, since it had been three weeks or more since the last nasty call. However, the moment I heard the click I knew what was coming, though as it turned out, the program had been changed.

It was opera this time, but something I did not know, or know well. Because the click had alerted me I was listening intently from the beginning. It was a female voice, and it began with the words "*Senza Mamma.*" The aria was allowed to proceed for a minute or so, and I picked out a word or phrase here and there: "*E tu sei morto,*" "*un angelo del cielo.*" Then it was succeeded by something I did know: the concerted laughter of the merry wives in the garden of Master Ford at the end of the second scene of *Falstaff.* The laughter made my chest contract nervously, made me sense once again that someone was intent on making a fool of me. There could be worse things, of course. On the other hand it could be intended to lead to worse things. I put the phone down before the music had finished.

I couldn't get back to my red boxes for some time. I went through the characters in opera I could think of who had been "*senza mamma*"— without their mother. It was only some time later, as I was preparing for bed, that it came to me as these things do: seeming to come from the blue into an empty mind. It was Puccini's *Suor Angelica.* Nobody's favorite opera, but one which I'd caught up with once, on a holiday in the Naples area. I didn't have it in my collection. It was, I seemed to remember, Sister Angelica herself meditating on her illegitimate child—the child she had been forced to give up before taking the veil.

Nowadays, of course, she'd probably be in the Cabinet, and talking about her experiences in the *News of the World.*

The more I thought about it, the less I could imagine Lucy Mariotti going into a nunnery.

It was Friday before there was any lull in my government work, so I had good time, in the occasional quiet moments, to think how I was to approach Professor Frere. I agreed with Frieda Brewer that, from a variety of points of view including my own position in politics, honesty would in this case be the best policy. Frieda had rung to give me his name, address, and telephone number, and in the end I rang him from my old home in Milton, before going out to a constituency meeting.

"Two-six-seven-five-three-four-one," came a calm, solid voice.

"Is that Professor Frere? Simon Frere?"

"It is."

"Oh, hello. My name is Colin Pinnock."

Very tiny pause.

"Ah. You're not one of my former students, are you?"

"No, I'm not. I did English, but at Cambridge."

"Perfectly good place to do it."

I detected a defensive, temporizing feeling coming down the line.

"You don't know me, in fact, Professor Frere, but I think you did know my mother, Elizabeth Pinnock."

Another pause—perfectly understandable, as memory was being racked. Only I didn't think it was due to that.

"Now...I think that rings a bell."

"Secretary in the English Department at Southampton University."

"That's it! Now I remember. Goodness me, that was a long time ago."

"Thirty-five years."

"Is that really how long? Well, well."

"I know how long it is because I'm thirty-five years old."

This time the pause was long.

"Mr. Pinnock, I think we should meet and have a talk."

"I think so, too." I added quickly: "Maybe I should say, Professor Frere, that the talk won't be in any spirit of recrimination or blame. There's nothing whatever to blame you for. I just want to find out what happened."

"Ye-e-es. And you live where?"

"Mostly in London. I'm an MP—actually a very junior member of the government."

"Really? I suppose it's a con—" He stopped short. I felt sure he was going to say it was a continuation of the family tradition, but thought it either unwise or an unfortunate reminder. He rather clumsily amended it to: "I suppose congratulations are still in order?"

"They are. Many thanks."

"I'd be delighted to have an excuse to come to London. I'd like to see the new British Library. But I wonder, if, before we meet, I might write to you. You say there is nothing to blame me for but…there are some aspects of the affair that are very painful memories for me. I would prefer not to talk about them, though of course I'd feel obliged to answer any questions when we meet."

"That's perfectly okay—a very good way of proceeding," I said. "It will give me time to sort out any questions and identify any areas where I'm still uncertain. Mark it PERSONAL and send it to the House of Commons."

The letter came three days later, handwritten—the writing of a careful, punctilious elderly man. I took it along to Dean's Yard and read it sitting on a seat in watery midday sun.

Dear Mr. Pinnock,

I think it's best to come straight to the point. I have done many things in my life that were silly, mistaken, or just plain wrong, but the human brain is fallible and one learns to take most things in one's stride. The one thing in my life of which I am thoroughly ashamed is my involvement with Lucy Mariotti.

It began unexceptionably. I was a rising Shake-spearian scholar and she contacted me by letter about doing a Ph.D. thesis. She came down to Southampton at my request soon after to discuss possible topics. There seemed to be a solid ground of knowledge there, which was a credit to Sydney University. We talked about taking a look at the Shakespearian Apocrypha and she seemed to like the idea. She said there was another professor who was interested in supervising her—she said this not in a manner that invited me to beg her to work under me rather than any other, but at least giving the impression that she would not be displeased if I did. I simply nodded, and we left the matter in the air.

I next read of Lucy Mariotti in the newspapers. She'd told me for whom she was working, so as soon as the case became a national cause célèbre I scanned the newspapers for her name. When I found it, read the tittle-tattle about her involvement with Lord John, I felt rather sorry for her, truth to tell. Wet-around-the-ears young colonial being seduced by an upper-crust Lothario was how I interpreted things. It was some time before I found out that Lucy was no Tess of the D'Urbervilles.

She rang me one night at home, sounding desperate. She said the police were finished with her, satisfied she'd had nothing to do with the murder and did not know where Lord John had disappeared to. But she was pregnant, without job or money, and the press were looking for her. Did I know of anywhere in Southampton where she could go to earth until she'd had the baby and could start work with me on her thesis?

My wife overheard my end of the conversation. She was a wonderful woman, very compassionate, and she'd agreed with my interpretation of the situation—innocence seduced by sophistication. I didn't need to do anything more than raise my eyebrows to her. She nodded, and I asked her down to stay with us until we could find her a bed-sitter. She arrived next day with three large suitcases—maybe not all she had in the world, but all she had in this hemisphere.

For the first few days everything went well. She was wonderful with our children, helped around the house, was very grateful—perhaps too volubly so. The only problem was that she was virtually in hiding, so she was around all the time. Then my wife started to have doubts. Lucy had never made any bones about the fact that she was going to have her baby adopted. But when she overheard her on the phone say something about "when I get shot of the kid," her attitude hardened. She watched her when she was alone with our two, then six and four, and decided she didn't like what she saw. She'd been putting on an act. She decided she should be alone with them as little as possible, which was difficult because I had my job and my wife was doing a first degree in history. She began looking around for a bed-sitter for Lucy—quite difficult at that time of year, though it would become easy as soon as the students went down for the summer vacation.

Two things happened at about this time. She asked me if I knew anyone who wanted to adopt a child privately. I knew this meant, in effect, illegally. But I also knew your mother, and her desperate desire for children. I had no idea at the time that Lucy was going to insist that this was a money transaction. I don't know how much you know about this, but I repeat I didn't even consider the possibility. I was young, green, law-abiding, naive, call me what you will. One evening, by arrangement, I drove Lucy round to their home and left her there. When they drove her home the deal was apparently completed. Gradually as I learned that the transaction was such that the baby—you—was virtually sold I was very shocked. But your mother, Elizabeth, swore me to secrecy, and seemed to take that aspect in her stride.

The second thing, which perhaps I should have put first, was that I was becoming obsessed with Lucy. She was devastatingly pretty, in spite of being very obviously pregnant. No—not in spite of: because of. I had always found women in pregnancy enormously attractive. When my wife was having ours...but perhaps I don't need to go into that. This is not a psychiatric session, though it is in the nature of a confessional one. Having Lucy in the house was like living with an unexploded bomb. I don't pretend she found me in the least attractive. I imagine she regarded me in the nature of a particularly tough nut to practice on. The inevitable happened one day when the children were at school and my wife was at lectures. It continued for two weeks until I was quite sickened by her rampant carnality, terrified of my own growing enslavement to it.

One further thing happened before we rid our house of Lucy. She inevitably had to fetch the children from school from time to time and be alone with them in the house. One evening on a day when this had happened I was putting the children to bed when the eldest, Imogen, said to me: "Lucy must be awfully hard up. She was talking on the phone today about selling something and getting thousands and thousands for it."

Lucy had settled down thoroughly in the house, I knew her bedroom, I was sure she had no possession which could fetch anything like a thousand pounds. Except what she had in her womb. She could not have been talking to Elizabeth, your mother, who'd been at work that afternoon. In any case the bargain there had been struck. Whatever was happening I wanted no part of it.

My wife was something close to a saint, but she was no holy fool. She already suspected what had been going on. She found a bed-sitter in a house with an older fellow-student of history, and we moved Lucy there smartly, overruling all her objections. She became extremely peevish, I remember. When I helped her up to the room with her cases and ignored her disparagement of it, I said good-bye. I never saw her again, though I heard of her.

That is all I have to say of a personal nature. There may be other things I can tell you—I do not know, of course, just how much *you* know. You probably, a young man, regard my shame at the episode as slightly comic. I can only say the relationship with Lucy left me feeling soiled, and above all my marriage was never quite the same again. My dear wife, who died last year, never upbraided me on the subject, in fact we never talked about it. But it was always there—between us, between me and my children. It is here with me now. I hope when we meet we can talk about it as little as necessary.

Yours sincerely,
Simon Frere

The letter, inevitably, was much in my thoughts in the next few days. I rang Professor Frere and arranged to meet in a Chinese restaurant close to King's Cross Station. I knew it well, and knew it was little frequented at lunchtime. Meanwhile the story haunted me, not so much for what it told me about Lucy Mariotti as for what it told me about my parents—how very far they were willing to act out of character and convictions in order to secure the child they longed for.

I used my official car to get to our meeting. My driver looked disapproving. The King's Cross area, decrepit and riddled with prostitution, had proved near-fatal to the reputation of at least one member of the previous government. Certainly it's an area with few charms. Perhaps the opening of the new British Library will help to clear the locality up. Then again, it could make it worse.

In the street where the Silken Road is situated a middle-class person sticks out like a sore thumb. I was on the pavement giving directions to my driver when to return for me when an elderly man, small, trim of figure, in smart sports jacket and flannels, came along from the library direction. My driver (a conventional soul, as most of the drivers are) looked relieved it was a man I was meeting. The man guessed as I had guessed on the same basis, and we greeted each other like exiles in an outlandish foreign country. Then we dived into the ill-lit and depressing chinoiserie of the Silken Road.

"The food really is rather good," I said apologetically.

"It was considerate of you to choose somewhere so close to the library," he said, trying to sound at ease. "I can go back for an afternoon's work."

We took the menu, merely glanced at it, and ordered. Food was not what we had come for, nor drink. As the waiter drifted off Simon Frere sat back in his chair and looked at me.

"Let me just ask you before we start: you discovered recently that you were adopted?"

"That's right."

"So your parents—they're dead, are they?—never told you."

"No, they didn't. My mother's dead, my father is fairly far advanced into senility."

"I see. How sad. Your mother was such a nice woman, and though I didn't know your father well, what I did know I respected. But I feel they should have told you: it's unusual not to these days. You said on the phone you didn't want to blame—"

"No blame at all," I interrupted hurriedly. "I had a happy childhood and a very secure one. It was rather a shock to learn from your letter that I was *bought*, but in an odd way that increases my respect for them. They were brilliant parents."

He nodded, as if relieved but unsurprised.

"I'm happy to hear that. So good did come out of it in the long run. Yes, that does put my mind at rest.... What happened was really quite simple, and my part in it may have been dubious legally, but *morally* I have to say I had no problems with it. I was quite young at the time and I was acting professor, standing in for someone who had had what was then a revolutionary brain operation and was out of action for two years. Your mother had been the departmental secretary for six or seven years. Her longing for a child was well known. I well remember the day she and Claud were knocked back as potential adoptive parents."

"Because of my father's mild epilepsy, I believe."

"That's right. It was a devastating blow for her—for both of them, I'm sure. Elizabeth was the only one I knew at that point. I've never seen a woman more bowled over by anything other than a death."

At that moment the piled dishes were put on the little heater, hot plates were put in front of us, and we helped ourselves to bits of this and that. We bent our heads over our plates to eat, though neither of us, I suspect, would have noticed or minded if no food or drink had been brought along at all.

"Just to go off on to a side issue for a moment," I said, to start the conversation up again. "I understand it was too late for Lucy to have an abortion, at least safely. Did she give any sign that she'd investigated the usual abortion channels?"

"No." Simon Frere's mouth twisted into an expression of distaste. "She wanted money, lots of it." He sipped at his wine, probably as a pretext for delay. When he spoke again I felt sure I was going to hear everything he knew. "I said I had no moral qualms about what I did, and that's true, of the initial stage. But it occurs to me I did keep myself prissily remote from the later stages, when I'd learned money was involved. I washed my hands of the business, and I can't be proud of that. If you were to ask me—to put it brutally—how much you fetched, I wouldn't be able to tell you." He sighed. "As much as she could get, no doubt."

"I wonder what the market rate was for assuaging emotional desperation," I remarked. "When did all this happen? How long after the murder?"

"Some time in April she came to us, about five weeks after the murder, if I remember rightly. Once the police were satisfied she and Lord John were not in it together, and she no longer had any contact with him or knew where he was, they let her go, though they took her passport away. Not that she ever showed any desire to go back to Australia. They also cautioned her not to speak to the press, so as not to prejudice any future trial."

"When you found out she wanted to give the baby away, did you try to persuade her to go through the usual channels?"

"No, I should have but—"

"You thought of my mother?"

"Yes. I suppose you think I was playing God. Perhaps there was some element of that in it."

"You did explain to my parents who it was who was having this baby—someone notorious in the murder inquiry?"

"Most certainly, and who the father was. It would have been dishonest not to. They took the view that the parentage was immaterial, that any other view was medieval." He looked me straight in the eye. "That was the only time I really talked to your father, and I liked him so much, and respected him, too. I thought the baby would have a wonderful start in life with parents like that."

"I did. None better."

"And then I…pretty well washed my hands of things, as I say. They were so happy, you see. The sight of your mother rid me of any doubts I might have had. I set up a meeting for them with Lucy to sort out the details, and felt that my involvement was at an end."

"But it wasn't, I suppose."

"Not entirely. Soon after the meeting I heard that your father had applied for a job in the Midlands. I assumed things were settled, as Lucy had told me they were. When I heard there was money involved I was horrified and worried, but I thought your parents could probably afford the sort of sum Lucy·would be likely to be asking."

"I suppose there's no need to follow up Lucy's attempt to find a higher bidder for me, since obviously nothing came of it."

Professor Frere shifted in his seat, and put his fork down, having done little more than toy with his food.

"It's not quite as simple as that."

"Oh?"

I put down my chopsticks and gestured to the underemployed waiter for coffee.

"Later in the evening when my daughter mentioned Lucy trying to sell something Lucy told me she'd talked to Professor Marryott—Patrick Marryott, professor at my former department at University College, London. He was a faintly—no, decidedly—insalubrious man. She just dropped it into the conversation, but the implication was she was thinking of doing her thesis with him."

"Would that have worried you?"

"I was nearing the end of my…physical relationship with her, and I think by and large I'd have been delighted to be rid of her. But Imogen's talk about selling worried me very much. For your parents' sake primarily, but feeling revolted by the general sordidness and cupidity of it, I decided to call Marryott and see if anything was going on I ought to know about. He was avuncular, condescending, and when I asked if he was involved in any attempt to find parents for Lucy's baby he laughed and said he might be. What business was it of mine? I said it was very much my business because parents had been found here for the child and an agreement entered into."

"I suppose the trouble with agreements like that," I said thoughtfully, "is that being illegal they can be broken with impunity because the injured party couldn't go to the police or a lawyer."

"Exactly. Marryott said it was Lucy's baby and she could give it to whomever she wanted to give it to—my people, who sounded as dull as ditchwater, pretty much like myself, or the Hayden-Gryces if they were whom she preferred, or they were the ones who were offering the most money. And then I really got worried."

"Pretty unmistakable name. Why were you worried? Did you know them?"

"Yes, I knew them well. He was a professor of History, she a lecturer in Art. Childless, and blessedly so, but rich—a private income. The last people you'd entrust a baby to. Neurotic, perpetually rowing, frankly in his case on the verge of insanity. I was horrified."

"You'd got yourself into an ethical dilemma."

He smiled wryly.

"You think me a bit of a prig. But I'm glad you can see how I viewed the situation. I was in a moral quandary. Suddenly the clean hands you thought you had don't seem so spotless anymore. I agonized. I had a strong suspicion that if I talked to Lucy she'd laugh in my face. But the thought of having involved your parents in a situation where they were likely to suffer such heartbreak was intolerable. I told Marryott he had to put a stop to this: it was about as honest and edifying as a slave auction. He told me that this was Lucy's business, and it wasn't for either of us to interfere. When I said the Hayden-Gryces were thoroughly unsuitable parents he said I was being judgmental as usual and it was time I stopped playing God. I began to get angry, and he said: 'Look, Simon, you're in this up to your ears. If you want to ruin a promising career all you have to do is make a fuss and that will be the end of you in academic life.' I still wonder if I did the right thing."

"Did you contemplate warning my parents?"

"Yes. That was really the only alternative, wasn't it, and I did think long and hard about it. But in the end I didn't *know* what Lucy was intending, and warning them would have the same devastating effect as denying them the longed-for baby would if that's what turned out to be Lucy's decision. In the end I was a coward. I did nothing, as Marryott knew that I would."

"And Lucy?"

"By then she was in her bed-sitter, neither my wife nor I saw any more of her, or wanted to know any of her business—beyond that she'd honored her agreement with your parents."

"Do you think they knew she was negotiating with others?"

"No, I'm sure they didn't. They couldn't have hidden their apprehension. I expect she was aiming to have the child and then go in for some sort of Dutch auction. Frankly, there's nothing so sordid or insensitive that I would think Lucy incapable of it."

"So is that what you think happened?"

He shot me a sharp look.

"I wondered whether you knew. Since you'd found out so much about your natural mother I thought you would have learned this, too."

"Learned what?"

"Lucy Mariotti had twins."

Chapter Thirteen

Getting Serious

Howw did you know? I asked at last, my mind having in the silence since his news broke conducted a swift rearrangement of my mental landscape. "Did Lucy tell you?"

He shook his head vigorously.

"I told you I never saw or spoke to Lucy after she moved out of our house. No, it was your mother who told me. She'd resigned from her job, but she came to see me the day before she and Claud and the baby moved to Milton. The baby, of course, was a deadly secret, but I knew, and though I could see she begrudged me the ten minutes she spent away from him—you—to come to see me and thank me, she did acknowledge that I'd earned it, and I was happy to see her. She said you had transformed their lives, and I'm sure that was true. In fact, you could *see* it. I was surprised none of her colleagues in the office commented on the fact that she was a changed woman."

"Why did she mention Lucy having had twins?"

"I suppose because Lucy had. When she handed you over she told them, and added: 'Luckily I had a would-be parent in reserve.' Your mother was quite indignant. 'Did she think we were going to go back on the agreement?' she asked. 'It's the last thing we would have done. It's as if she didn't trust us.'"

"My poor mother," I said, going over in my mind examples of her beautiful naïveté about the wickednesses of the world. "She would never have been able to comprehend what Lucy had actually been contemplating doing."

"No, your mother always thought the best of people if that was possible. Though I remember her saying too, that last time I saw her: 'I wish she'd offered us both the boys, because I wouldn't trust her to be sure she'd found a really suitable home for the other little one.' All this was said *sotto voce* in my office in the English Department, with both of us behaving like gunpowder plotters."

I thought for a moment.

"Is that all the evidence there is for my being a twin? Because she could have been making it up—a nasty joke to twist the knife in a little."

He'd lived with this much longer than me, and thought it through.

"Oh, I don't think so. The fact of her having two is the only explanation for her not having tried to get more out of your mother and father. I'm sure she was intending to do that, but the second baby meant she could double the sum anyway. And Patrick Marryott mentioned it too, fairly obliquely. We met at a conference somewhere or other, and though I'd very much rather not have talked to him, he came up during the coffee break one morning. 'Wasn't Lucy a clever girl?' he said in his usual sneering way. 'Solved all the problems and maximized her profits without burdening your old-fashioned Liberal conscience.' 'All the problems except the babies',' I said. He shrugged. 'Oh, they'll be all right,' he said. 'Children with their natural parents often have far worse prospects of happiness.' Which was true, but totally irrelevant. I always felt strongly about that. When Hayden-Gryce's death was in the papers—in the late seventies it was—I thought, 'Well, that's one

of them out of the way who will have made his
life hell.' I asked Marryott if Lucy was working at
her research with him, and he said: 'Oh no. She's
pursuing her researches in quite a different field.'
'What field is that?' I asked. He chuckled. 'The
same field as the respected Dr. Kinsey,' he replied,
and the chuckle turned into a roar of laughter and
he went off."

"Who is or was Dr. Kinsey?" I asked.

"You're too young to remember the fuss his
books stirred up soon after the war," Simon Frere
said. "I think the best word to describe him is
'sexologist.' I took him to mean that she was using
her undoubted charms and attractions—maybe as
someone's mistress. A rich person's definitely."

"That sounds pretty likely."

Simon Frere had put down his cup, refused a
refill, and had begun to make preparations for
departure. The restaurant was still sparsely filled,
and our table was remote from any other diners,
which had made our talk much easier.

"I won't say I've enjoyed our session," Frere said,
"but it has been therapeutic. On the other hand
I don't think I'll want to go back over the events
we've talked about too much in the future. I was
at least cured of any desire to play God by them,

or try to cure the miseries of this mortal coil. I don't think I come at all well out of things, and I'd rather put them behind me. The ball is now in your court, and it's up to you whether you decide to play it or not."

"Personally I'm very glad you did try to cure the miseries of this mortal coil," I said.

"But remember you could have been the one who was sold to the Hayden-Gryces. Now, is there anything else you want to ask me about? Then I can put it all behind me, as I'm afraid I put you behind me thirty-five years ago."

I thought.

"I've always been puzzled why Lucy didn't have an abortion the moment she found out she was pregnant. That would have been perfectly possible then, wouldn't it, even if it was illegal?"

"Perfectly possible, particularly with the Revill connections. She would hardly have needed to go backstreet to get rid of Lord John's child. Actually, I did ask her."

"What did she say?"

"Said she couldn't contemplate it because she was a Catholic."

"Hmm. Did you believe her?"

"I did not. It was the sort of tricky, dishonest

thing she would say, daring you to scoff and then putting you down. I think the baby was a weapon she could use against Lord John—either to get money or marriage or whatever out of him, or to get him bad publicity. Of course after the murder the police were investigating her for some time, and she certainly couldn't have done anything illegal in that time. Probably by the time she was cleared in their eyes the possibility of a safe abortion no longer existed. Lucy certainly wouldn't have done anything that might have involved risk to herself."

"You said you were a tough nut she was practicing on. Practicing for what?"

For the first time he looked sour.

"There are many varieties of whore and grades of whore-dom. I don't pretend to know where Lucy Mariotti landed up, but it will certainly have been some variety of whore, whether amateur or professional. That was her aim, and that will have been her destination."

I nodded. That did seem to me likely. I fumbled for my wallet and went to pay the bill. As I was at the counter I heard the door go, and when I turned back Simon Frere had vanished—back, no doubt to the redbrick bibliophile's palace beside

St. Pancras Station. My car was waiting for me outside, and the official driver's mood lightened perceptibly the farther we got from the dangerous seediness of the King's Cross area.

∽∽∽

The following weekend I got through my constituency business as planned by teatime on Saturday, and I took the train back to London. I felt I needed a free Sunday to clear my head, to sort out the implications of the new facts that Frere had laid out for me: the details of the transaction by which I had become Colin Pinnock, and the fact that I had, or had had, a twin brother. I decided over breakfast to have an hour or two in the Tate—something I like doing in those little pockets of free time I've had since I came to live in London: I decide on two or three rooms, and do them thoroughly, helped by the fact that there are some rooms I never consider doing, and by the fact that the arrangement of the whole gallery is more flexible than it used to be, and the pictures are changed more frequently.

The phone call came about nine-fifteen. I could think of no one apart from Susan who might ring me up at that time on a Sunday, and my finger was on the "record" switch of my tape recorder as

I took up the receiver. This time it was an aria I knew: the soprano aria "*La Mamma Morta*" from *Andrea Chénier* (an opera I've seen three or four times, mainly to enjoy the belting-it-out-to-the-heavens duet at the end, with the protagonists in a tumbrel on the way to the guillotine). My persecutor cut the duet short, and it was followed by the laughter of Don Pasquale and Malatesta at the end of their patter-duet.

I remained perfectly cool. If it was the purpose of these calls to disturb and disorientate me, they had stopped working. I went to my complete set and checked the words of the aria in the libretto. Nothing seemed to be of relevance to me, beyond the fact that the soprano starts by talking about her mother's death, and my adoptive mother was dead—possibly my natural mother as well, granted that she seemed to enjoy living danger-ously. I was now registering a new fact: all the records played seemed old—scratchy and boxy. Much-played LPs, perhaps, or even 78s, with singers whose voices I did not recognize.

Try as I might I could make little of this, beyond the fact that my persecutor could be someone who scavenged in street markets and car boot sales for operatic records with "Mother" in them. No doubt next time it would be "*Mamma, quel vino etc.*" from *Cav*—with about as much relevance as the previous ones. Was this person anxious to alert me to the word "mother" because he/she knew I was investigating my parentage, or to stimulate my interest in doing so?

It was twenty to ten. I could be at the Tate for its opening. I locked my door carefully, went out into the nippy fresh air, and began toward the river. Ahead was a demolition site, which only last year had been a thirties block of Council flats. The scaffolding towered six or seven stories high, and it was as I was starting on the pavement edge outside it that I felt a sudden stab of alarm. I immediately looked up, and was conscious of a large shape, or two shapes close together making an indistinct mass, on the wooden slats of the third floor at the far corner of the building. The next thing I registered was a brick coming in my direction. It landed on the pavement several yards in front of me. Even if I had continued walking it would have been well off target. I turned, registered the light Sunday morning traffic, and dashed across to the other side of the street. From there I had a fair view of the site and the half-demolished block of flats. There was no sign of anyone, not even a disappearing back. I gave up any idea of investigating or giving chase. I had no wish in any case to be the target of more, better-aimed bricks. Cooler reflection, as I stood there in the chilly morning sun, suggested that a brick that landed that far ahead of me had not been meant to hit, merely to frighten or to warn. It wasn't something to take seriously. Yet.

As I resumed my walk to the river I thought I could make a good guess at who had done the throwing. I was beginning to get an idea too as to what his relationship to me might be.

My mind wasn't on the forties abstract painters that day, nor even on Stanley Spencer. Often I have a meal at the Tate when I make these visits, but that day I just had a cup of tea and a bun, then took a taxi back home. I kept my eyes skinned on the people outside the Tate and the people in the streets on the journey home, but I got no sight of the slack-jawed young man.

I reported both the phone call and the brick to the police at the Palace of Westminster, who received my report with their usual barely suppressed skepticism. I record that here only because the incident with the brick was in fact the turning point, the moment when the psychological pressure became a real physical threat. Even the Westminster police, eventually, had to take notice. I rang Susan the following evening with a couple of things I wanted her to do. I could have rung Frieda Brewer, particularly as one of the things concerned Professor Marryott, whom she had actually met. I told myself I was closer to Susan, wanted to keep touch, but looking at my reactions to my dinner with Frieda I realize now that I had been repelled by her determination to bring up a child entirely on her own terms. Coming from a small but conventional family unit I found it a distasteful decision—cold and egotistical. The child was secondary, her creation, and perhaps mainly her plaything. I reacted to her desire to have a child without any paternal strings attached to it roughly as I would to a couple who wanted a blond-haired, blue-eyed child, and who had a tame scientist in tow who could supply it.

One thing I could say about my upbringing was that I was never secondary. Another thing was that I was decidedly not a mail-order child, but one who was accepted as what I was, with all sorts of unpropitious factors in my background taken totally in my parents' stride. Again and again I had felt during this unexpected journey to my origins how lucky I had been. Professor Frere's remark, though, struck a chill: I could have been the other twin.

"Susan, I've got a couple of jobs for you," I said.

"Good. I like to keep busy, especially on this little job, which I'm enjoying. I thought you might have been seduced into employing the American's researcher."

"Too high-powered and inhuman. You know how that scares a man."

"True. Being high-powered is aphrodisiacal, except when it's a woman who's high-powered."

"I don't know that that's true, on reflection. Think of all those male politicians who claimed to find Mrs. Thatcher sexy. Anyway, I await Ms. Brewer's bill with trepidation, and return to my first love—research wise, I mean. The first subject of investigation is Professor Marryott."

"Oh, he was mentioned in Elmore Hasselbank's article, wasn't he? One of Lucy's academic friends."

"That's right. And probably much more to her taste than the one I talked to last week—Simon Frere. A nice man, and a man with a conscience. Reverse those two descriptions and I suspect what you'd get would be Professor Marryott. He was a professor of English Literature at University College, London. I say 'was' because he's died since Hasselbank's article appeared. I'd like to know anything about him, but particularly if he has a widow."

"That shouldn't be too difficult."

"The other couple are the Hayden-Gryces."

"I always love names like that. It makes everything so much easier."

"Also London University in the early sixties. He a professor of History, she a lecturer in Art. Frere's memory is that he died in the late seventies."

"Right. Got that. And what's the connection?"

"They adopted my twin."

"*What?*"

"That's right. We were two. I've learned a lot since we spoke last. Come round when you've got the info and I'll bring you up to date."

That was Monday. She rang me on the Wednesday evening. No slouch, Susan. She said she wanted to talk to me, but not in my flat.

"Why? Scared of the seducer's couch?"

"No, because I'd like to see you on a lunchtime at a little and pretty nasty pub in Peckham."

"You make it sound so romantic. Tomorrow is a dead Thursday."

Dead Thursday is one of those days when there is no important government business to be done and everyone drifts off for an early weekend in their constituency or with their wife or mistress.

"That sounds all right. I'll be home all morning. Just ring me and tell me when you'll be there. The pub is called the Cock and Pheasant, and it's in Potter Street. If you come in your official car, I'd have it wait in the car park just off the High Street and make your own way. A car like that would be noticed."

I decided not to use the car, and had my A-Z in my briefcase, but as it turned out business caught up with me and, having phoned Susan and made a date for twelve-thirty, I found I had to use the car after all and brave my driver's disapproval of any suburb less swish than Chelsea or Kensington. The fact that I got out before my destination and told him to wait in the car park only increased the chill. It was getting to feel as if I conducted my life under the chilly gaze of a minister of the Free Church of Scotland.

The pub was indeed seedy—cold, dirty, silent, and ill-patronized. I got myself a pint and went to sit with Susan, who had commandeered a distant corner and was sitting there apparently absorbed in that day's *Daily Mirror*. She was dressed scruffily, an option that was hardly open to me. I briefed her quickly on all I had learned since I'd seen her last. Her eyes were bright with interest.

"The plot thickens," I commented with originality.

"Yes—it's becoming a rich, heady concoction."

"Well, throw in your twopennyworth of spices."

"Right. Well, let's take the Hayden-Gryces first. I did some research into his written work and found something that could even be marginally relevant to my own subject: a study of professional families in Lincolnshire towns in the latter part of the nineteenth century."

"Fascinating."

"Colin, don't play the tabloid vulgarian—it doesn't suit you. I know you have to suck up to the gutter press, but that doesn't mean you have to imitate it. Anyway, there was one Hayden-Gryce in the directory, living on the borders of Hampstead and Finchley, and I rang the number. An elderly woman's voice answered: high, intense, a very unrelaxing voice that rather sent my hackles up. She agreed she was the widow of Professor Harley Hayden-Gryce, and I rather incautiously said I thought I'd met her son some years ago."

"Why incautiously?"

"Well, you didn't actually say your twin was a boy, but I thought if it had been a girl you would have mentioned it. Anyway, the reaction came back like a whiplash: 'Well, if you're unlucky enough to meet him again, tell him not to get in touch.' Still in this high, power-drill sort of voice."

"Oh dear. Sounds like Frere was right in his forebodings."

"Very much so. There's nothing much more. I mentioned this article, said I was having difficulty getting hold of it, wondered if she had an offprint from the journal it appeared in. And she just broke in on me: 'Oh, for God's sake, look at it in a library like anyone else.' Then put the phone down."

"Nice type, obviously."

"That's what I thought. Though of course she was right: it was one of my thinner pretexts. Now Marryott. There are some spelled like that in the telephone directory, but not too many. I rang University College and spoke to someone in the English Department office—said I needed to speak to Patrick Marryott's widow about a reprint of his book on the Problem Comedies. She said, 'Samantha Marryott, oh yes, she lives in Pe—' Then she stopped, obviously reined in by someone else. She must have put her hand over the receiver, then came back and said: 'Actually I've just been reminded that we don't give out addresses or telephone numbers. If you would care to send a letter to us here we'll make sure it is forwarded to her.'"

"It wasn't too difficult. A London suburb beginning with P—not many of those."

"If she was living in London at all, of course," agreed Susan. "But I went back to the directory, found an S. Marryott in Peckham, and decided to go along and have a look for myself. The address was Two Underwood Lane—little terrace cottages from the early nineteenth century, mostly prettified up. I parked some way away, and as I was approaching I saw a woman leaving Number Two. There was a neighbor raking up leaves in the tiny apron of front garden all the cottages have, and I asked her if that was Mrs. Marryott who had just left. 'Oh yes, that's her,' she said, with a touch of grimness. 'Widow of the university professor?' 'That's it. Married him when she was twenty-one and he was fifty. Now he's dead, and she's even more firmly wedded to the bottle than she was when he was alive. She's on her way to the Cock and Pheasant now—goes there every lunchtime without fail. You can set your clock by her—five to twelve, to be there on opening time. What a waste of a life.'"

I looked around the saloon bar as casually as I could. There were not many candidates to choose from. Sitting on one of the bar stools and slumped over a drink on the bar itself was a woman running to fat, with dry-looking blonde hair and makeup that had been put on with a shaky hand and a bleary eye.

"That's her," said Susan. "And I thought that if anyone was going to get anything out of a sexy middle-aged lush, it would have to be a man, Colin."

CHAPTER FOURTEEN

Priapus Academicus

The next day, Friday, was the first reading of a Private Member's Bill of no particular interest to me (or to anybody else except the private member in question). I was due in my constituency for a meeting that evening, but lunchtime could be free. This time I managed to do without my driver, took the underground to the Oval, then a bus to Peckham High Street, which was bustling and invigorating with early weekend shoppers of every age, class, and race. To turn off it to get to the little street in which the Cock and Pheasant was situated was to go back to the dispiriting fifties (or so it seemed to me, who knew the decade only through black-and-white films shown at unearthly hours on the television).

When I got to the pub my quarry was already

planted on a bar stool—a regular and valued customer, obviously, in a drinking place that had few of those. She was wearing old green and brown checked slacks and a purple jumper. Both had seen better times more recently than they had seen the inside of a dry cleaner's. No amount of makeup could disguise the fact that her face was becoming puffy and raddled, looking like a collection of old string bags on a hook in the scullery. She gave off a smell of carelessness and hopelessness, of being already, and prematurely, at the end of the line.

I took up a position at the bar beside her, but there was no sign of a landlord or a barman.

"Marvyn's down the cellar fetching tonics," my neighbor volunteered in slurred tones.

"Oh well, no hurry," I said, making a pantomime of looking around me at the near-empty barroom.

"Looking for someone?"

"Oh, just my researcher. She said she might be in, and might not."

Her cheeks bobbed as her mouth twisted in scorn.

"Researcher! Another frigging academic!…That the girl you were with yesterday?"

"You're a sharp one," I commented, mentally adding, "Sharper than you look." She disclaimed the compliment, her scorn now seeming to turn away from academics on to herself.

"You notice new people in a dead-and-alive hole like this. I only come because it's cheap. Cheap and nasty go together, don't they? Here's Marvyn now."

Marvyn was the sort of barman who announces in his own person that you're in a pub on No Hope Street, and not too far from the end of the road. Below his rolled-up sleeves his arms were tattooed with the dismal record of his loves and his enthusiasms—Sharon and Sinead sharing space with Chelsea Football Club and Barry McGuigan. He had two rings in one ear and a stud in either nostril, and he took my order for a pint of best without comment or interest. Drink would have to be cheap here, because there was no other reason for coming.

"Will you have one with me?" I asked my companion.

"Wouldn't mind at all," she said, brightening up and actually turning to look at me. "I'll have a gin and tonic." She sipped again at the one she had got, still two-thirds full.

"Same again for the lady," I told Marvyn, who went about it with the inscrutability usually attributed to the Chinese.

"Forget what I said about academics," she said in her new mood. "There's good and bad in all professions, isn't there?"

"There certainly is," I said heartily, refraining from saying there had probably been some quite delightful public executioners. "I'm Derek Barton, by the way."

"Samantha Marryott." She smiled, with the last shadows of a coquettish expression.

"So how did you come by your jaundiced view of academics then, Samantha?"

She let out a short bark of laughter.

"I married one. It never fails. What's more to the point, I stayed married to him—stuck it out for years and years, till the nasty old prick died. I could have got out, got myself a life. 'Stead of which, having trapped myself, I stayed in the trap. Tell you what, we were barmy, my generation."

Since by my guess she probably grew to adulthood in the late sixties or early seventies, I didn't think fidelity to the matrimonial ideal was something she could blame on the zeitgeist. However, I feigned agreement.

"You've got a point there."

"Know what they say about the past being another country? Well, that's bang on, in my case. He got me when I was a slip of a thing. Wouldn't think that was possible, to see me now, would you?" She made facial gestures in the direction of a simper, and I made the expected noises of demurral. "I was in my second year, and green as a hothouse plant. You wouldn't believe it, but I regarded all the teachers with awe, and a professor was God himself. I said I was green, didn't I? You sleeping with your researcher, then?"

I fielded the wicked ball as best I could.

"Not at the moment."

"So what do you mean—you used to be or you're hoping to be? Oh, forget I said that. Pretend I didn't ask. Soured by experience, that's me."

"By your experiences with—what?—Professor Marryott?"

"That's him. That was him. It's like looking through the mists of time. When he started putting the hard word on me I was flattered. Can you imagine it? I was a pretty twenty-one-year-old—no, I was a *gorgeous* twenty-one-year-old—and I was flattered this overweight fifty-year-old with the prick he couldn't control wanted to get me to bed. What the hell did I think he'd want from me? To hear my gems of wisdom on image clusters in *Much Ado About Nothing*? I was a little fool, and he knew it and took advantage."

"But still you got him to marry you."

Her eyes glinted with cunning.

"I had that much *nous*...." Then she suffered a revulsion or reversal of feeling and banged her glass down. "God, listen to me. You'd think I was incapable of learning, wouldn't you? It wasn't *nous*, it was stupidity. If I'd had any brains I'd just have slept with him like everyone else. To hear me talk you'd think marriage with him was a big deal."

I let her gaze into the depth of the bar pools for some seconds.

"I've never been married. I don't know whether marriage with anybody is a big deal."

That interested her.

"Have you not? Nice-looking, well-set-up chap like you." There was a suspicion of a leer behind her remarks. Perhaps she had caught it from her husband. Or perhaps their leers had brought them together. "But then, probably you've made the right decision," she said. "You'd be wasted in a marriage."

Her moment of introspection was over, and

she'd gone back to her gin and tonic.

"I'll take that as a compliment. Is that what happened in your case? I suppose you found it restricted you too much."

This time she definitely did leer.

"You're joking! When I had a husband like mine? Not so you'd notice, I can tell you."

"Still, it's obviously left you bitter."

"Bitter? Too damned right I'm bitter. Look, I knew what he was like from the day I sat in the lecture room for his first performance to my year. On the fucking *ethos* of Shakespearean comedy. Some people lecture to individuals in the audience: one at the front, one in the middle, one toward the back. Patrick didn't do that. He picked out in the first five minutes the first batch of students he intended to bed, and then he lectured to them. He was famous for it. I had been around for a year, so I knew the score: I'd heard all about it long before I went to his lectures and tutorials."

"So you weren't quite as green as that hothouse plant."

She giggled.

"It's a good line. And makes me feel less bad about it."

"I bet you were in his first batch."

"Top of the list. Half of that fucking *ethos* lecture was addressed to me. If I'd had any sense I'd have opened my legs and said, 'Hello, good-bye,' to that damned thing of his and had done with it. That's what all the others did, except for those who kicked him in the relevant part and got bad marks for their pains. Instead of which I took it as a challenge. I'd got to get a ring and a white wedding. Have you ever heard anything more daft? Well, I was punished for it. What is that thing at the end of *Vanity Fair*? 'Which of us—'"

"'Which of us has his desire? or, having it, is satisfied?'" The question suddenly struck me with the force of a wet towel across my head. It was relevant to her, but it was just as relevant to me. I could hardly restrain myself from going out into the fresh air and analyzing what it was about the quote that bore so strongly home. My parents had got what they desired, a child, and in spite of Thackeray they had been satisfied—joyful, grateful, fulfilled. I had got what I desired, political office, and I was not satisfied. In fact I was so little satisfied I was haring off on the track of my birth and origins to hide from myself the emptiness of my life. Samantha Marryott had not noticed my reaction: she had merely nodded, as recognizing an old acquaintance she had thought about often.

"That's the thing. I got caught by getting what I wanted. I had him dancing with frustration—he needed a bowler hat stuck on his crotch by the end of that year. And at the beginning of my third year I went down the aisle all in white—that was a laugh—and we were the happy bride and groom. And that's when my troubles began."

"A lot of women marry rakes, thinking they can reform them."

That struck no chord with her. Perhaps it was too Victorian an idea.

"I don't think I *thought* at all. I don't think I even *liked* him—not then, and certainly not later. I soon found I was a brief pause between fucking students and fucking more students. I can't say I lost much sleep over it. I went out and did likewise. But he was in a different position, wasn't he? Being a professor. Ten years later and he'd have been up on a disciplinary charge about that. In fact ten years later he was lucky to wriggle out of one. He turned his attention elsewhere after that. In fact he'd always kept his eggs in more than one basket."

"Sounds like the sort of man they wrote dirty songs about in my boyhood days."

She threw back her head and emitted that mirthless barking laugh again.

"Tell me about it. I don't remember songs but there were jokes and limericks and slogans in the loos. He preened himself on that, wrote them all down when he was told about them. He always said when he retired he was going to write a late-twentieth-century version of *My Life and Loves.* 'Frank Harris has nothing on me,' he used to say. As it was he was too busy fucking to do much about it. When he died I found notes and parts of one chapter. I chucked them straight in the Aga."

"You don't seem to feel any jealousy toward the women."

"Good God, no. How can you feel jealousy toward so many? Contempt if anything, and pity.…Toward his whore I suppose I felt a bit differently."

"He had a regular mistress as well?"

She screwed up her face in distaste.

"I suppose you could describe her as that. But she was a whore for all that—a regular cash-on-the-nail whore, with a little stable of subwhores.

Patrick didn't pay, though."

"I suppose he counted as an honored guest."

She pouted and shook her head.

"He'd helped to set her up. If you could have shares in a brothel he'd have been the majority shareholder. This had been going on for years before he married me, and it went on for years afterward, too."

"Was this a former student who decided bodily prostitution paid better than intellectual prostitution?"

We both laughed. We were both academic insiders, or so she thought.

"Search me. I just knew her as Mrs. Labelle. Corny, wasn't it? Ran a genteel and exclusive establishment in Kensington—none of your Soho or King's Cross knocking-shops for *her*. The clientele was practically handpicked: politicians, aristocracy, show biz, high-flying academics. Well, it wasn't *exactly* handpicked, a lot of the customers heard about it by word of mouth. Connoisseurs of outré experiences tend to recognize their own kind, and pass the message on when they've discovered a good thing."

"Ah, so this wasn't just a run-of-the-mill brothel."

"Not at all. The more out-of-the-way the taste the more welcome you were. Madam entertained in the wider sense: you spent an evening there, rather than twenty minutes. The conversation was good, deals could be done, contracts made, similarity of tastes established—all this while this fantastic witty and erudite fucking *talk* was going on around you. Upstairs anything went and tact and discretion were assured. Oh, from what I heard it was a very clever establishment, filling a real need—Patrick's own words."

"Sounds like a prototype of the Groucho Club."

We both giggled.

"You're a fun academic you are," said Samantha, putting a hand on my arm. "You must really wow the students. Anyway, money had been put into this business, and in the early years of our marriage money came out of it. We didn't always live in a squalid little hole in Peckham, you know. But then the trade figures at Chez Labelle started dipping—"

"Fashions change," I commented sympathetically.

"That was it, partly, and moral habits, too. Cabinet ministers could get what they fancied in private life, without paying sky-high prices. Good conversation became even more of a lost art, and most people wouldn't know how to make it, or respond to it. Anything went in most spheres of life as far as kinks were concerned. When the going got tough Labelle got reckless. I never heard the details. Patrick might boast to me when things were going well, but he clamped up when things were on the slide. You hear things though, and from what I heard I gathered that Madam was being questioned about blackmail allegations. All the rooms in the establishment were of high-class hotel standard, and she'd bugged the phone in one room and got something on an Opposition spokesman on something or other. When she tried it on with him he went straight to the police. That busted the reputation the place had in the sexual underground for total discretion. So that was the end of a nice little earner for Patrick—for Patrick and me, if I'm being absolutely honest."

"Did you ever hear what happened to Mme. Labelle?"

"No. I wasn't likely to. Patrick's first instinct, if anyone associated with him was in trouble, was to pull up the drawbridge. She was out there and he was in his battlemented stronghold. The most he'd do would be to wave good-bye. There were other people banging on the door at the same time, other—to mix the metaphor, as Patrick wouldn't fail to point out if he were here—other pigeons coming home to roost. His career came to a halt. He was already a professor, so there weren't many upward avenues left, but for a time, as I've said, there was a question of a disciplinary inquiry, perhaps of him losing his chair. In the end everyone decided it wouldn't be worth the stink, and things were swept under the carpet, as they usually are in universities. Frankly, students were bought off. Patrick by then had a taste for the good life, but gradually we outspent our resources, and by the end his pension wasn't doing much more than covering our drinking costs. Our lives took a nosedive. It was a squalid death, Patrick's."

"Sad, sad," I commented, while feeling it was totally deserved.

"So that's the story of my life," said Samantha. "I don't suppose you wanted to hear it, but you did. Thanks for listening. How about telling me about yours?"

"Nothing near as Shakespearean to tell," I said.

"Big things can follow from an affair with one's

researcher." She looked around the near-deserted pub. "Doesn't look like she's going to turn up."

"Doesn't look like it," I agreed.

"Why don't you come back with me? Tell me your story. Everybody's got a story, somewhere."

"Why not?" I said, thinking of any number of reasons. She put an arm around my waist and I put an arm around hers, and that way we supported each other out into the scruffy street. She turned in the direction of Underwood Lane. I hadn't wanted to give her the impression I'd scraped acquaintance with her to wriggle her story out of her. On the other hand there were limits to what I was willing to do to cover my tracks.

"I've got a bottle in the car," I said.

"I've got bottles at home," she said, but she seemed interested.

"Best malt whiskey," I said, disengaging myself at her front gate. "Back in a tick."

She waved as I disappeared around the corner. I expect she guessed. I sent her a card addressed to the Cock and Pheasant, saying I'd found my car had been wheel-clamped and I'd had to deal with it to get to a later engagement. I signed it Derek Barton and I said I hoped we'd meet again pretty soon. If you tell one lie you might just as well tell two, or so all politicians think. Anyway, I shouldn't think Marvyn passed the card on.

That weekend I rang Matthew Martindale to bring him up-to-date on what I had been doing. On our one meeting I'd had a feeling for him that amounted almost to regarding him as a brother, and I didn't want to lose that feeling. He seemed to have something of the same. It was late Saturday, the children were in bed, and he called Janet over to listen to my news, because he said she was interested.

He responded with the sort of immediate and wholehearted interest that is loved by any storyteller—or any political speechmaker, come to that, though I can't pretend I've ever aroused it. His reaction to my stalker, to the telephone communications, and the information from my father's cousin were just what was needed to hearten me, and when I told him about Professor Frere's account of Lucy's pregnancy he said: "Now you *know* who you are." The revelation of the twin brother provoked a sort of three-way conversation, with Janet full of excited speculation. Oddly enough, when I happened to mention that I probably wouldn't be using Frieda Brewer anymore as my researcher, partly because she was contemplating a book on the Revill case, Matthew exploded.

"Bloody woman! What kind of mind do these muckrakers have? Why can't she let the story die a natural death?"

He sounded like an aristocrat of the old school, confronted by a piece of impertinence from one of his estate workers.

"I don't think she's a muckraker," I said patiently. "In fact she's not a journalist at all, just someone journalists use. She's intrigued by the whole business, and thinks there's a book in it."

"That's muckraking, whether she's a journalist or not. What business is it of hers?"

"I'm afraid it became a public matter when your father murdered your mother."

There was a second's silence.

"You think I'm overreacting?"

I was heartened to hear a woman's laugh at the other end.

"A little. I can hear Janet agrees with me. You know the subject gets raked up periodically, Matthew. It's a minor national scandal. Eventually someone was bound to write a book on it, and Frieda's would at least be scholarly and sober. I'm surprised, actually, that something much worse hasn't come out before this."

"Oh Lord," said my brother. "It's like something hanging over you—something you know in your heart is eventually going to happen—like your daughter's first love affair, or one of the children experimenting with drugs. The fact that you know it's going to happen doesn't make it any easier when it does."

We talked for some time, on and around the recent revelations. When Janet heard I was speaking from Milton she made the obvious but sensible suggestion that I should have a systematic going-through of any family papers in the house. Then Matthew told me that he and his sister had talked about me and what I was doing. She had promised to trawl through her memories to see if there was anything there that might be of use to me. We ended with declarations of an intention to meet up again.

That was Saturday night. On Sunday I slept in, visited my father, and then took to the road. At one o'clock I made a detour off the motorway to avoid the revolting and expensive eateries which are the only option for the traveler in a hurry. I found a cozy village pub to have a traditional lunch in and read *The Observer* while I tucked in at leisure. When I got to London I went on spec to call on Susan, found her in, and we went over all sorts of possible leads in the Revill case, then went out for a light Indian meal.

I arrived back in Pimlico about ten. I left the car ticking over in the street while I went and unlocked my garage. Then I drove the car in, came out, and turned to swing the door down and lock it. It was as I was bending down that I felt the knife. It was the oddest of sensations because before it became pain it was almost a sensuous feeling, and I could picture the knife—so sharp, so thin that it almost felt like a needle going into my back below the ribs, and once in being twisted. I clutched the door handle I was locking, cried out for help, then fell forward onto the cold concrete, feeling the wet sensation of blood soaking into my shirt. As I cried out for help I was conscious of steps running away, but of none running toward me.

CHAPTER FIFTEEN

Memories of Upper Brook Street

When I awoke in hospital I was attached to a device involving pulleys which enabled me to lie in something close to a resting position but left my lower back swinging free. When I asked the nurse how I had got there she said what I needed was rest. True enough, but not easy, and when I finally dozed off it was with the help of a narcotic, something I abominate. What I had was sleep rather than rest. I dreamed my old dream of fleeing along dark streets that progressively narrowed and enclosed me.

I learned what had happened the next evening. The man who had called 999 was someone whom I had helped a year or two before with some small business matter—the sort of thing that often comes up in constituency surgeries. He had come to me because he had found the then MP for my part of London "useless." Anyway Ron Price, who lived in the same block as me, had more than repaid me when he had driven up, seen my unconscious body, and immediately called help.

"I thought you were a goner," he said, sitting by my bed with an ease he'd never showed before when talking to me. "You do when there's all that blood, don't you? I felt your pulse though, and it was still pretty good, so I dialed nine-nine-nine on my mobile."

I'll never sneer at mobile phones again, nor even at those fatuous and gabby users on trains who broadcast the trivialities of their lives or businesses to those unfortunate enough to sit near them. I could even imagine getting one myself, I thought, particularly in current circumstances.

"What time was this?" I asked.

"Ten, quarter past maybe."

"No point in asking whether there was anybody nearby at the time."

"No—you'd been there a while without being spotted."

"Ten minutes at least."

"Oh, the mugger would have been long gone. Did he get very much?"

"Hardly anything," I said, without a pause. "I was intending to go to the bank today."

Whether "hardly anything" is any less of a lie than "five hundred pounds" would have been, I don't know. Anyway, it added verisimilitude to his presumption about my attacker. The Metropolitan Police constable who was sitting in my room in the Pimlico Hospital didn't raise his eyebrows. I had already been questioned by Scotland Yard and together we'd established that nothing had been taken from me.

I had a visit too from PC Marrit of the Palace of Westminster police. I'd always liked him, felt he was reliable and straight-forward, and to tell the truth had rather resented his skepticism, and that of his fellow policemen, about my stories of being marked and persecuted.

"A bit less cynical about all this now, are you?" I said, wincing as I tried to get up straighter and look him in the eye.

"Cynical, sir? You've no cause to say that, I'm sure." He relaxed a little and almost winked. "Mind you, we've always got the odd nutter in the House of Commons—the odd self-important crank or the teeterer on the verge of outright paranoia. We know the problem, and we have to look at all the stories they bring to us on their own merits, not seen through the eyes of the people bringing the story. We had an MP once who firmly believed he was being targeted by alien forces from outer space."

I grinned. I knew whom he was talking about.

"Good to know I've ranked comparatively low in your nutter gradings up to now."

"A very mild skepticism is the most that you can charge us with."

"But that's all changed now, I hope."

"Ye-e-es." He was going to concede, if he conceded at all, reluctantly. "Mind you, muggers who've got out of their depth, young lads who've done something serious they didn't really intend to, quite often do run off empty-handed."

"I assure you this man did not suddenly find himself out of his depth. He was waiting for me, he chose his moment when I was at a disadvantage, then struck out of the blue, as he had obviously intended to."

Marrit nodded.

"Yes, that does seem to be the view that the

Scotland Yard people are taking. Why did he strike *there*, do you think? Not by your garage, I mean, but that part of your body."

I felt gingerly round to my lower back.

"It was what I was presenting to him."

"It was hardly a deadly area."

I was recovering so fast I had to agree.

"I'm no anatomist, but I'm sure you're right. But the fact that it wasn't deadly squares with everything that's happened so far—pinpricks at first, metaphorically speaking, then getting more and more serious. And then that feeling of the whole thing being slightly ridiculous, calculated to raise a guffaw rather than real concern. Stabbing me just above my bum squares well with that."

"It does." He looked me in the eye. "Your worry is that the increasing seriousness is going to end up with something that is absolutely for real, isn't it?"

"Yes. That's what I'm beginning to think."

"And why the long buildup?"

"To relish the slow process of first making me uneasy, then really worrying me, and finally terrifying me. The psychology behind the whole campaign is entirely consistent. A quick kill wouldn't supply him with half the pleasure."

"Equally it could be someone who is having difficulty working up the nerve to do the ultimate thing. Someone lacking in confidence, basically rather timid...." He saw a flicker in my eye. "Do you have anyone in mind, sir?"

"Possibly. It's no more than a suspicion, an alternative scenario." I thought and made a decision. "I find I have a twin brother. We were both adopted, but separately. I think he is the man who has been following me. Not very bright, I would guess, or maybe psychologically scarred. He was adopted by a totally unsuitable couple, but a cultured one. It would explain his readiness with operatic excerpts. They rather suggest he may have an obsessive resentment both of his mother—his natural mother—and of me."

"Of you, sir? Why?"

"Adopted into a happy home, successful quite young, getting into government and starting on the career ladder there. It could feed an unbalanced mind."

We chewed over this for some time, and I gave him my brother's surname, though with the cavil that if I were called Hayden-Gryce, and if I had a justified resentment at my adoptive parents, I'd have changed it either formally or informally. He promised to check police records, and I suggested he check not only both components of his name but perhaps Revill too, and even Mariotti. The total silence my parents maintained on the subject of my origins was probably not reproduced by the Hayden-Gryces, who had obviously been neither sensitive nor restrained. They could have thrown the facts of his birth at him, taunted him with them, and in the process given rise to all sorts of obsessive fantasies.

"No improvement in my daughter's school yet," he said, as he got up to go. "They're still the same collection of wankers peddling the same no-hope philosophies."

"Give us time!" I said. "You can't work change in institutions in a few months."

"Oh, I'll give you time," he said, grinning evilly. "Until the next election."

I had other visitors in the four days I was in hospital—friends, colleagues, my minister, Susan. I also had one who was entirely unexpected. I was in a National Health hospital but in a private room with a guard, for obvious reasons. He mostly sat tactfully (and boringly for him, I'm sure) on an upright chair outside my door. On my third day in he came in and over to my bed, holding a card, and looking a little bemused.

"There's a lady outside, says you don't know her, but she thinks you'll speak to her if you feel well enough."

I took the card. It said Caroline Martindale, with an address in Notting Hill and the words Millennium Modes in the bottom right-hand corner. My heart skipped a beat.

"Yes, I'd very much like to talk to her," I said. "Please show her in."

She came straight over and shook my hand carefully, then stood at the foot of my bed.

"Good of you to see me," she said.

No, it was good *for* me to see her, satisfying at last to see my half sister. I don't know what I'd expected of someone in the fashion trade, but it was nothing like Caroline. She was slim, almost skinny, and was dressed in a floppy jumper—not dirty but definitely not new—and a calf-length skirt. Her hair was tidy but no more, and she had no detectable makeup on. She looked like a lady of the manor caught at the wheel of her Land Rover on a very busy morning, but her body language contradicted such a figure: her gestures were unconfident—sharp, unexpected waves of the hands, exaggerated twistings of the mouth. She seemed unsure whether she should have come, uncertain of her relationship with me and how to talk to me.

"You're thinking I'm not your idea of a fashion buyer," she blurted out after letting herself be inspected in silence. With a jerky movement she pulled out a chair and sat by my bed. "We don't go around in our spare time looking like fashion plates, you know."

"I'm sorry. I must have been staring rudely. It's just—"

"I apologize for 'Millennium Modes' on my card. That really is naff. It was my partner's idea, and *not* one of his better ones. We act as buyers to a lot of the chains, and for a few definitely exclusive shops. I *see* so much fashion I prefer to dress as a drab when I don't have to sustain an image."

"Actually you look very good," I said. To me she did.

"Horse manure," she said, cheerfully and without rancor. "You wouldn't think I'd been a model for a while, would you? In the early seventies, in the wake of Twiggy and a lot of other skeletal types. Worst time of my life. Sheer slavery. Treated like a carcass and dressed up like a pantomime dame. I think I only got jobs anyway because of who I was, and the scandal. Well, let's get down to business. As soon as I heard about you from Matthew I wanted to see you, and when I read about the attack—"

"You thought you'd better look me over before it was too late."

She nodded, keeping the tone light.

"Well, something like that."

"Actually, I thought your brother was a bit unforthcoming about the possibility of our getting together. I wondered whether he was being protective."

"He was. He is—very. He thinks I live on the edge of a nervous breakdown. Like a lot of nervy people, I'm very tough because I have to be. I suppose I'm nervy because of what happened to my mother. Or perhaps it's earlier than that— the breakdown of the marriage, the fact that my mother didn't care whether I lived or died. Did you think Matthew was being protective because it was actually me who killed my mother?"

My eyes widened involuntarily.

"Nothing of the kind! Don't be absurd. But I was a bit suspicious because he said you traveled all over the world on business, but also said he was in London the day my picture was in the *Evening Standard* because he was meeting you from New Zealand."

"A tarradiddle. Quite harmless. He was gaining time, wanting to think whether he would tell me about you, whether I should be encouraged to speak to you. Protective, and awfully old-fashioned, you notice. Actually he picked up a copy of the *Standard* in Wellingborough to glance at the final election results and he saw the picture there. He got on the phone to me straightaway."

"Why?"

"He thought if I saw it I might get an awful shock. Actually, I'd registered your by-election victory years before. He was out of the country at the time and I wasn't, and I saw you on television. There wasn't a lot of coverage, was there? I suppose that was because the Tories lost every by-election going at that time. But I saw the declaration of the count on television, and an interview with you afterward."

"What was your reaction?"

"I thought you had to be a relative somewhere along the line. It wasn't just the likeness to Matthew. I remember my grandfather quite well, you see, and I've grown up with pictures of him as a young man—in his robes for the 1937 coronation, and so on. The resemblance is unmistakable. I didn't think you were a sin of his old age, but I knew that resemblances often skip a generation, as they had with Matthew. The possibility that you were the nanny's child occurred to me, still more so when I read reports of the by-election in the papers next day and saw how old you were. Born in the year of the murder."

"But you and Matthew, when you talked, decided to do nothing about it."

"Of course. We didn't know whether you knew, whether you would want to know, whether it might even be a hindrance to a political career. And Matthew, of course, being protective, tends to shield me from all mention of the murder."

"You seem to have talked about it quite a lot at the time."

"That was the frightened ghoulishness of young children. Over the years Matthew has changed from being the younger brother to being the older one, if you get my meaning."

I was getting a weird feeling.

"It seems funny to me, talking to someone of about my own age who knew my mother."

"Well, don't think of me as about your age,"

she said, with one of her sharp, dismissive gestures. "I'm not. Did you sense when you were talking to Matthew that he didn't really know your mother?"

I considered.

"Something like that. He was so young."

"I suppose what I mean is that he doesn't really *remember* her. What he remembers is us talking about her after the… after our mother's death. I think he may have given you a slightly wrong impression of our relationship with Lucy Mariotti."

"Too harsh, you mean? After the murder you blamed her for it and you couldn't find things to say nasty enough about her?"

"Not even as simple as that. The fact is we definitely liked her when she first came. We'd had a couple of those square, hardfaced tyrants who seemed to be just waiting for the time when concentration camps would be set up in Britain. Too free with the hairbrush by half, and devoted to bed-with-bread-and-water punishments as well. Lucy was a wonderful change after those two. She was pretty, she was funny, she played with us, stimulated us, read us the sorts of books which actually fed our imaginations, not books which someone in a library thought children ought to read."

"So, not all bad then."

"Except that it was an act," said Caroline, sharp and downright. "I suspect Lucy of acting much of the time, a congenital role-player. The act she put on depended on what people wanted of her, and deeper down what could help her to get ahead, get what she wanted."

"That tallies with a lot of what I've heard about her—from a man who helped her during her pregnancy, for example."

Caroline nodded vigorously.

"What she wanted in this case was to get her claws into our father. I see that *now*. She saw that he loved us, saw that he thought Mummy neglected us, even positively disliked us, so she wormed her way into his heart by being wonderful with his children."

"I think Matthew would say she never really fooled you."

"Probably he would. He's remembering the things we said about her later. Children are much more easily fooled than sentimentalists like to admit." She shook her head, remembering. "We thought she was wonderful. Then she got her way, got him into bed with her, and from then on we were surplus to requirements. Except when he was there we were treated with benign neglect."

"Ah, so you did see through her before things came to a head. Children are not so gullible then."

"We didn't exactly see through her. We judged her on how she treated us. I think that's what children always do. We hated her because she just switched off her interest in us."

"Ah, but did you realize that she was no longer interested because she'd got what she wanted and was sleeping with your father?"

"No-o-o." But she had to think long and hard about that. "That came later. Remember this was a large and traditional house. We were upstairs on the second floor for much of the time—though being children we often broke loose, came downstairs, and noticed things. But no, we didn't know Lucy and Daddy were sleeping together. We did know something was very wrong with our parents' marriage, and had been for some time. Our sympathies were all with our father, because frankly Mummy was a hard, cold bitch and we felt for her just nothing....We did know Daddy slept alone."

"Ah."

"Without realizing its significance. In any case I think in aristocratic circles it's quite usual, or was then, to have separate bedrooms, with separate dressing rooms, linked but apart. You *came* together when you felt like it, of course, but you slept apart. But I think our parents slept together when I was young. At some stage Daddy moved out."

"I'd gathered Lucy moved into a household where the marriage was in a sticky state—perhaps on the rocks. It seems like a recipe for disaster."

"It does, doesn't it? We were far too young to understand that. We would never tell Daddy how we felt about Mummy, never tell him how she neglected us and never wanted us near her. He *knew*, of course, and we would have liked to tell him and talk about it but sensed he would shy off the subject. In fact I think the reason we—or I—realized the marriage was on the rocks was because after a time we never talked about Mummy with him at all. It was a subject we all avoided by common consent."

"So what was the situation in Upper Brook Street in the months leading up to the murder? Your father had a separate bedroom, but was stealing into Lucy's room. Lucy was pregnant, and perhaps was happy she now had a hold or a bargaining lever to use with your father. And your mother was on her own—but perhaps, someone has suggested, had a new man in her life."

"All that may be true, but most of it we didn't know about. A lot of what I *think* I knew I got from the article by that American in the *Observer* color supplement. As to whether Mummy had a lover, we just wouldn't know. We hardly saw her. We certainly didn't know Lucy was pregnant. We did sense that Daddy was fond of her, then sense something stronger than that....But I think that in the weeks leading up to Mummy's death something changed. The situation wasn't as clear-cut as you make it."

"I just have the broad outlines in my head—at least I think I have."

"My memory of the weeks leading up to the... murder—I hate saying it—is that the situation was very fraught. Our father wasn't his usual self. Nervy, irritable, tense. When Matthew and I talked about it afterward we wondered—in childish terms—whether Lucy had found another man. But she must have found out that she was pregnant by then, and this could have been a way to bring things to a head with Daddy: 'I'm having your child. What are you going to do about it?'"

"A reason for divorcing your wife, not murdering her."

She got quite animated at this.

"Ah, but you're talking as if the...murder was something planned and premeditated. I don't see how it can have been, unless it went badly wrong. I think it must have been a spur-of-the-moment act of rage, something totally out of character, brought on by—something, I can't guess what. And then the only thing Daddy could think of to do was get out, disappear, whatever."

"Kill himself?"

"Maybe."

"If Lucy Mariotti was sticking out for marriage, then divorce would hardly have been a problem. Divorce might not have done any good to your father's political career, but it sure as hell wouldn't have been as bad for it as murder."

"You're still talking as if this were premeditated. I'm quite sure it wasn't."

"Point taken. In any case most people seem to think your father's political career wasn't all that important to him."

"It wasn't. Fishing and shooting are what he really enjoyed doing."

"And of course after divorce there would have been another step, and one he may not have been willing to take: marriage to Lucy."

Caroline thought.

"You mean he could have seen through her by then?"

"Yes. Everybody agrees that Lucy was clever—cunning, devious, ingratiating. I bet it was due to Lucy that they all three went round to parties and theaters together—putting up a front. But I have the impression it was the sort of cleverness that after a time *showed*. You realized she was so pleased with herself and her own cleverness. She gave herself away. Professor Frere, who took her in after the murder, thought that. If your father felt himself trapped in one bad marriage, he may not have wanted to walk straight into another."

"Yes....Somehow the feeling I got, though I may be mis-remembering, of course, is that he was as...hot for her as ever. Sorry, I can't think of a nicer way of putting it."

"I suppose you didn't get any ideas about what might have happened by what you saw on the night of the murder, or the day afterward?"

She raised her eyebrows.

"You're joking. We heard nothing, saw nothing, knew nothing. We slept through all the to-ings and fro-ings of the night itself, and when we awoke the next morning we found that the police had taken over the house."

"How did you find out?"

"We heard noises, went out onto the landing, and—I still have the picture in my mind—immediately saw a policeman and Mrs. Gould the housekeeper. She was normally rather a remote figure, not someone of any great importance in our lives. Obviously she had been waiting for us to wake up. She ran forward, bundled us back into our bedroom, and said there'd been a bad accident. Said our granny and grandad Martindale were on their way to take us to their home, and they'd explain. We'd to stop in our room, she'd bring us breakfast, and we'd to wait for them. That was what happened. They came, obviously very upset, but pulling themselves together for our sakes. We were dressed by then, and we were hurried downstairs—I'd never *seen* so many policemen, and never have since—and out into their car, with cameras clicking from behind the police cordon. I thought I saw Lucy being driven away ahead of us and I thought, 'So *she's* not dead then,' because we'd talked about it while we waited and we'd decided that somebody must have died. As soon as we were well under way Granny Martindale explained that Mummy had had a terrible accident and was dead. All I remember feeling was that I was glad it wasn't Daddy. I expect I showed it, and hurt Granny."

"Were they fond of your mother?"

Caroline considered.

"No, I don't honestly think so. I think Granny was hurt because it showed how badly they'd failed with her upbringing. With her education they went for class rather than warmth. They were very careful in choosing our schools."

"Did they tell you about your father?"

"I remember asking, and they told us he'd had to go away, and we wouldn't be seeing him for a while. We accepted that then. It was all part of this big disaster that had happened. It was only later, when we started to overhear whispered comments and conjectures, that we began to get clues and to piece things together."

She stopped, and I lay there wondering if there was anything else I wanted to ask her. In a way what she told me was illuminating, but also infuriating: she had been so close to events, but kept from knowing about them. She took, or rather snatched at, the cue of my silence.

"I must go. It's not fair to tire you with all this dragging up of the past. It will be good when we can meet and talk about something else, won't it?"

"It will."

"What you should be worrying about at the moment is not the past but the present. You're going to have to get yourself better security. Shouldn't that be easy now you're a minister?"

I pursed up my lips in distaste.

"I've always wanted as little as possible. I don't choose to invite someone into my life. You come from the class that had servants. You're used to having outsiders around you all the time. I come from the class that keeps themselves to themselves."

"Well, you're going to have to keep yourself a bit less to yourself, and have someone beside you. Promise! You politicians are so lacking in common sense! You're under threat, so you need protection. I don't want to lose you now that I've found you."

I nodded a promise and she darted out. I lay there, thinking not of my security, but of something she had said. She'd talked about her father fishing. I'd never seen him as a country person before, and the family certainly hadn't had an estate on which to practice rural pastimes. Neither she nor Matthew had talked about being in the country with him. Had she been speaking not of the government minister of 1962, but the man he had become since? She had said: "Fishing and shooting are what he really enjoyed doing." If she really thought of him as dead, wouldn't it have been more natural to say "were what he enjoyed doing"? Had there been an infinitesimal pause between the "are" and the rest of the sentence? Had she begun to say "are what he really enjoys," and then hurriedly amended the sentence to cover her tracks?

Had she inadvertently been about to speak of him not in the past but in the present?

CHAPTER SIXTEEN

The Abbot of a Very Small Establishment

Caroline rang me on my second day back at work. Somehow I was not surprised. Nor did her slightly odd manner disconcert me. The bright tone and roundabout way of speaking, hinting but not saying, were things I instinctively understood. I was on the verge of becoming in reality a brother to her and Matthew.

"Back to work so soon! You must be a glutton for it."

"I enjoy my work," I protested. "And of course it's piled up."

"Ah—then you won't want to see me again."

"On the contrary, I'd very much like to. And I always make a habit of taking time off at some point in the day."

"Really? That is sensible. So maybe we could meet at lunchtime. Are you a great one for lunch?"

Her intonation told me this is what phoneticians classify as a question expecting the answer "no."

"Not really. But a walk always clears the head."

"I do agree. If only fashion shows would give us breaks to do the same! Places do get crowded at lunchtime, though…"

"I'm flexible. I could make it for two to three."

"That sounds good. Let me think. What about Green Park, near the station at two?"

"I'll be there. And the day?"

"Tomorrow?"

And that's what we fixed on.

My driver who, with his Wee Free mind could find reasons to disapprove of anything, even an hour in the park on a chilly day, looked dour. He left me by the tube station, and when I slipped into the park I was hailed by Caroline from one of the seats along by Queen's Walk. Before I got to her she had begun to march determinedly away from Piccadilly and away from the more frequented paths. When I gained her side she looked around her, but was not quite satisfied. We walked on. I suppressed any desire to comment on or ridicule her precaution. She had had decades of concealment. Finally she turned to me, still trying to hold herself as casually as possible. I was close, but not too close. We could have been lovers ending an affair.

"You picked up my slip, didn't you?"

I thought for a second, then nodded.

"I noticed something that seemed a bit odd."

"I thought I'd covered it over rather cleverly, but I saw something waft over your face—suspicion, or maybe puzzlement, I suppose."

"I thought you very nearly used a present tense where one wouldn't be natural." I came close to her, my face earnest. "That's never been my main interest in going into all this."

"I know. I'm glad. But Matthew and I had talked it over even before I met you, and we've discussed it again since our meeting. Oh damn—that man is looking at us. Could he be Secret Service, following you?"

I repressed the instinct to say this was Green Park not Gorky Park, and we walked on to where there were still fewer people.

"I think if he was Secret Service he wouldn't be looking at us," I said lightly. "They have artificial eyes implanted where nobody would suspect them to be."

She grinned, but nervously.

"I expect you think I'm paranoid, but we've had to be very, very careful over the years—in fairness to him, apart from anything else. We never go over...*there* with the sole purpose of seeing him. We've never had anything more than one-or two-night stays with him all these years, and you shouldn't have any longer."

"I wouldn't want any longer, but I would very much like to meet and talk with him."

Her voice went still lower.

"We wondered when you could get off."

I thought.

"The injury helps. The permanent secretary is urging me to take a few days off to recuperate. The end of next week and the weekend would be fine."

"I'll check. We thought you might go with Matthew and the whole family. You could go with them in the car to Fishguard: the ferry over to Rosslare is best. Matthew's family all go regularly, and the children love it there. A day off school isn't a problem. I'll ring Matthew this afternoon."

It seemed in the spirit of our communications with each other that I make no comment on the destination, though my brain was ticking overtime with interest. I just nodded.

"It sounds a wonderful idea. I came away from Chatstock wanting to know them better."

"They liked you, too. Now, there are ground rules. You never mention his name. The children know nothing—they know him, but they don't know who he is. In general it's best only talked about indirectly. You're there to recuperate, and you're going fishing, or walking or shooting. Once you're there with him you both make your own rules, feel your own way. But I must make this clear: he will *never* talk about the murder."

"I see."

"He is old—seventy-odd. He lives with it, but he lives with it *alone*. I must have your promise on that."

"You have it."

"Matthew can give you better directions than I can. You'll find Matthew's already told him about you. The village will have heard that a relative is coming, but the less splash you make in the neighborhood the better. Oh, and *never* talk about it on the phone—not even, if it can be helped, in the coded way we have, and that's too complex for you to learn in a hurry. It's evolved over years and years of concealment. Is that understood?"

"Absolutely."

"Bye, Colin."

And with one of her quick, geometric waves she was off. I walked around the park sunk deep in thought for the half hour before I was due to be picked up. My thoughts were predictable. I now knew what I had only suspected for a few days: that I had a father alive. Naturally as I walked I wondered what he would be like. Perfectly futile thought, but perfectly understandable. My other thought was trite, too. I wondered whether I had murder in me—whether we all had the capacity to kill, given the right, or horribly wrong, circumstances. When I got back to the Ministry I ordered a great plateful of sandwiches and ate ravenously.

That night the phone rang in the flat. I had no fear it would be my phantom caller again. That phase, I believed, was over, and the plan now was to leave me with the uneasy feeling that a new and more deadly period had been entered. In the event it was Matthew.

"Colin! Good to hear your voice. I'm told you're well, but not entirely well. Is that right?"

"Pretty much so. I function, but I get tired."

"What you need is a few days away. Easily said—is it easily done?"

"I don't see why not. I am a minister—what I say should go, though I'm not sure it always does."

"What about the weekend after this one?"

"Sounds fine."

"I wonder, would a short family break tire you too much? The kids have pretty nigh inexhaustible energy as you know, but we could all do with a weekend away."

"It would please me no end—old bachelor that I am. And there are plenty of ways of getting away from you all if you become too much."

"You know the children. I think I can promise they will become too much. You can get away on a Thursday, can't you?"

"Yes, anytime after midday."

"Be down here by three o'clock then, and leave all the arrangements to me. Just come, and we'll set off."

So that's what I did. I went up to Milton to do

constituency work that weekend, but canceled for the following one. Everyone was very understanding, because the fact that I'd been "mugged" had been widely publicized in the local papers. People seemed to take it as proof that I was not a cosseted minister, but went about my business pretty much like a normal person, as an old lady put it to me. I went to see my father, who just recognized me. I was cautioned against seeing his weakness as a sign that his ordeal was approaching its end. I called in on George Eakin and brought him selectively up to date. His gratitude and interest made me feel a louse about holding out on him over several vital details, but the secrets were not mine to confide. I suppose those feelings of guilt were akin to feelings Matthew and Caroline must have had very often over the years.

My reunion with the Martindales was joyful, and the drive in a crowded station wagon to Fishguard was very jolly, full of singing, traveling games, and dreadful children's jokes. That night, very late, in a large and comfortable cottage not far from Wexford, Matthew got down a road map of Ireland, pointed out a village near the coast of County Kerry, and gave me directions thereafter. He went over them twice, and had me repeat them. He said that a Land Rover had been hired, and he'd drive me to pick it up next day in Wexford. We left after an early breakfast, and before the middle of the morning I was driving through the lush southern counties of Ireland, toward the Atlantic coast.

I found the village of Kilrose without any difficulty, and stopped off to pick up provisions, something Matthew had suggested. As soon as I left it the road became quite rough. It was still tarmac, but it was narrow, with dirt sides onto which I had to drive when a rare car or lorry came in the other direction. One had to be vigilant for the occasional pothole. The lack of people was eerie. It was as if the Famine had struck only last year. The strangeness of the landscape was only added to by the occasional house: one story, new, smart, and clean as a this-year's model car in the showroom, and almost as unused. Country retreats, I guessed, for politicians, businessmen, or Common Market functionaries. They served to underline rather than lessen the emptiness of the area. The sheep, grazing on the sparse grass in among rocks and heather, raised their heads as I passed, gazed at me blearily, then got back to business.

Matthew's directions were simple and clear. I turned off at the top of a gentle incline five miles out of Kilrose. The moment I did so I was grateful for the toughness of the Land Rover I had hired. Matthew had known that anything less could have met with problems. The path was rocky, pitted, and what I could have done if I'd met with another car, beyond reverse and back right down the road, I couldn't imagine. But Matthew had told me that there would be no other car, and there wasn't.

When I'd driven a little over a mile the path veered to the left and I saw in the distance a cottage—little more than a hut. It was of stone, with a door set in the middle and small windows on either side. A plume of smoke was rising from the chimney. The path got no better as I approached, but I was able to pull up right outside the cottage door—it faced the path because here it ended. There was no other car there. I turned off the ignition and got out. Heather, with greener patches, stretched out to infinity, with not another cottage in sight. The place seemed deserted, but as I turned toward the little stone structure, intending to bang on the door, I was hailed from some way away. My heart stopped as I turned. On a little knoll a couple of hundred yards away there stood a man—an old man, thin but erect, his voice strong. I made toward him through the dead heather and rocks, stumbling from time to time. He, coming in the other direction, had all the confidence of decades of familiarity. As he got closer I saw that the thinness was not fragility but a spare toughness of frame. He showed his years most in his lined face, but the lines gave it an immense and imposing individuality. His hands were gnarled, but his walk and his carriage belied his years. He came up to me and I could think of nothing else to do but stretch out my right hand. He had other ideas, and he embraced me and I, awkwardness gone, hugged the old man close.

"We're more open here," he said, "more emotional. Not a bad thing." The voice had a slight, soft Irish burr. He broke away and held me at arm's length to look at me. "How like Matthew you are!" he said wonderingly.

"I know," I said, my voice breaking as I spoke to him for the first time. "When I look at him it's like a slightly wrong mirror image. And we're both like your father."

He pondered that. Everything he did was slow.

"I think of my father as much older—and he

always was remote to me. It's Matthew you call to mind."

"And there must be something of you because it was that that brought your name into the whole matter—my shape, the way I sit or hold myself: there must be something."

"I probably wouldn't know, would I? I don't see myself. Well, well, this is a wonderful pleasure. I'm sorry I wasn't here to greet you. A sheep has been off-color. Come in, come in."

He gestured toward the cottage. I stopped by the car.

"I bought some provisions in the village. Matthew said they would be welcome."

"They will, they will. I hope you've got some bread. I can make my own, but it's very hard on my old hands. People are very good about getting things up to me, but you can't expect them to come more than once a week or ten days, can you? Leave them a moment. Nobody's going to break into your car and steal them."

He led the way through the door and into the one living room of the cottage. It smelled strongly of the peat fire which smoldered away in the open fireplace against the far wall. The furniture was old, smacking of the secondhand shop—a small table with two unrelated chairs, an armchair and a little sofa, a gas lamp, a bookcase—small but nearly full. My father filled a kettle from a jug of water and put it on the hob, then went about preparing a cup of tea. I was conscious that if I had volunteered to help him I wouldn't have known what to do, without electricity or gas.

"I think, you know, it's best if you just call me George. Everyone calls me that. It's not a common name in southern Ireland—too Hanoverian I suppose. I've told them in the village I'm expecting a visit from a relative, but if you call me Uncle George you'll involve yourself in a lie, and so often one sinks deeper and deeper in, doesn't one?"

"Yes. But politicians never learn."

He looked at me sharply.

"Odd you should be a politician. Though perhaps not, because I never was, really. Not giving my heart and soul to the cause, or letting it dominate my waking thoughts. Can't offhand remember how I slipped into it, but I think it was someone suggesting my name for the Worthing constituency. So much of life is pure accident, isn't it? Shall I call you Colin?"

"Please."

"Nice name. I like it."

"I don't know what surname you use. I should have asked Matthew."

"It's Green. I wanted something anonymous, something that didn't stand out."

"Of course....I didn't slip into politics by accident, by the by. I pushed my way into it. It's what I've always wanted to do—or thought I wanted to. But it was accident I got such good parents, and I'm grateful for it."

"Good, good...." His lined old face was troubled. "I gather from Matthew you had a twin, who wasn't so lucky."

"No."

"It's very sad. I wish there was something I could do....Sometimes I feel so helpless and useless."

"Kettle's boiling," I said cheerfully.

The tea when it came was without milk. I had some in the car, but it seemed to be how my father preferred it, or maybe how he thought it ought to be served. He reached up to a high shelf and took down an old biscuit tin and two tea plates. He offered me some homemade oat cakes. When I bit into one it tasted like a particularly brutal kind of blotting paper. I wondered if he had made them, or if they were a tribute from a friend in the village. I could imagine him having female admirers—similarly old, but attracted by his manner and his gentleness.

"What do you do in your spare time?" he asked.

"At the moment I have very little. Though I have been going into my origins as you know." He nodded, looking down at the floor. "When I was an ordinary MP, just occasionally Opposition spokesman, I went to the theater and the opera a lot."

"Ah. Yes, I once enjoyed that. You don't fish?"

I wished it was something my other father had taught me, though probably he had never done it himself. It would have made a fanciful bond between my two fathers.

"No, I don't fish. I've never had much chance to. I'd rather like to learn."

"It's a form of meditation for me. Perhaps it could help you, too. People in politics always need something to relax them—to be always politicking is dangerous. I warn you—I'm not one of your great fishermen who boast of their enormous catches. It's just a background to thinking, and of course a source of food. It's what I most enjoy eating. The differences between fish are so much more subtle than those between meats."

"Perhaps you could take me tomorrow and show me how."

"I'd like that very much," he said, with a warm smile. "I would be proud if I could say I'd introduced you to a quiet form of relaxation. Opera is too much like the House of Commons."

After our tea we had a walk in what was left of the light. The landscape was grand with a touch of monotony, and empty. Always that emptiness. I was touched by a vision of my father as almost the only effort at human habitation in all that loneliness. He asked me a lot about my upbringing, and I told him about Claud and Elizabeth, how they had longed for a baby, how generous and loving and protective they had been, how I had given a new meaning to their lives and how they had given themselves to the business of making my life good and fulfilling. He told me a little about his own childhood, but that meant mostly about prep school and Eton.

"It's an odd sort of upbringing," he said, in his gentle, uncomplaining voice. "I don't think any other country sends away its children like that, do they? Unless they've caught it from us in some of the old Empire places. Even when I was at home I barely saw my father or mother. In the holidays they arranged a series of treats, but they never came with us. Wouldn't you have thought they would have wanted to? I realize now—because now I have time, and now I can think things through—that I had all those strong feelings and affections and no one—just no one—to fix them on."

We were straying near forbidden territory. In the dying light I looked into his face and decided I should retreat rather than advance.

"Do you have friends here?" I asked. "In the village?"

"Oh yes: we're a wonderful little community really, and we all know each other. I go down shopping when I need to, sometimes have a drink in the bar, and they come up with things, or if they haven't time leave them at the end of the land, by the roadside. They know I'll potter down there every other day or so, and find them. That's my world now. I don't want a wider one. I have no idea of the name of your boss, the Prime Minister—nor the name of the Irish Prime Minister either, come to that. They don't matter to me. They probably matter to far fewer people than they imagine they do. It's very good for you to have your world contracted to such a little scope.

Much easier for you to aim at serenity."

When we got back to the cottage he lit the gas lamp and cooked on the fire two fish that he'd caught that morning, which we ate with boiled potatoes and carrots. Then we had rice pudding from a tin. We had instant coffee afterward, and later on an Irish whiskey. We steered off forbidden topics, and I told him about Susan, and why things had gone wrong between us. Only at bedtime, which was very early, did anything disturb the atmosphere. He insisted that I must have the bed, and he would sleep in blankets on the floor. I protested that I was a young man, I could sleep anywhere, and he said it was what he always did when his children came to visit. When I saw that it was beginning to distress him I gave in, and watched him put on his pajamas and pull a bundle of rough blankets around him.

Lying there in bed in the darkness I looked at the shape he made against the wall in the little room and it made me think of him as a holy man, the abbot of a very small establishment, maybe one who, as his flock had died or one by one made their way back into the world, had attained a greater peace on his own.

When I had finished shaving next day in a bowl

of hot water, I went into the other room and found the fire lit, or perhaps revived from the day before, and eggs being boiled and bread toasted on the end of a fork. It felt like being a schoolboy again, but pleasantly so. My mother had always insisted that you mustn't start the day on an empty stomach, and I never did, though I quite often do now. Sitting at table, breaking the tops off my eggs and cutting my toast into soldiers, I noticed two rods had already been selected and were by the door beside a large wooden box.

"My bag of tricks," my father explained. "You would really like to do a bit of fishing, wouldn't you?"

"I'd love to—unless there's something in the way of provisions you need me to fetch in the Land Rover."

"Provisions? You've brought enough to last me a month!"

When we set off I didn't volunteer to drive. Probably the car couldn't have got within miles, and in any case it seemed as if selecting the right spot for the weather and the season and then walking there was part of the pleasure. The going was rough, as all the going for acres around was rough, but after about three miles we came to a patch of rich green on the banks of the river Feale, and here we settled, selected our bait, and the man I called George gave me loving and earnest tuition in the first stages.

It was only after two or three hours, much of it spent in companionable silence or in the passing on of basic tips, that we talked at all in the usual sense. The fish seemed remarkably uninterested in our advances to them, but I didn't comment on this because I sensed this was part of the process. I was always careful what I said, because I intended absolutely to stick to my word and not pump him for painful details. So I just said:

"This must be one of the most peaceful spots on earth."

"I think it is."

"Idyllic, but almost empty."

"It's idyllic because it's almost empty. We should get over the feeling that man is an essential part of a landscape."

That put a new shine on my meditations about emptiness. But I thought he was probably speaking personally as well.

"I suppose so," I said. "Is that what made you choose it?"

"I don't think I did anything so positive as

choose it....You'd like to hear how I came to disappear so completely, wouldn't you?"

"Only if you want to tell me," I said humbly. "And only what you want to tell me."

"There's nothing painful about that, and nobody that could be hurt now. That's not true—or I don't *know* it's true—about...the other business. It's a matter of wonder to me— always has been—that no one guessed before, how it came about. That night...after I'd left Upper Brook Street...I walked and walked the streets for some time—an hour, two hours. Then at some stage I found myself—literally, because I hardly knew what I was doing—near my brother's flat by Holland Park."

"Your brother's!"

"Yes." He looked into my face, and saw that I'd heard about his brother. "I don't know why anyone should be surprised by that. When I came a little to myself and realized where I was, I had to make a decision: was I going to give myself up, or was I going to try to disappear."

"But...but everyone says—"

"That Bertie was so ineffectual, did nothing with his life, that we weren't close? That's true enough, except perhaps the last. You know, when you grow up in a household where the usual close parent-child bond doesn't operate, and where you're sent away to pretty fearsome schools, the younger generation has to stick pretty closely together because their brothers or sisters are all they've got. I hadn't much in common with Bertie, that's true, but in fact in all the early years we were very close."

I considered that, in the slow, contemplative way that the life here seemed to induce.

"I can understand that," I said, "at least now you've explained it I can. But it seems rather pointless to go to him, when he was by all accounts so ineffectual."

"You've forgotten the crucial fact about him."

"What's that?"

"That he was a homosexual. At a time when practicing homosexuals were prosecuted and imprisoned."

"I'm sorry. I'm being thick. I still don't see—"

"Don't worry. It's a world away, from what I can judge, sitting my life out here in this wonderful wilderness. There's no reason why someone who has grown up in a different moral climate should understand. This persecution of homosexuals was intermittent: for months, years even, nothing much would be done, then some rule-bound little jackanapes at Scotland Yard or in the Home Office would decide on a big swoop, or the arrest of a high-profile victim to encourage others to lie low. The consequence of this was that there was a well-established machine for getting people out of the country when the authorities began to get active. Often the person who would be 'vanished' was the boyfriend of a high-profiled person who'd been targeted, someone who might be bullied or tricked into giving evidence against him. Without evidence, no prosecution. The boyfriend could either be got to a bolt-hole in the country, or in especially important cases they could be spirited out of the country: to the Continent, to some country where homosexuality was not illegal, to the States, to Ireland."

"I see. So you went to your brother—"

"I knocked him up in the middle of the night, him and his boyfriend of the moment, told him… about it, and he was immediately on the phone. By dawn I was in a car speeding to Wales, by the time the news broke in the country as a whole I was on a fishing boat on the way to Ireland—to the Republic of Ireland, of course."

"That was the place you chose?"

He shook his head.

"Not really. I'd always liked Ireland. The family still had some property here, though not a good deal, and so I'd been several times with the children. We still have it, and it's the excuse for Matthew and Caroline to come over. It's a long way from here, in County Wexford…but of course—"

"That's right. I was there last night."

"You would be. Silly of me. It serves its purpose better by being pretty distant from here. No, though I'm fond of the country, Ireland chose me: I could get into the country pretty easily without going through any passport control or customs. We landed in a tiny fishing village in the South, I was picked up, and in no time I was on my way to my bolt-hole in Limerick."

"Did you literally go into hiding? Go to earth?"

"Almost literally. Never went out except in the dark, and so on. I was the guest of the Catholic Church, unbeknown to it. My host was a dignitary, very highly regarded, and if they knew about his activities in respect of less serious criminals, they kept quite about it. The laws against homosexuality were quite as Draconian here as in

Britain, but of course it went on, and sometimes it was winked at. The Church, in particular, did a lot of winking. I believe my host was a holy man, but without the gift of chastity. I know he wrestled with his failing, but I think he wrestled knowing he would lose. A lot of people do, and not just silly, self-deluded people. I knew his habits. I'm quite sure his activities never involved children. I would have found that intolerable. In fact, at that time he was my only friend."

"But were there no questions, with all the hue and cry going on in Britain?"

"They were two countries wide apart then. America was closer. They've been forced together a bit since. There were no questions because hardly a soul knew about me. My friend's housekeeper was told I was a Catholic Englishman who had suffered a nervous breakdown. She was a comfortable body who hardly did more than pass the time of day with me. My friend and I prayed together, we talked, endlessly. He is the only person I have talked with about…Anyway, at the end of that time, when the hue and cry had died down a bit, when attention had shifted to poor old John Profumo, a very much lesser sinner, we had to decide what I was to do with myself."

He paused, and in the silence I gently said: "And you chose the greatest possible solitude and seclusion."

"Yes. I couldn't consider any kind of monastic institution—for many reasons, not least the difficulty and danger for them. In any case I was not then of the Catholic faith, though I am now. My Irish host knew of this place, and Bertie arranged the buying of it—for quite a small sum, in cash. I came here with a new name, looking I think ten years older than any picture anyone had seen of me in the newspapers, and I've been here ever since."

"Forging the right lifestyle for yourself."

His gentle eyes twinkled.

"You use expressions I wouldn't use. How pretentious language has become! But I think you're right, if I understand it. I had to find a way of life that…suited. Not suited me, but suited my situation, my state, what I had done. I can see why anyone—even you, if you were not such a gentle person—might feel I should have gone to jail, paid for what happened, even hanged, because people *were* hanged at that time. I had to have a way of life that showed—not to the world, but to myself— that I understood such feelings, even shared them.

I think probably I have failed in that."

"Because your way of life is so good?"

He looked at me appreciatively.

"Yes. You are very perceptive. It is so good—far, far better than anything I ever knew before. It was hard at first, not because it was lonely—loneliness was what I needed above all else—but because I had to learn to do everything, and learn on my own, from my mistakes. Now anything else would be hard—impossible, in fact. I dislike the traffic in the village—I, a Londoner! I'm a creature of silence, and the open, but it's no longer a punishment. It's a gift."

That seemed to be the moment to stop. By coincidence the fish began to give signs that their sluggish curiosity had been aroused by the bright goodies we had been dangling in front of them for hours, though they were still inclined to tease and swim away.

"They're like stay-at-home voters," I said, watching a departing tail. "You work your guts out to get them to the polling station, and then as like as not they spoil their ballot papers or vote for the other chap."

But an hour later we had caught a meal for ourselves, my contribution being a modest-sized but succulent-looking trout. I slit its throat with qualms, but I knew that if I'd had a few more days at it, I'd have done it quite unthinkingly.

As we were packing up to start back home, I took up the subject of his disappearance again.

"I don't think you should blame yourself because your life here is so good, George. The instinct to punish yourself is not very healthy."

"On the contrary!" he said, with the decisiveness of someone who has really thought his situation through. "People use words like 'masochism' about the instinct to judge yourself, but it's nothing of the sort. It's the people who can't do that who are in danger—the people who do dreadful things and afterward just shrug and say: 'That was bad, but it's no good crying over spilled milk, the best thing is to get on with my life.' Those people are not much above animals. We have to judge ourselves for what we have done. Anything else is chaos. And if we judge ourselves, we have to punish ourselves as well."

I didn't want to argue with him. He felt so strongly about it, and his views were based on so painful a personal experience that anything I said would be by comparison jejune. I nodded, and we started back to the cottage, he walking confidently, I stumbling now and then, but after a while finding my feet on that strange terrain. My father was thoughtful all the way home, but as soon as he began to prepare a meal, and particularly as he put the fish into the frying pan, he began to regain his sparkle. Once we were at table he was eating with relish.

We talked a little, in the gaslit semidarkness, about politics. He asked polite questions, which often showed he knew nothing at all about what had gone on in that last thirty-five years. I said there was a big row brewing up in my party over the question of reducing state benefits for single mothers.

"I know I've no experience, beyond my first few days, of being the child of a single mother, but somehow I take it personally. I keep asking how you can penalize a single mother without penalizing her child, but no one gives me an answer. And is it right to force a mother back to work if she genuinely feels her child needs her around precisely *because* she is the only parent? If my mother had been a different sort of person to Lucy, if she'd kept me, wouldn't I have wanted her around as much as possible? Wouldn't she give me the security I otherwise wouldn't have?"

I was a bit on my soapbox, rehearsing a speech I probably would never give. But my father had not followed the last bit, because his attention had been distracted by the name.

"Lucy!" he said softly. "How exciting she was. You feel you've never really lived before, because you've never known such excitement. What a snare it is, that feeling! It becomes the be-all and end-all of living. The truth is it's only peace that lets you live to the full, lets you appreciate existence and its potential. Excitement is destruction."

As I lay in my bed that night, seeing again the form of my father in his bundle of blankets, I tried to see him not as the holy man I'd envisaged last night, but as the man who had engendered me, a man so excited by a new passion that he had felt as if he'd never lived before.

CHAPTER SEVENTEEN

A Frightened Man

All that took time to absorb. My journey back to County Wexford the next day had been uneventful, after affectionate farewells from my father. We knew we were unlikely to meet often in the future, but we also knew that when we did it would be from liking and not from duty. My gradual integration into and acceptance by Matthew's family was something of great moment for me, but it was the fragile bond with my father that was more poignant.

Then it was back to the daily grind. I was conscious, back at my desk within the Whitehall machine over the following week, that I was having difficulty concentrating. Working toward *possible* legislation in the year 2000 or 2001 doesn't easily present itself as a vital or a life-enhancing task. I kept thinking of my father, of what a gentle and lovable person he was, then speculating how that was to be reconciled with the fact that he had made no bones about being a murderer.

Or had he quite said that?

I shook myself. I was doing what Matthew had warned me against: trying to prove he hadn't murdered his wife. It might be that he hadn't said explicitly to me that he had done it, but he had said that many people might feel he should have been hanged.

Outside the Department my life was eerie. Or rather, I was creating eeriness out of nothing. Because nothing was happening—no telephone calls, no near accidents or minor onslaughts, no identifiable shadowings. Yet I had got myself into the psychological mood in which I would almost have welcomed any of those things, maybe as a proof that there was still someone out there who might yet put himself or herself in a position where he might be identified or even arrested. Something happening seemed a precondition to someone being caught.

On the Friday morning, when I left the Department to climb into my official car on my way to the Blind School in Worcester, I thought I saw my stalker in a crowd of commuters arriving at work farther down the street. It was a glimpse only, if that, and when I looked back and strained my eyes to pick him out he was gone, or at any rate indistinguishable. I got slowly into my car, and didn't bother to report the matter. Even I could see that the police, however convinced they now were that the threat to me was a real one, had enough on their plates without taking cognizance of possible sightings of possible threats.

All this time I was aware of, even part of, political rumblings. The question of benefits for single mothers was assuming the status of a trial of strength—not between the government and opposition, but between government and their own backbenchers. It was becoming a litmus test of machismo, a contest of political wills: we've said we're going to reform the benefits system, and by God we'll take the difficult decisions involved— that was the line emanating from Downing Street. Puzzled, and often emotional, backbenchers wondered why the new ministers were so keen to cozy up to their traditional enemies in big business and so enthusiastic about clobbering those people at the bottom of the social scale they traditionally should have been keenest to help. As a test of political muscle it was frustrating to those of us on the lower rungs of government because it was a matter where one might have least expected disagreement.

When I had dinner at Susan's in midweek, and went over all the events of my visit to Ireland, it is significant that, even with so much of absorbing interest to communicate to her, before we had finished with the main course we had turned to the single-mothers issue, about which we both felt strongly.

It couldn't help coming up at work. I said to Margaret Stevens one day in the corridor:

"It somehow seems futile slaving away for the disabled when everyone whispers that they're the next who are going to be clobbered."

She nodded.

"I do understand. But I always say that when you're on the bottom rungs of government you need to keep your eyes firmly on your own brief. It's only when you get higher that you can afford to raise them and take in the wider picture."

"I'm sure that's wise, but I'm not sure I can do it."

It was when I had just arrived back at the flat after engaging in some minor politicking with discontented backbenchers in one of the Palace of Westminster bars that my phone rang.

"Mr. Pinnock?" said a strong male voice.

"Yes."

"This is Calham Road Police Station here."

Calham Road was the nearest station to the flat—small, but old and bleak rather than homely.

"Oh yes?"

"We've brought a man in. He was loitering in the vicinity of your flat, and we'd been alerted by the police at the Houses of Parliament about your being targeted."

"That's right," I said, able to talk about it now without a suspicion of being paranoid. "I think it's pretty clear now that I have been, by someone or other. There was certainly a young man stalking me some weeks ago, but he hasn't been in evidence recently." There was something about the policeman's voice that had sounded cautious and a bit puzzled, so I went on: "Is there something that you're not telling me, something that's worrying you?"

There was some hemming and hawing at the other end.

"Not exactly worrying us, sir. More a case of

something we didn't expect. The fact of the matter is, as soon as he was brought in the man asked to speak to you."

That floored me. There was a moment's silence as I thought it through.

"What you're saying is that, without your mentioning my name, he asked for me."

"Yes, sir. Of course naturally we don't go fetching people the moment we're asked to, particularly important people like yourself." I laughed and he laughed cautiously. "But of course his asking for you made us wonder, and when we'd probed a bit he told us that, though you don't know him, you are in fact his brother."

"Ah....He's someone, I'd guess, who's a bit unstable mentally."

"We think so, sir. Have to be a bit careful about that these days. He's certainly very nervous—frightened even, and tends to babble on in a way that we can't follow. Can I take it then, sir, that there's nothing in this talk about being your brother?"

"Not exactly. Look, I can be with you in ten minutes—"

"If that's convenient we'd welcome it, sir, but I suggest we pick you up. Just to be on the safe side. From what the police at Westminster have said, it's not a good idea for you to be walking the streets alone at night."

I had no problem agreeing with that. There was a ring on my doorbell within five minutes and I was driven to Calham Road Station by a glum young man who looked as if he was reconsidering his career choice. Most politicians like talking to people, or else feel obliged to, but to my tentative remarks he responded as if I were trying to put something over on him.

At the station I was met by the man I had talked to on the phone, a thickset, stolid type, though with intelligent eyes.

"I'm Detective Sergeant Porter," he said, taking me toward the cells. "He's through there in a custody cell at the moment. I should warn you he's fairly…disturbed."

"Yes. That was my impression the only time I got a good look at him."

"You've seen him but you've not talked to him?"

"Never. What does he say his name is?"

"He doesn't, sir. He just says: 'I don't know.'"

"Cunning? Or part of the mental disturbance?"

"Hard to say. Could be a bit of both. Being mentally disturbed doesn't stop you being cunning."

"Of course not. I think, you know, I'd better talk to him. Does he display any hostility toward me when he mentions my name?"

"None, sir. Quite the reverse."

"Can I talk to him alone then?"

He shook his head.

"I don't think we can take that risk, sir. But we can leave the door open a bit, and I can be outside."

That seemed in every way the best idea. I nodded my agreement. The duty sergeant took up a heavy bunch of keys and led us along a corridor to the last cell. He opened the door and I went inside, followed by Sergeant Porter. When we looked through the flap the man had been sitting on a bare bed, gazing vacantly ahead, but as I came in the eyes took on a dim species of life. He got up and started toward me, but very unconfidently. Then on a swift gesture from Sergeant Porter he backed away, his eyes clouding up again. I began to regret I'd agreed to a police presence.

When he was again sitting on the bed, his jaw drooping, as little threatening as it was possible to imagine, Sergeant Porter went outside, nearly but not quite shutting the door behind him. I worried a little, after that bad start, and thought for a moment, trying to get the tone right.

"Hello. I hear you want to talk to me," I said. He nodded.

"What's your name, then?"

He hesitated. Clearly it was a question that disturbed him.

"She called me Tim," he said at last.

"Right, Tim. And who is 'she'?"

"The woman I was given to."

There were definite vibrations in the voice. Hatred, I thought.

"I don't think you like the name, do you?"

"I don't like anything that came from her."

"I see. Do you have a name that you do like?"

The face screwed up in thought.

"I called myself Tony for a time. That was when I was on my own....She called me 'Pits.'...Did you know you had a brother?"

"I know now that I was born with a twin."

"When did you find out?" he asked eagerly.

"Quite recently."

"Did you want to meet him when you knew?"

"Very much."

"Because it's me. I'm your twin."

"I thought you might be. But of course I want to be quite sure. You do understand that, don't you? I want to be quite sure that it's you who are my twin." A pause, and then a sad nod. "Why have you been stalking me?"

"Stalking?" He became agitated again. "What's that, stalking?"

"Following me around, dogging my footsteps, being threatening."

His face showed its liveliest emotion thus far.

"I haven't! I've never threatened you! I just wanted to talk to you. I wanted your help—and to help you, too. But I couldn't pluck up the courage."

I looked into his cloudy eyes, and the confusion, the uncertainty, and the fear I saw there sent a pang to my heart. This really was a man who barely knew who he was.

"I see," I said gently. "I believe you. I used the wrong words. But you see I knew you were following me and I couldn't understand why, and that's why I felt threatened. I didn't realize you wanted my help."

"I was frightened. I still am."

"Are you homeless?"

He shrugged.

"Sometimes. There's hostels and things."

"I suppose you thought I could help you to find somewhere to live."

He shook his head.

"No. Why should you do that? I don't worry about living on the streets. I'm used to it."

"But it can be frightening."

"Not as frightening as being with *her*."

I chanced my arm, though I'd so far been trying not to prompt him.

"Do you mean being with Mrs. Hayden-Gryce?"

His eyes became still more confused, and he struggled with a thought.

"Yes. She was frightening."

"But these days you don't have much contact with your mother, do you?"

He flushed indignantly.

"*She's* not my mother. She told me that often enough." The voice had raised itself as he retreated into his past, his childhood. "'Thank God you're not mine,' she used to say. 'I couldn't bear to think anything of me went into the making of a pathetic piece of nothing like you.' 'Thank God you're not my mother,' I would say back, but I couldn't think of anything to call her. There aren't words bad enough. I was never very good with words. They made me so I couldn't think....." He suddenly looked at me with something close to accusation in his eyes. "You had good parents."

"Yes, I did. Very good parents."

"It's not fair. You don't know what it's like. The nagging and the shouting and the—the *scorn!* Them wishing you'd never been born, wishing they'd never taken you on."

"No, I don't know what it's like, Tony."

His mood changed. He smiled hesitantly.

"I like you calling me Tony. Not like her calling me Pits. 'Give me your chips, Pits,' she would say. 'Food's wasted on a lump of idiocy like you.' She was horrible....I'd been quite happy there till she came."

There was definitely something there I was failing to understand. I decided I needed to go at things obliquely.

"Tell me about your home life when you were growing up. It's difficult for me to imagine, coming from a good home."

He struggled with his memories, and also I think with an undercurrent of resentment at our different fates that went against his basically gentle disposition. In the end he could only come up with his former protest:

"It's not fair! She shouldn't have given me to people like that!"

"No, she shouldn't," I said, and waited.

"He was as bad as her, or worse. Day in, day out they were screaming at each other, or sniping, or really fighting. They enjoyed it, you see."

"I expect you're right."

"Of course they did, or they wouldn't have stayed together," he said, with a child's logic that nevertheless rang true. "They enjoyed it, and they enjoyed having me there, to use as a weapon, or so they could turn on me together. They always said I was stupid, but I understood."

"Children always do, I think."

"*I* did," he said, with an odd sort of pride. "They often talked about putting me into care. Often I wished they would. It couldn't have been worse than living with them. Care could have been *nice*. It got worse when *he* died. I thought it might be better, but it wasn't. She didn't have him to scream and shout at anymore, only me. After a few weeks I couldn't take it anymore, all the shouting, the frustration, the drink. I got out."

"Did you manage to get a job?"

"A job? No, I've never had a job. Who'd employ someone like me? I never had any friends who might get me one. And it was just when unemployment was beginning....Sometimes I had a room to myself."

His eyes lit up briefly. I couldn't doubt for a moment how much he had needed a haven.

"That must have been nice. Peaceful," I said.

"It was. Peaceful—that's the word. That was in places where they'd accept people on Social Security. But there weren't many of those. In between I slept rough, went to one of the hostels, begged a bit. It wasn't so bad. You get friends when you're sleeping rough. People get to know you, get used to having you around, help you....But you sort of lose control. Of yourself. You don't care anymore. You get involved in things...."

The picture was beginning to take shape in my mind.

"Was this when you were sent to the place where you were happy at first?" I asked gently.

"Sort of." He thought. Retrieving that part of his past was obviously a problem. "There was a big fight—half the dossers under the bridge against the other half. I wasn't involved! I was frightened! But the police took me in with a lot of others, and then someone went into my history, contacted *her*, and then I was sent to this place. And it was good. I felt secure—you know? You know how that feels, don't you? Like nothing bad could happen to me."

The very way he said it showed it had been an illusion.

"But it did."

"Yes, it did. She came."

"The one who called you the Pits?"

"Yes. My mother." He looked at me and I saw naked, unashamed fear in his eyes. "Our mother," he said distinctly.

Slowly the face crumpled, and he began crying, his whole body shivering. I sat with him on the bare bed and put my arms around his shoulders, hugging him to me.

It took time after that, and closeness, and encouragement, before he began to recover himself, and more time still before he could begin to talk about it. "You need to know," he said. So gradually the details came out. When his mother had come in and had found out his name—he was calling himself Tony Gryce then—she had immediately been interested. When she had begun probing, asking about his background and his parents, she had gradually realized who he was.

"I'm your mother!" she had suddenly announced one day. "I'm the one who gave you away. And you're the sod who ruined my life."

When he had said that Tony looked up at me, his mouth screwed up as if he was about to cry.

"And then it started up all over again," he said.

"What did?"

"The picking on me. The scorn. Just like *her*. It was like she had it in for me—though it was *her* who gave *me* away. She kept saying I ruined her life. She'd expected to marry our father, but he disappeared, and after we were born—I don't know, she never really told me, but things must have gone all right for a time, because she often said, 'When I had my own business,' so it couldn't really have been us who ruined her life, could it?"

"No, it couldn't."

"But she thought so. Thinks so. The story's never quite the same, nor the story of why she got sent there, but it's never her fault. While we were in there together she made me her slave. 'You owe me that,' she kept saying. She liked humiliating me, liked making me do…really nasty things for her. Everyone was too busy to notice for a long time. It got so bad, so unbearable, that I—"

"Tell me. Then we can forget it."

"I tried to—you know—do away with myself." Something in my face must have suggested I didn't take his suicide attempt seriously, because his voice took on a tone of protest. "I did try, really, not for show. But they didn't allow us any of the things I could have done it with properly. So they found out about what she was doing and separated us, and after a time they decided I'd be better off outside. They had medicines, drugs, that they said could control what was wrong with me. They found me a room with some others—others like me, and they said I would have a social worker I could go to, and I had to go to hospital regularly to make sure I was taking the drugs. It was all right for a time."

"What happened to make it go wrong?"

He frowned, trying to remember.

"They sort of lost interest. I don't think they had the time, and they had worse cases than me. The place I was in broke up. Then I was back on the streets, odd nights in hostels…"

"And that was when she found you again, I suppose?" I hazarded.

"Yes. It wasn't difficult. We'd talked in there, and she knew the sort of places I'd go to."

"I don't quite understand," I said, "why she would want to make contact again, if she said you—we—had ruined her life."

He shook his head in a shared bewilderment, as if at some fathomless wickedness.

"She liked having a slave, someone to scream at, abuse. She *enjoys* it! And then after a time...she started talking about you. She was obsessed with you."

"When was this?"

"Earlier this year. I think she'd lost interest in me, got all the fun she could think of out of me, and I often got away from her. But eventually she'd find me again, and she'd go on about you. It was when the election was on, and she'd pick newspapers out of the bins and read all about it, and it used to drive her mad. She'd go on about how you'd got it made, you were going to the top, you'd ruined her life, and wasn't I jealous that you should have everything so good when I had nothing. I felt sure she wanted to use me against you. She's *mad*, you know. Not like me, confused. But *mad*. And dangerous."

"I think you're right."

"She said you were away fighting the election. I knew you were an MP—she'd gone on about that often enough. I think our father was a politician sometime long ago. She said when you came back she was going to start having fun. She and I, she said. She'd begun to be interested in me again."

"Did she know where I lived?"

He looked at me.

"You don't know?"

"Know what?"

"She lives there, too."

∽∽∽

Suddenly several things became clear. She knew my habits because she had had every opportunity to observe them.

"She badgered them in the housing department," Tony said. "She was released into the community like me, and she was living in a hostel. But she went on and on, back and forth to their offices. There was a man there, someone in charge, that she said she'd got something on. Something in his past. Finally they gave her a tiny flat in your block. It's the floor above you. And the flat immediately above you is vacant, and she can get in—she can get in anywhere, it's like magic—and she listens to you. She can't hear what you say or anything, but she listens to the music you're playing, knows when you're in, and follows you when you go out. She's been in your flat, too."

"I know. But she can't any longer."

"Yes, she swears about that. But she still listens from the flat above. She laughs and chuckles about what she's doing to you. And she uses me. She talks about 'our' plans, and how you've got it coming to you from 'us.' That's why I'm frightened. That's why I've been trying to talk to you. But you're an important man and I didn't know if you'd listen, and she *scares* me so, and in the end I've tried to get up courage but—"

"So when you've been watching outside the Department or my flat, when you've followed me, you've really been wanting to talk to me, to warn me."

His expression became beseeching and earnest.

"Yes! Plucking up the courage. I don't talk to people easily, you see. If someone talks to me first it's all right, but to go up to someone I don't know and start talking to them…" He shook his head sadly. "And I did want to warn you. I wanted to like you because you're my brother, someone I never knew I had, my twin, but I didn't see how you could like—someone like me. Most of all I wanted to warn you about *her*."

"What would you have said if I'd come over in the park and talked to you?"

"I don't know." He looked down, shamefaced. "Maybe I'd have run away. Like I did when I saw you in that shop. But if I'd stayed I would have said that our mother is mad and is trying to kill you. I'd have said she's spinning it out because she enjoys it so much, and wants to—to savor it. She loves power, you see, and new experiences. She says she's a connoisseur of sensations, but I don't really understand what she means. 'I like trying out new thrills,' she said to me the other day. I'm afraid she's planning to kill you, as something new, and doing it slowly. Or—"

"Or what?"

He thought, seeming to cringe slightly.

"It was after I watched you in the park. It was last week or maybe the week before. Time doesn't mean much to me. She'd forced me to be with her, and we were watching your flat from a distance. She said on a Sunday you often walked along Mill-bank to your office, or one of the galleries. She'd watched you, you see, for months."

"She was right. I do."

"And when you came out of the flats we ran on

ahead to that building site and stood on the scaffolding—just round the corner from your path,
out of sight of you coming down the road. And
then she put the brick that she'd left there in my
hand, and said I had to throw it. She wanted it to
hit you on the body, but not on the head. I was
terrified. How could I be sure not to hit your head
and kill you? I didn't want to hurt you at all."

"So you threw it well before I got there, to be
sure."

"Yes. There was nothing she could do—we both
had to run for it as soon as I'd thrown it, and I
got away from her. But she was livid, and she's
made me pay since. And I'm afraid—"

"Yes."

"I'm afraid she's going to make me do the killing."

∾ ∾ ∾

When I'd said what I could to comfort and reas-
sure him, I slipped out into the passageway where
DS Porter had been listening. We agreed that his
story was convincing, that it hung together, and
that there was in any case nothing to charge him
with even if we'd wanted to. But what to do with
him was a problem.

"We can't just turn him out on the streets," I

said.

"It's the only home he has," Porter pointed out.

"I've suddenly found a brother, and I'm not leaving him with the dossers, or having her make him her instrument against me. It would be a lot easier if you'd taken her in."

"We'll get on to that now. Do you know her name?"

"Her name, her birth name, is Lucy Mariotti. I don't think she's ever been married, but I can't be sure. And I wouldn't think that her birth name is the name she goes by. I know that at some stage she went by the name of Mrs. Labelle, but that was at a time when she was running a high-class knocking shop with all tastes catered for. I rather think she'll have put that persona behind her." I poked my head back around the door. "What name does our mother go by these days?" I asked the man I had to try to think of as Tony.

He looked up at me eagerly.

"Mrs. Flanders. Didn't you know?"

I raised my eyebrows.

"We've never met." I turned back to Porter. "Right. Mrs. Flanders, on the fourth floor of Ruskin Terrace, Fairwater Flats. Let's get that under way while I think about Tony."

It was quickly done. Two cars went round, but there was nobody in the flat. A neighbor who kept a weather eye through her spy-hole on comings and goings said she'd gone out that afternoon and hadn't come back. That left the problem of Tony still acute. Only one solution occurred to me. When we took him back to the custody sergeant to get him discharged, I said:

"I think the best thing is for you to come home with me, Tony."

His habitually unfocused eyes became sharp with fear.

"No. She can get in there."

I shook my head decisively.

"She can't. You said so yourself. I've had the locks changed, and bolts put on."

"She could get in if she really wanted to. You don't know her. She can get in anywhere."

"But she can get at you if you go back on the streets."

"At me. But in your flat she'd have both of us."

I could see after a minute or two of to-ing and fro-ing that there was no chance of persuasion.

"I wonder if we could go to my old girlfriend's,"

I said. "Does she know about my girlfriend?"

Tony shook his head.

"No. Says you haven't got one. Sneers about that."

So I rang Susan, explained about Tony and how wrong I'd been about him, and she agreed at once to put us both up. "Safer for you, too," she said. I felt an overwhelming urge of gratitude to her for her common sense and compassion. There are not many women who would take in a mentally disturbed man she didn't know without question. We were driven to Chiswick in a police car, and it was promised that a general eye would be kept on her flat. More could not be afforded, but more was probably not needed.

Tony took to Susan at once. By the time we got there she had a shepherd's pie in the oven. It was so late I found I wasn't hungry, but Tony ate greedily. Susan opened some tinned fruit, and that was equally acceptable. "I'm hungry, but I'm used to that," Tony explained. He asked for tea afterward, had several cups, and talked about his friends among the dossers. By mutual unspoken agreement we kept him off the subject of his mother. I'd told Susan over the phone that she terrified him. By midnight Susan had found him a pair of my old pajamas still in the flat, and he'd gone to bed in the spare room. His breathing was regular and very noisy, as if he had serious sinus problems, but we took it as an audible sign of returning confidence.

We slept together that night, the first time in nearly two years. I'm not sure how it happened, but I do know I didn't ask and she didn't invite me. It happened because somehow we had got back on to that wavelength of understanding we had been on when we had first come together. I know too that it felt good and was good.

CHAPTER EIGHTEEN

Mother and Child

For the next ten days I stayed at Susan's flat. It was a bit messy, having to tell the national party apparatus, the constituency people, and the ministry too that my address and telephone number were temporarily changed. It seemed to give them a warrant for the surveillance of my private life. However Margaret Stevens for one expressed pleasure when I told her that I was back with my girlfriend.

"Good for you to have a proper home life," she said.

Against all the odds, in spite of all her experience of marital breakdowns and sexual hoo-ha in the lives of her political masters, and against a backdrop of media guffaws about the Foreign Secretary's private life, she still believed in domestic bliss as the proper basis for a political career. It was the only time I knew that sensible woman to come to a conclusion that was totally contradicted by all the available evidence.

Tony stayed at the flat with us. He never went out, was scared to, so we shopped for him and bought shirts, underwear, casual trousers, toiletries. I was at work all day and into the evening, so for long periods he was alone in the flat. We got the impression that then he was happiest—in his own space, doing his own thing, going at his own pace. He hardly ever watched television, but he read, disliking anything exciting or disturbing, happy when he chanced to find in Susan's collection the sort of book where people in the country went about old routines, made mildly humorous conversations, were as close to their animals as to other humans.

We didn't look for miracles, but over the days we felt we saw very gradually an increase in his confidence, a new sense of something approaching well-being. He talked to Susan more easily than he talked to me. When they were alone in the flat he told her about life on the streets, the characters he'd known there. He never talked about his adoptive parents or his real mother, and Susan took care never to allude to them in the most indirect manner. She found out he could cook a little, and encouraged him to learn new things. He liked thinking he could do something to, as he put it, "pay us back." When I came back at night he gave me the sort of quiet I needed after a hard day at the office and in the House. I think he did this from a sort of awe, regarding me as a Great Man. Susan was similarly considerate, but suffered from no such delusion.

I had been neglecting my constituency, though they knew of my "mugging" and understood, or thought they did, why they were seeing less of me. On the first weekend in December I decided I had to fulfill my promise to myself to continue being a good constituency MP even though I was now a minister. In the ordinary course of events Susan might have come with me, as she often had in the past, but we both agreed she had to stay with Tony. I drove up on Friday morning, had lunch with my agent, and met with other party notables in the afternoon. I managed to have a quiet word with George Eakin, and brought him broadly up to date. What I told him worried him.

"So there's someone out there, who's apparently your mother, yet is out to get you?"

"She's an old woman—a bit mental," I said.

"And that makes it better? And she's not old—not if she was in her early twenties when she had you. So what have you done about extra security?" I hemmed and hawed, and he regarded me with a mixture of fear and contempt. "Well, if you've done nothing, I'll have to. I'll be ringing you up tonight to see you're all right."

I shrugged and nodded. After that I visited my father in the nursing home, but the months since the election had seen him steadily declining, and he barely recognized me. The only thing I could do for him was sit by his bed and hold his hand. I was back in the old family home in Connaught Avenue by seven, preparing for a "surgery" the next day and wondering whether to have a takeaway for supper or just rustle up something on toast.

There was nothing much on television. The British are so good at making television programs that nobody has noticed the sharp decline in the content. Vacuity certainly ruled that Friday night. I had all my old LPs though, many of them unplayed since I'd gone up to Cambridge. I put on Sir Adrian Boult conducting Schubert. I'd seen him once as a child in Birmingham, and loved the way his puppet-on-a-string gestures produced such tremendous results.

It was in a pause before the last movement that I heard a noise from upstairs. Something had been dropped on the linoleum floor.

My reaction, I admit, was unwise. I should have ignored it, convinced the intruder I hadn't heard it, then gone out to phone 999 perfectly casually, as if I were ringing up a friend. Instead I instinctively reached over to turn off the gramophone, then darted out into the hall where the phone was.

"Get back in there."

The voice, plummy yet harsh, came from the top of the stairs. I sensed a shape there in the darkness, could dimly see legs. I was on the point of dialing 999 anyway, but reconsidered. If she had a gun it might be the last thing I would do. I withdrew my hand from the phone, turned, and went back into the sitting room, feeling like a dog withdrawing from a fight. My mind was numb, and before I could plan out even a sketch of possible action, footsteps came tumbling down the stairs. I retreated farther into the room.

It was the face I saw first. The hall was lit by wall lamps, and one just beside the sitting room door illumined it. The face was raddled, the cheeks all faded pouches, but the lips were newly painted with a gash of scarlet for a mouth, and the whole was haloed by a mop of dyed red hair, the curls seeming out of control, like a shrubbery gone wild. Below the face were slack chins, and below that a body that was a heavy mass of flesh. But it was what that bulging mass was clad in that was the most grotesque sight: a shiny satin frock, something that must have been enormously sexy a quarter of a century ago, now many sizes too small for her, emphasizing her grossness and restricting her movements.

My mother had brought her wardrobe with her.

As I looked at her the gash of red in the center of her face expanded into a horrible smile of anticipated and longed-for revenge. To drive home the desire, her hand came round from behind her back: in it was a fearsome knife—the sort of knife a professional chef would use: long, razor-sharp, deadly. As she pointed it in my direction she saw my eyes widen, and her smile became still more full of relish.

"Yes. Not a toy knife this time. A real slicer. You'll feel this going in, won't you?"

The accent was genteel: a chilling, ruling-class tone with not a trace of Australian left. I started toward her, but the knife hand sprung forward, and when I hesitated she gestured commandingly toward my father's old chair. I sank back in it gratefully, as if given a reprieve and an opportunity. She read my thoughts, or imagined she did.

"Oh, you haven't reached your time yet. That would be too easy. Relax. It will come. I am a woman who makes things happen. All you can do is wait for what's coming."

The arrogance of her voice, tinged with madness, unnerved me. Anything I could say would have sounded feeble, but perhaps not quite as feeble as what I did say.

"What do you want?"

She laughed, contemptuously, as if my cliché was symptomatic of the quality of my mind.

"Nothing you can give me and still live," she said. She poked her horrible face forward, its ravenous eyes glinting. "*I want your death.*"

I worked hard to regain my habitual coolness, to treat her as I would treat any other disturbed person I might encounter.

"You've been working up to my death for

some time," I said, my voice emerging, against the odds, as calm and matter-of-fact. She seemed flattered.

"Yes, I have. Have you felt it? That nice, satisfying, upward curve toward *that*. At what point did you sense where it was to end? First there were little pinpricks, humorous gestures, then a brick thrown, then a stab wound....Finally there will be that slashing attack that will leave you gasping and bleeding and dying."

"That will leave a great hole in your life. Nothing left to live for."

Her eyes glinted. She had faced that.

"I will find something. Someone. But you had to be first. I've been meditating it for months. Everything leads up to your death, so it has to be. It's the end of your road. You'll die in the boring little suburban dump those boring little suburban people brought you to."

"Maybe boring people make rather good parents. I've no quarrel with what you did when I was born."

For reply she shrugged her fat shoulders, bursting out of their shiny prison. Whether or not I had a quarrel with her, her gesture said, was quite immaterial.

"Why?" I asked. She laughed.

"For being born," she said.

Argument with such a proposition seemed useless, but the conversation had to be prolonged.

"You haven't killed Tony."

"Pits?" She sneered, revealing brilliant white teeth, the only good sound things left in her body. "Pits is hardly worth killing. An afterthought, something that popped out unexpectedly and made a bit of money for me. Someone who has a life that's hardly worth snuffing out. I shall need Pits after—"

She looked at me, greedy relish again lighting up her eyes.

"If you can find him," I said.

That brought her up short for a moment.

"I thought you must have spirited him away somewhere. I haven't seen him in any of his usual haunts." She brandished her murderous weapon and laughed. "I shall find him! No one can hide from me."

The madness was becoming more manifest by the second. Being confronted by homicidal lunacy must be one of the most unnerving experiences possible. You know that reasoned argument can have no effect, but it is almost impossible to think

up an alternative to it. In desperation I tried surprise.

"Sir John has managed to hide from you pretty
effectively," I said. The effect was extraordinary.
For a moment I thought she was going to kill
me there and then. The body stiffened, the hand
gripped the knife more firmly. Everything spoke
of outrage, that I should know such a fact.

"He's alive?"

I raised my eyebrows.

"I thought you knew everything."

Her mouth twisted with rage.

"Where? Where is he living?"

"Somewhere safe from you."

"Tell me where your father is!"

My heart thumping I tried a trick. I swung my
eyes round to the picture of my parents on the
sideboard, and her eye involuntarily followed
them. But I was saved from springing and wrestling with her by the phone ringing. I sat back in
the chair, my heart thumping, grateful not to have
been a dead hero. Surely that was George?

"Shall I answer it?"

She shook her head.

"Do you think I'm a fool? Do you think I'm
mad? People have—but they've learned. And don't

play games about who your father is."

"*That's* my father," I insisted. "I'm sure you're aware he is in a nursing home."

"I'm not talking about him. I'm talking about your real father. The man whose prick made you."

"How nicely you put it! By the way I've never understood how you came to get pregnant."

She spat on the carpet.

"I told him I couldn't have children, after a botched abortion I'd had in Sydney. The abortion was true, the rest wasn't. I made out it was the tragedy of my life."

"I see. So I don't have to feel I was unwanted."

Her eyes widened in scorn.

"I didn't *want* you! I had other plans. I was going to be a person to reckon with—as I became! Oh no, you were just a counter. I would have used you if I'd wanted him to marry me. I was in a situation full of possibilities and I didn't want to make up my mind till I had a full hand of cards. I knew I could get rid of you if I decided I could do better."

"I see."

"You owe your damned existence to the police," she said, not in a mood of reminiscence, but one of anger. "They kept such a close watch on me after the murder that I couldn't do anything about you."

"Nice," I commented.

"Everyone has abortions these days! I was punished because I couldn't have what every chit of a girl has now. It's your fault! You're to blame!"

"I do seem to have had a variety of possible fates," I said, declining to take this point of view up. "Extinction, adoption, or becoming the acknowledged son of a lord, though admittedly only one with a courtesy title."

"The situation got rather messy after you were conceived," my mother admitted, still waving the knife but holding it as firmly and menacingly as ever. "Being the acknowledged son of a lord wasn't on the cards for very long after he put you in me." She paused, remembering back, and with anger. "That stiff-necked prig bored me. God, *how* he bored me! He was passionate, he was besotted, and any girl can take a lot of that, but he was so damned *righteous*. As long as I wanted to keep the marriage option open I had to be so good, so domestic, so loving to his brats. The appeal of that role wore very thin."

"So I heard from his daughter."

"Dull little Caroline. What's she doing now?"

"A fashion buyer. Quite a glamorous job."

The news seemed to inflame her. Her face showed a mixture of surprise and hate. I realized that my becoming a minister had probably inflamed her in the same way. I had done the sort of thing she had wanted to do. People she despised being successful stirred up resentment at the ruin of her own hopes, augmented her collection of grievances. However, she swallowed, and with a dismissive gesture of her left hand put Caroline aside and reverted to herself.

"I'm a connoisseur of emotions," she said, throwing her head back in a ludicrous gesture of conceit. "It's been my great strength and great joy. It's been what has marked me off from other people. They operate within a tiny spectrum. I operate over the whole range."

"Really?" I said, raising my eyebrows again. "I'd have thought it was quite narrow. You like having the power to hurt, annoy, disturb. You enjoy creating disorder. I'd have thought the psychology books would have had a quite simple word that pinned down your particular mental disorder."

"Disorder? It is not a disorder! It is an intellectual distinction."

"What you will. It's in the eye of the beholder, I suppose."

"Are you trying to annoy me?" She waved her deadly wand closer to my face. I shrugged.

"From what you've said about your plans I've nothing to lose."

She smiled on being reminded of them, and regained some of her equilibrium, or what passed for it in her.

"Actually my great strength has been understanding other people's more outré emotions, and responding to them. When I had my business I catered for every taste under the sun—I or one of my girls or boys. Whatever the preference was, we could accommodate the customer. It was a house of great resort, especially for the gentlemen. And I'm not using the word 'gentlemen' as any vulgar madam might. The cream of society came to me: men at the top of their professions. Politicians, judges, writers, media people—they all would meet and talk in my establishment. It was really a salon, a drawing room: the conversation was daring and witty, and ranged well beyond your understanding. When they write a history of London life in the seventies and eighties my house in Kensington should be at the center of it."

"You'd like that, wouldn't you? Perhaps the author will devote a special chapter to Mme. Labelle's esoteric and high-class knocking shop. When did you change your name to Mrs. Flanders?"

"When the police had become a lot too interested in Mme. Labelle. You *have* found out a lot. You get the allusion?"

"I suppose so." I decided to continue annoying her, because she seemed to get a spice out of a duel. "Though Moll Flanders wasn't a whore or a madam. That's a vulgar error. She was a serial bigamist."

She quivered with aggravation at being corrected.

"Smart alec! Pedant!"

"You're an English graduate of long ago. Something we have in common. You should have known that. Bigamy was never in fact your line, was it? You can't be a bigamist until you've first been married."

"I was never so daft. I've told you why I decided not to have Lord John. If I was bored with him as a lover, it wasn't likely I'd find him very interesting as a husband."

I chanced my arm with something I'd guessed

from Caroline's and Matthew's account of the household.

"And by then Lady John had come into the picture, I suppose."

She gave another of those annoying moues at my not needing to be told something. But then she grinned evilly: even if she could not announce it as a revelation, she would enjoy talking about it.

"I told you I was a connoisseur of sensations. That was a situation I could relish! She should never have married. A lot of women did at that time who shouldn't have—for security, for children (though that certainly wasn't *her* motivation), or because they didn't understand their own inclinations. The Revills' marriage was over long before I went to live with them, though I'd have put the final nail in it if it hadn't been. When I heard from Lord John why he thought the marriage had broken down I thought: there could be a bit of fun in this for me! In fact, I knew I'd enjoy having it off with both of them."

"I said you like creating confusion and disorder," I said.

"I certainly did that!" she said, with pride and pleasure. "We found it so easy at first, Veronica and me. He was at the Ministry or at the House of Commons most of the time. The children were upstairs in the nursery, playing quite happily on their own. Their snotty little noses went unwiped for a bit. So while they were playing up there, we were playing down below, in bed. It was *too* easy. I think the housekeeper suspected, but she was sort of semidetached in the household anyway."

Not so semidetached, I thought, that she didn't blush at the recollection of her suspicions when Frieda Brewer was questioning her.

"To spice it up a bit," my mother went on, "I started telling him the old headache story and going to her bed at nights. He began to get an inkling, but was too much of the gentleman to try to catch us together. His damned codes, his *honor*, really screwed him up, the poor fish. Anyway, at heart he didn't *want* to know, to have his suspicions confirmed."

"Why not?"

"Because he was wild about me. I was giving him what he'd never had in his life before."

"Poor man," I said. That was unwise. It caught her attention, and drew her away from her reminiscences.

"Lucky man." She licked her lips and did a little semicircular walk around the room, waving the long, sharp knife. "I'm going to find him, you know. I know what you're doing, but I haven't forgotten him. *You* come first, but *he* will come next. Even if I have to alter my plans and play with you a bit before I kill you, I shall get it out of you where he is."

"Even you can't believe that. A man who knows he's going to die is under the least possible compulsion to tell the truth. I'll lie, and I'll be dead before you can check it out."

She thought this over.

"Perhaps this is going to be *much* longer drawn out than I planned," she said at last, injecting a threatening tone to her words, which did not hide an inner uncertainty. "And why not? All the more enjoyment for me." I registered that no plan seemed to be springing to her mind.

"You were just playing with them, weren't you?" I said. "With Lord John and Veronica. As you want to play with me with that knife. As you've been playing with me since the day I became a minister."

She laughed.

"I loved listening upstairs to you playing musicals and opera, then playing you things over the phone from my old collection. I had an enormous collection at my establishment. I always tried to please my gentlemen, find out what their tastes were, give them what they wanted. Often I had to plunge deep to find out what they *really* wanted but didn't even know themselves they wanted. That was fun. Then I could play with them."

"That's it, isn't it? The pleasing them was a preparation to playing with them, and the playing got nastier and nastier."

"Maybe. They put themselves in my power. I never went after them."

"But you do nowadays, because it's become a need. Tony never put himself in your power. You went after him."

"I didn't go after him. We landed in the same institution. That was no great coincidence. There are hardly any asylums left, even in London. They keep you in the home area, so that relatives can visit. Pits and I were Central London people." She laughed harshly. "There weren't many keen relatives to visit people in there, but no one had fewer visits than Pits and me."

"He should never have been in an institution at all."

She flushed.

"I'm the one who should never have been in an

institution! Pits is feebleminded. That's why he was there. They got it right for once. They couldn't have got it more wrong with me." Her eyes glinted with grievance. "They were leaned on, of course. I was arrested for pestering a government minister. I wasn't pestering him. I was blackmailing him. He must have leaned on the police to have me quietly put away, and the police leaned on the psychiatrists. Mind you, psychiatrists are sadly limited people. They were too stupid to understand a really creative imagination."

"Your talent for disorder, you mean?" She twisted her mouth.

"I've worked on people all my life. I've made them into my puppets. Twisted them to my will, which was so much more daring than their own. That's a sign of greatness, not of madness. But you can't expect the hoi polloi to understand that."

"But you deny you twisted Lord John into murdering his wife so that he could marry you?"

"Haven't I told you I'd given up that idea almost as soon as you were conceived?" she almost shouted. "By then I had much bigger plans. I was going round with him and Lady John and meeting all sorts of more exciting and more influential people. They were people whose interest really counted, people who could get my career into liftoff. I'd already made inquiries about an abortion, got the name of a society abortionist. The killing of Veronica was the last thing I wanted at that point. It was an accident."

"An accident?"

She laughed outright, an ugly, sneering sound.

"Oh, don't get your hopes up. He killed her all right. It was an accident from my point of view. I just wanted to enjoy an extension of my little game—get some added spice out of it. On the surface, as I've said, we were all three very friendly: civilized, modern people. Lots of people in their circle thought I was sleeping with him, but they saw us together and thought it was a mutually acceptable arrangement as far as Veronica was concerned. Nobody realized just how close we all were, all three of us. We went to parties together, to Covent Garden, to the theater. One of the plays we went to—"

"Don't tell me!" I cried. "It was *All's Well That Ends Well.*"

"You're too sharp for your own good," she spat, stalled.

"Not bad for one who was brought up by boring little people," I agreed.

"Any fool can get a university education these days," said my mother scornfully.

My eye thought it caught a light down by the front gate. George? Or George and a police presence? I tried not to look at it, make her aware of it.

"The play with the bed trick," I said thoughtfully. "The one where the husband thinks he's in bed with the woman he's been leching after, but in fact it's his scorned wife, because the women have got together and arranged a substitution. You wanted to stage a Shakespearean play in modern terms."

"I told you I collect outré situations," the witch said, with ludicrous self-satisfaction.

"But surely Veronica took some persuading? If she'd discovered she was a lesbian, why should she go back to sleep with a husband she felt revulsion from?"

"Because one of the things that united us was despising Lord John for the stiff-necked, upstanding, moral sort of prig that he was. She liked the idea of humiliating him more than she disliked the idea of sleeping with him. The thought of him finding himself in such a ludicrous situation was gloriously funny to both of us."

I thought.

"But there was a difference from the play, wasn't there?" Her hideous face flickered. She didn't like anyone being a jump ahead of her. It meant she wasn't in total control. "In the play Bertram had not slept with either woman before. Lord John had slept with both."

With the sudden mood flash of madness she had forgotten me and was back in the past. Her fingers, though, kept their tight grip on the flashing knife. Outside I thought I caught the dimmed lights of cars arriving.

"It was over as soon as it started, wasn't it?" I pressed her. "A great disappointment. He knew practically the moment he got into bed with her that it was his wife in his lover's bed."

Her voice came, loaded with reminiscence and venom.

"I waited in Veronica's bedroom. I'd told him he'd be welcome in mine that night, after several nights of 'headaches.' It was nearly midnight when I heard his door open. He slipped down the corridor and into my room—he knew it all so well that he never needed to switch any lights on. I waited a second or two, and then tiptoed down the corridor and stood listening outside my room.

He was talking to her, telling her he'd missed her, me as he thought, and he climbed into bed and was starting to go into his routines—how I hate men with routines!—when suddenly I heard a bellow of rage, something I'd never heard from Lord John, never expected to hear."

"Did it frighten you?"

"Of course not. It amused me."

"It excited you, I should think. The outraged aristocrat was more your type than the gentle moralist."

"Maybe, maybe," she said impatiently. She was back in the past, and didn't like being interrupted or contradicted. "The next thing I heard was her laughter. She hardly ever laughed, and only to wound. I joined in from the door. The bedside light came on, and he stood there, naked, seeing us both—*me too*—taking the piss out of him. That was the moment he snapped. The next thing I knew he'd thrown himself on Veronica and his hands were round her throat."

"Didn't you try to stop him?"

"I might have done, but it was over as soon as it started. Sometimes it is. Don't suppose you knew that. I didn't. The technical term for it is vagal inhibition, and even the police admitted that was what must have happened. She was dead within seconds."

Something struck me, a hope.

"Are you sure? Are you sure she wasn't still alive when he left the house, and you finished her off?"

She stared at me, her face eaten up with contempt.

"Haven't you been listening? Are you as dim as your brother? Can you imagine any reason I would have for wanting her dead? You're just a simpleminded fool, wanting to cling to the idea that your father is not a murderer. That cow's death destroyed all my political ambitions—that and your birth. Oh no, he killed her. The police admitted, but only after days and weeks of questioning me and testing my story, that he might not have intended to kill her, that if things had gone normally with an attempted strangulation he would probably have given up long before she was dead. It was not much more than a moment of rage on his part, but it was enough to kill her."

I clung to my shadow of an idea.

"The police kept on at you for a long time, by the sound of it."

"Of course they did. I was the only witness.

At first they thought it was some kind of plot between John and me—lovers against the wife. I told them at first it was just a row between John and Veronica, which grew so heated he tried to strangle her. It was spur-of-the-moment stuff and they knew it. They wanted to know how come a row between those two had finished up in my bedroom. Then the forensic people discovered that Veronica had not just been in my bedroom, but had slept, or lain, in my bed. That really got them going! In the end they got most of it out of me."

"And in the meanwhile Tony and I were growing, growing, growing in your womb."

She threw me a glance of hatred.

"Like parasites on a tree. Eventually they conceded I'd had nothing to do with the murder, and they left their tail off. I'd been living in a bed-sitter under an assumed name, with a copper at the front door and a copper at the back and a copper's sister-in-law as my landlady. When I finally managed to get to the abortionist I'd intended to use at the time of the murder he said it could only be done with potential damage to myself. He wasn't going to take the risk, and I sure as hell wasn't going to either. *So you lived.*"

She said it like a threat. I ignored that, and nodded. She wasn't Veronica's murderer. I had really only toyed with the idea as a way of prolonging the discussion.

"You can't expect me to be sorry to have lived."

"Pits is! And I'll make him even sorrier before long. You won't be so smug and self-satisfied about your successful career when I've finished with you either."

She looked at me and started fingering the knife. I could only cast around desperately for something to delay the final confrontation.

"And did you never see Lord John again?"

"Never. I soon stopped laughing, when I saw her lying there on the bed and not moving. I'd always felt a bond with Veronica. There was no morality nonsense about her. I looked at him, he looked at me, and we both bent over and examined her. He just said 'My God!' in that stifled aristocratic way of his. Then he rushed out of the bedroom. I was trying resuscitation, but I could hear him putting on clothes in his room. Then I heard him rush downstairs and slam the front door. I thought he was going to the police. Getting any life back into Veronica was hopeless, and I suddenly thought:

What if he tries to shift it all off on me? So I rang the police myself, wanting at least to start with a few Brownie points. And I've never seen him or heard his voice to this day....Oh, but I'd like to! I've scores to settle with him, too. And I will settle them. You're going to tell me where he is."

Caressing the knife she took a step toward me, her eyes flaring with rage and a sort of lust. Her love for herself, her sensual feeling for her own primacy and prowess, was almost erotic in its intensity.

"He's where you can never find him," I said.

"I can find him. You've seen him, haven't you?"

"Yes."

"Then I shall. You *liked* him, didn't you?"

"Yes."

"Weaklings together. *Where?*"

"In a sort of retreat."

She laughed harshly.

"A monastery! I might have known. There was always a monk lurking there, a passionate monk! That's my speciality: the secret self that every man keeps hidden from the world, but which I can unlock. That was the brilliant thing about my establishment: winkling away at that secret of the inner soul."

"You're off-beam as usual," I said. "He's not a monk. He lives quite alone."

"Better and better," she said, licking her lips.

"In any case, you can't put any blame on him. You said yourself that what happened was virtually an accident."

"He killed her. Whether he intended to or not he killed her, and that ruined my life."

"And I ruined your life," I said, as if it were a litany, "and Tony ruined you life. Why don't you face it: *you* ruined your life."

"*No!*"

It was bawled out. That was her core dishonesty, the thing that she had never faced up to, that her delusions were a refuge from.

"You planned your whole life, step by step. And you blew the plans one by one. That's why you have to thrash around and blame other people. That's one of the forms your madness takes."

"*I am not mad!*"

"Once you got the job in Upper Brook Street," I said, "you began to make plans. Lord John was the first in your sights, and he made easy game: a frustrated, sad man whose marriage had been empty and was now in ruins. You soon realized Lord John was never going to fly high in politics, but you were well in by then with him and his wife—they took you to parties, places where people of their kind were seen and did business. You met people who were at the top of all sorts of concerns and walks of life, or who were getting there. Lots of avenues were opening to you. And then you blew it."

"I didn't," she snarled. "I was just having a little fun."

"But that was exactly it," I said, seeing that the needling was working. "You've got a trivial mind, a mind that went for present fun rather than future prospects. You were never going to go anywhere significant, not on your own account, and not by clinging to any man's coattails either. You liked trivial power, manipulating people, creating chaos and confusion in their lives. So you set up this silly, cruel little joke of getting Lord John into bed with his wife. *You* ruined your life."

"Men ruined my life! You, him, others. Always men!"

"You can't ruin someone's life by being born. A baby has no moral responsibility. Some people never develop one, even when they have apparently grown up. You had quite a nice little business, a high-class brothel that gave every customer what he wanted. Their dreams came true there—their sexual dreams. It was obviously a business you thoroughly enjoyed and were suited to running. But when attitudes became so permissive that your establishment began to lose its function you blew it again by resorting to blackmail. The only possible basis for an enterprise like yours was total discretion. You ruined your own life."

"No!"

"And you became more and more desperate, madder and madder, and you cast around in your own mind for people to blame. Always other people to blame. Because you're the kind who can never accept responsibility for what they've done, never acknowledge the burden of guilt for what that has meant—for themselves and for others."

"You should have been a preacher."

I leaned forward.

"I know where Lord John lives."

I was fairly sure by now that a rescue force was in place outside the house. That was reassuring, but it didn't create total confidence. There was still that time between them trying to force an entry and actually getting their hands on the madwoman and her knife. There was the reputed strength of mad people, too: I was reasonably strong, reasonably agile, but for how long could I fend her off? Her and that knife?

I had decided my best card would be to get her off balance. In fact I couldn't think of any other card.

"*Where* is he?" she whispered.

"That's for me to know and you to find out."

She came a step forward, the knife held firm and threateningly.

"Where?"

"A cave beside a monastery in northern Greece," I said. Her eyes glinted, but suspiciously. "A mud hut in the rain forests of South America. A ruined hovel on the edge of a bog in the Republic of Ireland. On the top of a pillar in the Sahara Desert—"

Her face became redder and she waved her weapon.

"Stop playing with me, or else—"

"You've played with people all your life. I must have inherited it from you. I've already told you where he is, as a matter of fact, but you're too *stupid* to understand me."

I flung the adjective at her. She howled with rage, I prepared to sidestep, but as she hurled herself forward there came first a great ripping sound as the purple satin of her dress split across the shoulders, then a second later a massive concentration of lights, bursting suddenly through the sitting room window, followed by the sound of feet battering at the front door. She stopped, confused, and I threw myself on her, gripping her knife arm with both hands, twisting it round, the satin tearing still further into rags, but she still clutching her hideous weapon with all her strength and pushing it closer and closer to my face, my eyes. It was only as uniformed men burst into the room that it fell useless to the floor and I could push it aside as she threw herself at my throat.

It took three of the policemen to subdue her, and even after they had handcuffed her she was aiming kicks at them with her stumpy legs and spitting in their faces. Bruised and shaken I followed them through the hall and out into the garden, which arc lamps were illuminating as if it were a film set. George Eakin was standing there with several of the local top police brass. He came forward and put his arm around my shoulder, and together we watched my mother, howling and screaming obscenities, being driven away and out of my life forever.

CHAPTER NINETEEN

Recalled to Life

Lucy Mariotti was sectioned that night, and very soon certified unfit to plead to any of the charges the police had lined up for use against her. Unfit to plead, unfit to do anything except rail, blame, lament, assail. I was sent regular bulletins on her, though I made no particular inquiries. Unless she was threatening me she was nothing to me. Mother in name, mother by a crass accident of biology, beyond that—nothing. If I were inclined to worry if anything of her had gone into my makeup, I would have concluded that her contribution was balanced by that of my biological father. The local newspapers merely recorded that a woman, released into the community some time ago from a London psychiatric hospital, had been arrested for causing an affray at the home of local

MP Colin Pinnock. That seemed to me to get it about right, though at the time what she caused seemed rather more than an affray. At any rate she was now nothing more than "a woman."

But Tony was more than just a man. He was my brother, and a confused, pathetic, nearly broken individual. Susan and I talked with him about Lucy, made it clear to him that she was now locked away in a secure institution, tried to convince him that there was no danger of her being released back into the community. But that was the sticking point. It had happened before, and he could not believe it would not happen again. We meditated setting him up in a small flat or bed-sitter, but that overmastering fear of his mother didn't augur well for the experiment succeeding. It suddenly occurred to me that, just as I had made contact with our father, so he should, too. I felt that the serene old man could act as a calming influence—him, his way of life, and the remote place that he led it in.

I am not a sentimentalist about nature. I know it can be as red in tooth and claw on these islands as it is down the Amazon or in the African bush. You only have to watch sparrows fighting over a nut container to know that. But I did sense that peace, quietude, and natural beauty could have a positive influence on a troubled mind. I arranged it through Matthew and Janet as before. They took him with them to Wexford, Matthew reporting that Tony got on well with the children, but seemed somehow bewildered by family life, couldn't take it in or become part of its dynamics. Matthew drove him alone to Kilrose, then left him with our father.

He is still there. Report says that he is, if not happy, then more contented than he has ever been. He walks, fishes, tends the sheep, goes to town to get provisions. He meets people there, and slowly has made friends with them. His "holiday" has stretched to three months now, and he is welcoming the approach of spring. The seasons always meant a lot to Tony, having been on the streets. Sometimes I feel guilty about my father. Solitude suited him, he flourished in it, it was what temperamentally he was most fitted for. Then I remembered his nagging sense that he had not expiated what he had done, and felt that caring for his emotionally scarred son was part of that expiation.

Meanwhile I had been thrown, straight after my mother's arrest, into the political fray. The issue of the cuts in benefits to single mothers, after simmering for weeks, boiled over into a vote in the Commons. It was a defining issue, and I don't blame the MPs who thought it was too soon to forsake their own party and their own longed-for government. But I resigned my position in the Department of Education and later the same day voted against them. The vote was not just a single vote, it was part of threats to cut benefits for the disabled, it was the courting of sleazy businessmen, it was the abolition of student grants for tuition, it was the awfulness of Prime Minister's Question Time—all cheap point-scoring and ducking the issues—it was the feeling that everything was being labeled "New" but nothing had changed. It was, in short, general discontent and disillusion.

I resigned on December 10, in the early afternoon, and it made the later editions of the evening papers. By the next morning the papers were crowing over the fact that almost all the new women MPs in our party voted to cut the benefits. I was relegated to a short paragraph. There resteth my political career.

As soon as I resigned the Downing Street Misinformation Machine started spreading it around that I would have lost my place in the next reshuffle anyway, and that I had been distracted by family matters and had for that reason performed indifferently as a minister. I cherished a letter from Margaret Stevens, expressing sorrow at my going, and including the words "Politics do make me sick sometimes." It was unlike her to be so candid, but I suppose the approaching date of her retirement loosened her tongue.

"There's life after being in government," I said to Susan a week or two later, when I was settling into being just an ordinary MP again.

"There's life after politics," Susan replied.

And that was a question that was bubbling around in some deep recess of my mind. I'd been approached soon after my resignation to work for Opportunities for the Disabled, an educational charity—work on a voluntary, part-time basis, using what clout I still had as an MP. But I hadn't been there long before the director resigned, and I soon found they were interested in me as a replacement. I thought long and hard, as the cliché goes in political life, and I decided that I wasn't willing to do two jobs and do both inadequately. It occurred to me that I would probably do more real, practical good for the disabled through running the charity efficiently than I had done in seven months as a minister preparing for initiatives that might never get off the ground and might do precious little good if they did. I finally decided to accept the job and informed the Milton constituency that I would be standing down as their MP. I think their regret was genuine, but I resisted all their efforts to change my mind. I would always be a Milton man, would always cherish my links even after my father slipped out of life, but for the moment I was obliged to live and work in London. There was work to be done, and it was work worth doing.

When I proposed to Susan, which she thought very quaint, I made the proposal a double one. I asked her to marry me and raise a family with me. I felt we should be clear from the beginning that we both wanted both things. She accepted under the two heads. Margaret Stevens would have approved of our foresight and precision.

It was on our honeymoon in Italy that, one day, sitting at a table in a pavement restaurant in the main piazza in Sienna, Susan looked at me and said:

"Recalled to life."

She didn't need to explain. That was exactly what it felt like.

About the Author

Robert Barnard's most recent novel is *The Corpse at the Haworth Tandoori*. His other books include *No Place of Safety, The Bad Samaritan, The Masters of the House, A Hovering of Vultures, A Fatal Attachment*, and *A Scandal in Belgravia*. He has also recently produced a collection of short stories entitled *The Habit of Widowhood*. Winner of the prestigious Nero Wolfe Award as well as the Anthony, Agatha, and Macavity, the eight-time Edgar nominee is a member of Britain's distinguished Detection Club and lives with his wife, Louise, in Leeds, England.

To receive a free catalog of other Poisoned Pen Press titles, please contact us in one of the following ways:

Phone: 1-800-421-3976
Facsimile: 1-480-949-1707
Email: info@poisonedpenpress.com
Website: www.poisonedpenpress.com

Poisoned Pen Press
6962 E. First Ave. Ste 103
Scottsdale, AZ 85251